DOM CASMURRO

DOM CASMURRO

A Novel by
JOAQUIM MARIA MACHADO DE ASSIS

Translated from the Portuguese by
JOHN GLEDSON

WITH A FOREWORD BY JOHN GLEDSON

AND AN AFTERWORD BY JOÃO ADOLFO HANSEN

Oxford University Press
New York   *Oxford*

Oxford University Press

Oxford   New York

Athens Auckland Bangkok Bogotá
Buenos Aires   Calcutta   Cape Town   Chennai   Dar es Salaam
Delhi Florence Hong Kong Istanbul Karachi
Kuala Lumpur   Madrid   Melbourne   Mexico City   Mumbai
Nairobi   Paris   São Paulo   Singapore   Taipei   Tokyo
Toronto   Warsaw

and associated companies in

Berlin Ibadan

Copyright © 1997 by Oxford University Press

First published by Oxford University Press, Inc., 1997

First issued as an Oxford University Press paperback, 1998

Oxford is a registered trademark of Oxford University Press

Library of Congress Cataloging-in-Publication Data
Machado de Assis, 1839–1908
[Dom Casmurro, English]
Dom Casmurro / by Joaquim Maria Machado de Assis;
translated by John Gledson; with a preface by John Gledson
and an afterword by João Adolfo Hansen.
p. cm. (Library of Latin America)
ISBN 0-19-510309-2 (Pbk.)
1. Gledson, John, 1945– . II. Title. III. Series.
PQ9697.M8D613   1997
869.3—dc20   96-44126

5 7 9 10 8 6

Printed in the United States of America

Contents

Series Editors'
General Introduction

The Library of Latin America series makes available in translation major nineteenth-century authors whose work has been neglected in the English-speaking world. The titles for the translations from the Spanish and Portuguese were suggested by an editorial committee that included Jean Franco (general editor responsible for works in Spanish), Richard Graham (series editor responsible for works in Portuguese), Tulio Halperín Donghi (at the University of California, Berkeley), Iván Jaksić (at the University of Notre Dame), Naomi Lindstrom (at the University of Texas at Austin), Francine Masiello (at the University of California, Berkeley), and Eduardo Lozano of the Library at the University of Pittsburgh. The late Antonio Cornejo Polar of the University of California, Berkeley, was also one of the founding members of the committee. The translations have been funded thanks to the generosity of the Lampadia Foundation and the Andrew W. Mellon Foundation.

During the period of national formation between 1810 and into the early years of the twentieth century, the new nations of Latin America fashioned their identities, drew up constitutions, engaged in bitter struggles over territory, and debated questions of education, government, ethnicity, and culture. This was a unique period unlike the process of nation formation in Europe and one which should be more familiar than it is to students of comparative politics, history, and literature. The image of the nation was envisioned by the lettered classes—a minority in countries in which indigenous, mestizo, black, or mulatto peasants and slaves predominated—although there were also alternative nationalisms at the grassroots level. The cultural elite were well educated in European thought and letters, but as statesmen, journalists, poets, and academics, they confronted the problem of the racial and linguistic heterogeneity of the continent and the difficulties of integrating the population into a modern nation-state. Some of the writers whose works will be translated in the Library of Latin America series played leading roles in politics. Fray Servando Teresa de Mier, a friar who translated Rousseau's *The Social Contract* and was one of the most colorful characters of the independence period, was faced with imprisonment and expulsion from Mexico for his heterodox beliefs; on his return, after independence, he was elected to the congress. Domingo Faustino Sarmiento, exiled from his native Argentina under the presidency of Rosas, wrote *Facundo: Civilización y barbarie,* a stinging denunciation of that government. He returned after Rosas' overthrow and was elected president in 1868. Andrés Bello was born in Venezuela, lived in London where he published poetry during the independence period, settled in Chile where he founded the University, wrote his grammar of the Spanish language, and drew up the country's legal code.

These post-independence intelligentsia were not simply dreaming castles in the air, but vitally contributed to the founding of nations and the shaping of culture. The advantage of hindsight may make us aware of problems they themselves did not foresee, but this should not affect our assessment of their truly astonishing energies and achievements. It is still surprising that the writing of Andrés Bello, who contributed fundamental works to so many different fields, has never been translated into English. Although there is a recent translation of Sarmiento's celebrated *Facundo,* there is no translation of his memoirs, *Recuerdos de provincia (Provincial Recollections).* The predominance of memoirs in the Library of Latin America series is no accident—many of these offer entertaining insights into a vast and complex continent.

Nor have we neglected the novel. The series includes new translations of the outstanding Brazilian writer Joaquim Maria Machado de Assis' work, including *Dom Casmurro* and *The Posthumous Memoirs of Brás Cubas.* There is no reason why other novels and writers who are not so well known outside Latin America—the Peruvian novelist Clorinda Matto de Turner's *Aves sin nido,* Nataniel Aguirre's *Juan de la Rosa,* José de Alencar's *Iracema,* Juana Manuela Gorriti's short stories—should not be read with as much interest as the political novels of Anthony Trollope.

A series on nineteenth-century Latin America cannot, however, be limited to literary genres such as the novel, the poem, and the short story. The literature of independent Latin America was eclectic and strongly influenced by the periodical press newly liberated from scrutiny by colonial authorities and the Inquisition. Newspapers were miscellanies of fiction, essays, poems, and translations from all manner of European writing. The novels written on the eve of Mexican Independence by José Joaquín Fernández de Lizardi included disquisitions on secular education and law, and denunciations of the evils of gaming and idleness. Other works, such as a well-known poem by Andrés Bello, "Ode to Tropical Agriculture," and novels such as *Amalia* by José Mármol and the Bolivian Nataniel Aguirre's *Juan de la Rosa*, were openly partisan. By the end of the century, sophisticated scholars were beginning to address the history of their countries, as did João Capistrano de Abreu in his *Capítulos de história colonial.*

It is often in memoirs such as those by Fray Servando Teresa de Mier or Sarmiento that we find the descriptions of everyday life that in Europe were incorporated into the realist novel. Latin American literature at this time was seen largely as a pedagogical tool, a "light" alternative to speeches, sermons, and philosophical tracts—though, in fact, especially in the early part of the century, even the readership for novels was quite small because of the high rate of illiteracy. Nevertheless, the vigorous orally transmitted culture of the gaucho and the urban underclasses became the linguistic repertoire of some of the most interesting nineteenth-century writers—most notably José Hernández, author of the "gauchesque" poem "Martín Fierro," which enjoyed an unparalleled popularity. But for many writers the task was not to appropriate popular language but to civilize, and their literary works were strongly influenced by the high style of political oratory.

The editorial committee has not attempted to limit its selection to the better-known writers such as Machado de Assis; it has also selected many works that have never appeared in translation or writers whose work has not been translated recently. The series now makes these works available to the English-speaking public.

Because of the preferences of funding organizations, the series initially focuses on writing from Brazil, the Southern Cone, the Andean region, and Mexico. Each of our editions will have an introduction that places the work in its appropriate context and includes explanatory notes.

We owe special thanks to Robert Glynn of the Lampadia Foundation, whose initiative gave the project a jump start, and to Richard Ekman of the Andrew W. Mellon Foundation, which also generously supported the project. We also thank the Rockefeller Foundation for funding the 1996 symposium "Culture and Nation in Iberoamerica," organized by the editorial board of the Library of Latin America. We received substantial institutional support and personal encouragement from the Institute of Latin American Studies of the University of Texas at Austin. The support of Edward Barry of Oxford University Press has been crucial, as has the advice and help of Ellen Chodosh of Oxford University Press. The first volumes of the series were published after the untimely death, on July 3, 1997, of Maria C. Bulle, who, as an associate of the Lampadia Foundation, supported the idea from its beginning.

—*Jean Franco*
—*Richard Graham*

Dom Casmurro: A Foreword

Machado de Assis (1839–1908) is an anomaly among the great novelists of the nineteenth century: a Brazilian, but with no tropical lushness and grandiloquence to conform to "Latin American" stereotypes of his day (and of our day if the enduring vogue for "magical realism" is anything to go by); a realist, but one who constructed his greatest novels, including *Dom Casmurro*, in the willfully digressive style of the antirealist Laurence Sterne; a conventional, happily married civil servant, with none of the dramatic life of a Dostoevsky, or even a Dickens or a Flaubert. True, he shared what he called with typical discretion in a letter, "the same illness" with the first and last of these: he was epileptic (the disease manifested itself from about the age of forty on) and, just as importantly, a great-grandchild of slaves and a mulatto, a fact he was apparently not keen to advertize, having grown a bushy moustache over his thick lips.[1] Machado was obsessively discreet, with none of the vast quantities of revealing correspondence other novelists of the period delight us with, no diary (unless he destroyed it along with his letters), not even many revealing anecdotes.[2] Yet what the author did *not* leave tells us something: there was something to hide—a satirical contempt for what surrounded him akin to that of Jonathan Swift and which is often, I think mostly mistakenly, called pessimism.

In the tension between the notoriously polite and discreet public figure, founder of the Brazilian Academy of Letters, and the man who, in a story in a ladies' magazine, could drop an unmistakable reference to the rape of a twenty-four-year old bishop by the son of a sixteenth-century pope, lies both his greatness and the explanation of how late its recognition is in coming.[3] Machado is a subtle and astonishingly subversive writer as capable of surprising us as his own contemporary readers.

To have its full impact, Machado's fiction should be approached with as few preconceptions as possible. This necessarily implies that the role of this introduction is limited. I have concentrated on two subjects that will reduce the distance between us and Machado's place and time, and put the reader in a position as close as possible to that of Machado's own "dear reader," with whom he had such a playful, if wary relationship. First, I have given a brief introduction to the novel's historical and social background. This is a society which may actually look more familiar than it is, and since *Dom Casmurro* is narrated "from the inside," so to speak, by someone who shares many of that society's presuppositions, a more "objective," outsider's perspective is a useful complement, placing the reader on firmer ground. Second, I have sketched in some of the intellectual and literary background to Machado's work, bringing in issues which far transcend the Brazilian context. The local and the universal cannot easily be prised apart in Machado, any more than in Dostoevsky or Joyce, but it seemed useful to deal directly with issues which can make somewhat oblique appearances in the novel. In all this, I hope to increase the reader's enjoyment, and not spoil the pleasure by revealing too much.

Dom Casmurro was written in the 1890s, but for the first 97 of its 149 chapters remains in the 1850s, as the narrator, Bento Santiago, remembers his teens and his courtship of his next-door neighbor, Capitu (pronounced Cap-i-TU) Pádua. A contrast of the 1850s and 1890s tells us something about Brazil and about the social structure that is implicit in the plot, but in many ways taken for granted.[4] It also tells us something about the novel's peculiar realism.

In the early nineteenth century, coffee had overtaken sugar as Brazil's main export crop; both crops depended on slave labor. The country achieved political independence as an Empire in 1822, under a branch of the Portuguese royal family, the Braganças. Britain, which had sponsored the process of independence and had tried to force Brazil to abolish the transatlantic slave trade in the intervening years, finally achieved her aim in 1850 (although slavery itself was not to be abolished until 1888). The paradoxical result of this move was the liberation of funds that had been tied up in the slave trade and along with much of the rest of the world, Brazil (and Rio de Janeiro in particular), entered years of spectacular boom. In fact Machado contemplated describing the enthusiasm of these years in the novel, in a passage that he eventually deleted. This period was crucial to Machado's career as a writer, for it opened up a market for the arts and literature, which, narrow as it was by European standards, gave a determined and versatile young man willing to turn his hand to anything—hack journalism, poetry, short stories, drama—the small room for maneuver needed by a literary arriviste.

However, Machado's narrator, Bento Santiago, shows a different side to the decade (which is probably why the above-mentioned passage was finally omitted, as we shall see). The house on the Rua de Matacavalos is the product of a more permanent, stable social structure, largely brought about by slavery and the kind of economy and society it presupposed. Patriarchal (though Bento's father is dead, the father's eyes still "cast a shadow over him"), devoutly and excessively religious, careful in its finances, with its considerable wealth originally based on a plantation (probably producing sugar) not far from Rio de Janeiro, Bento's family is a typical representative of the land-owning aristocracy. A literal "aristocracy," at least in name, many of these wealthy people were in fact barons, viscounts, and marquises, and took their place in the hierarchy whose summit was the Emperor himself, the studious and discreet Dom Pedro II (1825–1892). When he appears in Bento's fantasy in Chapter XXIX, we should visualize his coach as a heavy, baroque affair, as antiquated as the Santiago family's own chaise (Chapter LXXXVII). The title *"Dom,"* given to Bento in the first chapter, and used for the title of the novel, was in fact reserved for the Emperor and senior religious figures; it is not the exact equivalent of the Spanish *"don."* (*"Casmurro,"* the adjective that completes the appelation and gives the title to the book, is explained in Chapter I. If any reader is so mischievous as to disobey Bento's instructions and look it up in the dictionary, he or she will find that it normally means "stubborn, headstrong.")

As Machado unobtrusively shows us, this is a very conservative and backward world, where leeches and emetics are still the common currency of medicine, and, as much to the point, where a mother's vow to make her unborn son a priest can be seen as acceptable. The Santiagos are only atypical in that the father is dead, and so the family is limited to one child, where the norm was for Victorian-style fertility, and in that they live in the city, though on money with rural origins.[5] (Even in this they represent a trend toward the concentration of power and wealth in Rio de Janeiro, continued in another way by Escobar, Bento's best friend in the seminary, with his "vocation" for commerce.) Chapters XCIII and XCIV, under the pretext of showing us Escobar's astonishing ability to count fast, tell us a great deal about what the Santiago family owns, which still reflects the conservatism of their class: buildings for rent, government bonds, and the hiring out of some of their slaves while others were sent out into the street to work with part of their earnings returned to their masters.[6]

It is perhaps a more exotic world than it appears at first sight. One very important member of the household, José Dias, requires more extensive commentary. He lies at the heart of the novel: he is the first to "reveal" to Bento that he loves Capitu, however unintentionally he does it, and his comments about Capitu's "sly and dissimulating eyes" and the probability that she is after "some local dandy" have an equally devastating effect on Bento. It is crucial, then, to understand Dias's position, which in turn explains his motivation. He is a dependent (the Portuguese word is *agregado;* literally, an addition, an adjunct, emphatically not, as another translation has it, a "friend of the family"), and could, as Bento says, be thrown out of the house from one day to the next. He might seem to be a kind of Brazilian Uriah Heep, worming his way into the household and manipulating it for his own benefit. It may well be that Dickens had some influence on Machado here; early on in his career, Machado translated *Oliver Twist* from a French translation and, later on, he learned English well and built a library that included a large number of books in English.[7] However, it would be wise not to see José Dias as simply "evil": he is a fully fleshed out character, perfectly understandable in social realist terms, as indeed, I would argue, are all the characters in the book. A couple of small details which might pass unperceived illustrate the point. First, in Chapter III, arguing that Bento ought to fulfil his mother's promise and go to the seminary sooner rather than later, José Dias remembers two liberal members of the Brazilian clergy, the Bishop Silva Coutinho, who presided over Brazil's first Constituent Assembly, forcibly dissolved by the Emperor Pedro I in 1824, and Father Feijó, Regent during Pedro II's minority in the 1830s, and who went so far as to argue against priestly celibacy. Second, in Chapter XXXV, José Dias remembers Pius IX's first political acts, "great hopes for Italy"—a subject no other characters latch on to, hardly surprisingly given that these first acts were unequivocally liberal. Later, he atones for his slip by referring to the conservative Pope's "august and most paternal heart." In other words, Dias is a repressed liberal, who generally keeps his opinions well hidden.

There is a certain poetic justice in the central position of the dependent or *agregado* in the novel. Machado himself, born the son of a housepainter and the protégé of a wealthy family, belonged to this "class," if it can be called that, and his earlier, more conventional fiction frequently returns to the topic. But it is not just a personal matter. The dependents, as Machado saw, embody some of the contradictions and paradoxes of the Brazilian social structure in much more revealing ways than slaves: slavery is not an obviously subtle relationship, as the brief conversation in Chapter XCIII demonstrates. The *agregados* were free, yet not free, as Machado's portrayal of less fortunate characters in other novels reveals, and so they show how domination works. In an immobile, conservative society, they are one of the few points of unresolved tension that can make a novel move: in a sense, along with the death of the all-powerful father, they allow the novel to have a plot at all.

The Pádua family represent a different kind of dependence, and indeed the rivalry between them and José Dias is in all likelihood based on that difference. Pádua, a civil servant as Machado was for much of his life, is dependent on the state, and the novelist goes to some lengths to show how little freedom of maneuver he has. His place in the bureaucratic hierarchy is so fixed that promotion, even after temporarily replacing his superior, seems out of the question. He owns his house only because by a lucky chance he won the lottery. Like José Dias, who never gives up the idea of an all-expense-paid trip to Europe, he has to make do with imaginary compensations. He is like his own caged birds. It cannot be overemphasized that there is an enormous social gap between the Santiagos and the Páduas: in the early version of this chapter, Dona Glória simply says that they came to know one another because she did them a favor; in the final version, accident in the form of a flood intervenes to take the sting out of the condescension. Capitu, perhaps the most famous female character in Brazilian literature, has her complexities and her charms, which would be spoiled by too much introduction, though it should be remarked that she, too, is the product of her place in society, and has a natural desire to climb the social ladder and to educate herself in such unladylike subjects as Latin.

By the 1890s, when Bento is recalling his youthful love, the European façade that can make us think we are reading a rather strangely constructed but recognizably European novel had, if anything, become more solid and convincing. Slavery had been abolished in 1888, and the Empire had fallen in the next year, giving way to a Republic. Rio de Janeiro was once again expanding and desperately trying to modernize itself to attract European immigrants: Bento himself is now living out in the suburbs, within easy reach of the train on which we first encounter him. His conservatism is eccentric, certainly: the visitor to Engenho Novo today can find plenty of houses built around the turn of the century (with façades that recall French Second Empire, Swiss chalets, and many homes that would best be called "eclectic"), but nothing as shamelessly nostalgic as Bento's folly. A retired lawyer, cultured, conservative ("I was always a little Muscovite in my ideas," Chapter XC) and perhaps more than a little snobbish, he prefers to shut himself off from the modern world, even as he shuts the window after thinking how everything has become the object of competition between the United States and Europe (Chapter LXIV). It is possible that he has come down in the world somewhat, at least relatively, because his house in the suburbs, whatever his personal reasons for having it built, is in a much less privileged area than the one in which he was born.

In sketching some of the historical background to the novel, I am not trying to argue that the essence of its message is historical or social, though it is true that unless something of that background is understood, a great deal of *Dom Casmurro*'s richness and subtlety will go unnoticed. But the novel's realism is much more ambitious than that. What might appear to be a domestic drama with a passing resemblance to *Romeo and Juliet* (though in a comic vein), can be seen as a commentary on the nineteenth century, described in Chapter IX of Machado's *Memórias póstumas de Brás Cubas* as "agile, skilful, vibrant, proud, a little verbose, audacious, learned, but in the end . . . as miserable as the other ones." Machado was aware, of course, that Brazil, along with the rest of Latin America, was a backwater that imported everything from philosophies of life to fashions in clothes from Europe. But he also knew that larger cultural—even spiritual—changes were reflected there, too, however distantly, and that they were as necessary a part of his subject as the streets, the characters, and the customs of his Rio de Janeiro.

To illustrate this, and to show Machado's ambition, I shall quote from the earlier version of some chapters of the novel (the only one we know of, published in the *Revista Brasileira* in 1896, when the novel was nowhere near finished, we can assume). This is Machado's picture of Rio de Janeiro in the aftermath of the abolition of the transatlantic slave trade:

Public life was festive, energetic and varied. The political revolutions had ended. Luxury was on the increase, money was in good supply, improvements were springing up. Nothing but balls and the theatre. One columnist of 1853 (if you don't trust me) said there were three hundred and sixty-five balls a year. Another in 1854 writes that all through the year everyone was off to see the shows. Private salons vied with one another.... The Italian opera had for a long time had its yearly program of events; in the previous decade more than one singer had sent our tenderhearted, enthusiastic populace wild; now there passed through a series of more or less famous performers, Stoltz, Tamberlick, Mirate, Charton, La-Grua. The dramatic theatre itself in its performances blended song and dance, arias and duets, a *pas de trois*, a *pas de quatre*, occasionally a whole ballet. There was already horserac-ing, just one club that attracted the cream of the city. The races began at ten o'clock in the morning and finished at one in the afternoon. One would go simply in order to see them [i.e., in contrast to the 1890s, when people went to bet. JG]. Europe was sending over its fashions, its arts and its clowns. Old-style carriages, *traquitanas* and *seges*, gave way to the coupé, and Cape-horses came in like victors. Brazilian songs and serenades went hand in hand with Italian arias. Ecclesiastical festivals were numerous and splendid; inside the church and out, there were widespread, sincere piety, local pilgrimages, and endless picnics.[9]

This passage was originally inserted, very awkwardly, in the middle of the conversation in Chapter III that now gives the main plot of the novel such a lively start. Its realism is that of the newspaper columns (called *crônicas* in Portuguese) that it quotes, the most famous of which were the work of Machado's predecessor, mentor, and friend, José de Alencar (1829–1877). The awkwardness is, in a sense, inevitable, for these developments contrast with the world inside the house, which is "monotonous and gloomy." Only through one of José Dias's plati-tudes—"the theater is a school of manners"—is Bento even allowed to go to the theater.

Between 1896 and 1899 an extraordinary transformation took place in Machado's plan, if I am right. He took one idea—that of the opera, which appeals so much to a sentimental Brazilian audience—from the plethora of detail in this passage and turned it into a theme pursued throughout the novel. It is the subject of the narrator's first major digres-sion, as he is flushed with enthusiasm at his new occupation of writing, and not "running out of paper" as happens later. In a simple sense, Machado is recognizing the fact that Bento is narrating in the 1890s, and that it is somewhat false for him to quote earlier journalists, but much more important than that is what has happened in the intervening years. The opera, from being a social event or merely a fact in the history of Brazilian culture, becomes a symbol of a whole mentality. From the first chapter, we see Bento going to the theater ("I'll give you a box, tea, and a bed; the only thing I can't give you is the girl.") In Chapter IX his friend Marcolini, the out-of-work tenor, insists that the Creation itself was an opera—*Paradise Lost*, perhaps?—and, what seems even more ridiculous, they argue about the accuracy of this absurdly anachronistic story and conclude that it might be true. What does this mean? Many readers must put the book down in despair when confronted by this frivolous brain-teaser. We would perhaps be wise to remember not only the enormous popularity of opera in the nineteenth century, but also the immense claims made on its behalf, especially by Wagner and his devotees. There can be no doubt that Machado has the idea in mind of the *"Gesamtkunstwerk,"* the total work of art in which words, music, scenery, and the theater itself are under the overall control of one creative genius (this theory is in fact mentioned in Chapter CI).

No story is perhaps more central to questions of truth, fiction, and belief in the nineteenth century than that of the Creation. Of course the chief agent of disbelief was the *Origin of Species*, which destroyed any notion that the creation story might be literally true. If it was not literally true: however, perhaps its message—that of original sin and the presence of evil in the world, at least—might be metaphorical, and true in that sense? Machado was, by all accounts, skeptical: no doubt he had read Darwin—"Reread your Spencer and your Darwin," as he says to the younger generation of writers appearing on the scene at the end of the 1870s[10]—but a more profound influence on him was Ernest Renan, whose *Life of Christ* was published in 1864.[11] Renan's whole thrust as a historian was to separate the mythological from the literally true, the first sentence of his book tells us that Jesus was born in Nazareth. Machado himself remained, as far as the scanty evidence can tell us, a radical skeptic: towards the end of his life, he published anonymously a short piece called "Christ's Passion," in which he tells the story of the Crucifixion as a purely human drama.[12]

In a sense, "The Opera" is the reverse of this plainness, an astonishing self-proclaimed fiction, complex, detailed, and absurd. Yet we should not be deceived: Bento does in a sense believe the story or, rather, he believes that what is seemingly true may contain all the truth we can have. This product of a seminary, and of an earlier decade when "there was widespread, sincere piety," has embraced a total skepticism typical of the turn of the century. In one of the very illuminating and witty *crônicas* Machado wrote in the 1890s, as *Dom Casmurro* was in gestation, he commented ironically on the fact that the Great Turk, as he prefers to call the Sultan, has sent the Pope a letter of congratulations on his jubilee: summing the matter up three weeks later, he tells his readers that "all beliefs have become confused in this unbelieving *fin-de-siècle.*"[13] This is Bento's state of mind, as it is expressed in this chapter: there is no ultimate system of belief, and everything can be relativized. His fondness for classical allusions, and the temptation he feels (in Chapter XVII) to compare a biblical saying to a myth about Achilles, form part of his cultured, skeptical, and somewhat cynical mind. Thus too, his friends have "gone to study geology in God's acre," joining the new science and traditional religion in humorous juxtaposition. The range of Machado's realism has undergone enormous expansion, from a journalistic description of an out-of-the-way corner of the world in the 1850s, to what is implicitly a characterization of a cataclysmic change in mentality that, in one way or another, affected people everywhere who were in the reach of Western culture. We should be careful, however: Bento's delight in what is seemingly true—a likely metaphor, as opposed to the truth—is not necessarily Machado's.

The dual chronological focus of the novel (1850s/1890s), which is maintained with unfailing skill and appositeness throughout, can produce problems, especially for the modern reader unaware of just how traditional Brazilian family life had been in mid-century, though in such chapters as LXXXVII ("The Chaise") these things are roundly hinted at. Equally, we may be in a sense over-familiar with more modern aspects of Bento's mind, which are overlaid, sometimes with seeming incongruity, on traditional attitudes. Capitu is at one moment (Chapter XII) a fifteen-year-old girl who dreams of dancing in the moonbeams over the Corcovado (the famous mountain in Rio de Janeiro on which the statue of Christ the Redeemer now stands). At another moment, in chapter XXXII, she turns into a devouring temptress, a siren ready to lure Bento to his destruction. This second image, a product of Bento's fertile imagination—or even an emanation from his subconscious—seems much more a product of the 1890s—with its several *femmes fatales,* its Eves, Medeas, and Salomés—than of the world of the 1850s Bento is trying to evoke.

One combination in which Machado takes particular pleasure is that of religion and money: in fact, the pleasure is partly due to the paradoxical links between the two things, and so between the traditional and the modern. God is described as a "Rothschild, only much more humane," because for Him, good intentions are legal currency. Escobar, whose "vocation" is commerce, takes his name, without a doubt, from the Jesuit casuist who is one of the main targets of Pascal's *Lettres Provinciales*. What Machado is saying is that certain forms and traditions of Catholicism habituate their devotees to a kind of calculating relativism, in which sins have values attached, and can be "paid for" quite literally, in the currency of prayers, paternosters, and Ave Marias: in this case, there is a fatally easy transition from the 1850s to the 1890s. It should be said, however, that the 1890s brought Machado—or, more likely, Bento—into a sharp awareness of the importance of money, and in particular of the reliability of "currency." The "Encilhamento," the boom and bust of the early nineties, which began with a licence to print money and ended in high inflation, corruption, and scandal, sent shock waves through the whole of Brazilian society, and undermined the reputation of the nascent Republic. Machado was probably one of the few people not be to taken in by the euphoria: even in his earlier novels, speculative financiers (one of them significantly called Cristiano Palha, literally translated, Christian Straw), are present, and indeed are more obviously corrupt than is Escobar, or are given greater opportunities to show their paces. Machado was no innocent in economic matters but, as numerous *crônicas* show, he was obsessed by the phenomenon itself, and aware of its deep social and psychological effects.[14]

* * *

Dom Casmurro was published in 1899, or 1900 depending on whether one takes its appearance from the French presses or its arrival in Brazil as the criterion. "Turn of the century" it undoubtedly is, but where does it fit into the development of fiction in that period, so often seen as the beginning of modernism? One could begin by making comparisons with contemporaries, with Henry James (1843–1916), for example, who shares a similar acute awareness of the role of the narrator, or even with later writers such as Marcel Proust (1871–1922) since Machado, too, especially in this novel, gives a crucial role to memory.[15] This latter comparison is much more problematic, for *Dom Casmurro* is about memory-loss, not memory recovery, as Lúcia Miguel-Pereira rightly points out.[16] Bento has failed, as he says in Chapter II, to tie the two ends of his life together.

A more valid route to an evaluation of Machado's place is to take the story back into the nineteenth century, and in particular to understand his relationship with and position within the realist tradition. There is no doubt of his profound admiration for the great masters of realism, notably Stendhal and Flaubert. Machado has Flaubert's concern with finding the exact word (which places some pressure on the translator) and Stendhal's psychological acumen and ironic familiarity with the reader (and a certain nonchalance about whether he is understood now or in fifty years time). But it is not so much affinities as negative reactions which cast the stronger light.

In 1877, Émile Zola published *L'Assommoir*, his study of the downfall of a French working woman, Gervaise Macquart, due to misfortune and hereditary alcoholism. It was an enormous, worldwide success, running into thirty-eight impressions in the year that it was published. In the next year, the great Portuguese novelist Eça de Queirós published his study of adultery in middle-class Lisbon, *Cousin Basilio*. Also in 1878, Machado published a review of Eça's novel, which is his most important work of criticism. It is a wounding attack, not so much on Eça himself (though he does accuse him of a servility to French models almost amounting to plagiarism), as on Naturalism, the movement to which both he and Zola belonged. . On the surface, Machado may seem to be disgusted by the crude details to be found in some of the scenes (and it has to be admitted that he plays the prude for effect) but, in reality, his objection to Naturalism is much more interesting than that, and his own prudery is largely for show. In neither sphere can he accept the materialistic determinism that underpins the novels: not only does it revolt his sense of human freedom that characters should be utterly predetermined by their ancestry (as in the case of Gervaise's alcoholism) it also makes for novels without tension, so long as one knows what the basic causes of their actions are. Human beings cannot be reduced to totally knowable and predictable creatures.

There may well have been personal reasons for Machado's rejection of Naturalism. A mulatto with epilepsy cannot have felt comfortable with doctrines that often reached daring conclusions about race and disease. But these reasons were, more importantly, philosophical and artistic. Moreover, Machado's opposition was the most obvious cause of the extraordinary artistic transformation he underwent at the end of 1870s, and that divides his fiction so clearly into two periods. The first period is that of his first four novels published in the 1870s, which are usually labelled "romantic," which approach problems parallel to those treated in *Dom Casmurro* (love across class boundaries, between dependents and masters), and which are told by a traditional third-person narrator.[18]

None of the five later works that constitute the second period, however, on which his reputation stands, have simple third-person narrators. The baby had had to go out with the bathwater: any real omniscience on the part of the narrator had become impossible to Machado, for it would imply that complete control which is itself determining, and deterministic. He needs at least the illusion of freedom: a first-person narrator is one way of achieving that, though one that brings its own problems with it. This means, not so much that he finds a new method, as that he is plunged into a process of continuous experiment, with one narrator who is dead, another who seems to be conventional but turns on the reader in the middle of the novel to tell him that he has been leading him up the garden path, another who writes a diary in which, of course, he cannot see what is going to happen the next day, and so forth. But—and this is a point which needs to be insisted on—none of these solutions makes Machado less of a realist. They are better understood as part of a search for a more consistent realism, and none of the novels illustrates the point better than *Dom Casmurro*. Its subject matter—a Brazilian family, typical of a place, a class, and a time, and typical in the way in which people interact both inside and outside that family is perfectly within the conventions of realism. What is more daring is that the narrator too from the first to the last word of the novel, in his attitudes, his narrative method, his language, is part of that realism. This has already been shown in the ways in which the 1890s color the view we get of the 1850s: the important point is that Bento is no more above the fray, removed into omniscience, than any other of Machado's narrators. Part of the unique fascination of this novel, in fact, is that he is so thoroughly grounded in his own physical and temporal environment: the glimpses of his suburban setting, as he opens the window to look at the children playing in Chapter LXXXV, or our first encounter with him on the train in Chapter I, are only the most overt parts of a subtle process that affects every sentence of the novel.

Machado's continuous experimentation after 1880 is driven in part by his rejection of Naturalism, and quest for a more coherent and searching form of realism. On one level, it might seem as though he had been revolted by Naturalism's excesses in other ways, too: in particular, two favorite subjects both in Zola and in Eça de Queirós, the Church and the priesthood, and sex, receive a much blander treatment than in the novels of his more aggressive contemporaries, or so it might seem. Father Cabral is certainly a tame object of fun beside the gallery of corruption and perversion of Eça's *The Crime of Father Amaro*, with nothing more than a little gourmandise and an overwhelming mediocrity to distinguish him. Bento's fellow seminarians are no worse and no better: the one who "they say has discovered a specific against yellow fever," a disease which made hundreds of victims in Rio de Janeiro every summer still at the end of the century, perhaps sums up their ineffective harmlessness. But when one thinks further, the novel contains at its heart an attack on the Catholic Church which goes far beyond the sins of any of its individual representatives: its whole plot revolves around the question of priestly celibacy. What interests Machado, one could say, is the perversity of the norm, the fact that it can be *realistic* at this given place and time, with the sanction of authority, to condemn a young man to forgo his most natural need and instinct, and be seen to be doing the right thing; even uncle Cosme, a ladies' man in his own youth, is reduced to bumbling apology when he attempts to protest.

With the issue of celibacy not only religion, but sex comes to the heart of the novel and, again, it is the perversity of the norm which reveals Machado's line of attack. Bento has "orgies of Latin" and is a "virgin with women": in other words, he has received what in British or American terms would be a Victorian upbringing—in the Brazilian case complicated by slavery and Catholicism—carefully shielded from his own most basic urges, repressed, and made to feel guilty about his urges. In the 1890s, he is still very careful that his language should be "chaste for the chaste, as it may be foul for the foul," though there is no doubt that his habits are more unbuttoned than they used to be: here, too, he is in tune with the *fin-de-siècle*. Chapter LVIII is perhaps the best example of Machado's "chastity": it seems to me to be a description of adolescent masturbation, but so brilliantly relayed that many readers would divine it rather than be conscious of it. (Many would not be aware of it at all and, most importantly, nobody could prove it.) Not only does this suit the respectable citizen Joaquim Maria Machado de Assis, with his position in society and his domestic peace to think of, it is also a perfectly realistic way for Bento to recount this moment in his slow and imperfect sexual development. He too does not entirely understand what is going on, nor does he want to face it. It has become something of a commonplace to compare Machado to Freud. Fortunately, the *Interpretation of Dreams* was published too late for speculation about influence to arise, though Machado had read precursors such as Eduard von Hartmann *(The Philosophy of the Unconscious),* and above all Schopenhauer.[19] But my suspicion is that, if anything, such readings legitimated what Machado already knew, through acute observation and common sense.

The subtlety and precision of Machado's observation of the psychology of his characters is perhaps nowhere so complete as it is here, so intricate and so sustained. This has a great deal to do with the fact that *Dom Casmurro* inhabits the world of adolescence. As we see his characters (particularly Bentinho and Capitu, of course) try to understand and manipulate the adult, social world in which they appear to be pawns, we understand both that world and him. Thus the vital importance of gestures, of the tone in which people speak, which can be supplicating or demanding, or any of a hundred shades in between. Why does Capitu suggest that José Dias, apparently the young couple's greatest enemy, the one keenest for Bento to go to the seminary, could be their greatest ally? How is it that she knows that that might be so? Why does Dona Glória cry in Chapter III? Why does Capitu fix on that event in particular? As we ask and answer these questions—keeping out of the reckoning as far as possible the idea that people are "good" or "bad"—we too begin to build up the jigsaw of this world, to which Machado gives us most of the pieces. It is a very different activity from reading a Naturalist novel, in which we know to a much greater degree how people will act. Our judgments of the characters are defined, very largely, by their interactions, their perceptions, the power that they have—or would like to have—over one another.

* * *

It will be useful to say a few words about the translation, though in general it must stand on its own merits. I have made considerable efforts to be both accurate and readable with a writer who, without any deliberate virtuosity, is perhaps as subtle in his nuances as any in the Portuguese language, and who keeps an equally guarded familiarity with both the colloquial and literary linguistic registers, something that is basic to his irony. In general, I have erred on the colloquial side, most obviously in the use of elided forms (you're, can't, shouldn't, etc.) in narrative as well as in quoted speech. In Portuguese there are no equivalents for these elided forms, so we have no way of knowing whether Machado would have approved: admittedly, English-language contemporaries would not have used them. I have used them, I confess, to convey the carefully cultivated conversational quality of the narrator ("Listen," the narrator says to the reader at one moment), and to make the novel sound more natural to a modern reader. I have made efforts to stick to Machado's own punctuation, which some might think makes an excessive use of semicolons, because there is considerable evidence that he gave punctuation a great deal of care: the run-on effect caused by the paucity of full stops is thus deliberate. When Machado quotes the Bible, I have used the Authorized (1603) version.

Most importantly, I have used the notes, rather as I have used the introduction itself, to reduce the modern English-language reader's distance from a novel that is, after all, a domestic drama, and that, as we have seen, cannot within its own parameters of narration be too explicit or explanatory. It seemed a misuse of space to tell the reader the story of *Othello* (to give one obvious example) and not to give some idea of the geography—physical and social—of Rio de Janeiro in the late nineteenth century. Notes have been kept to a minimum but, to exclude them, as both the previous translations (by Helen Caldwell and Robert Scott-Buccleuch) have done, seems unrealistic and unhelpful. I would like to thank Cristina Carletti, whose excellent notes for the 1994 Editora Scipione edition of *Dom Casmurro* were extremely useful. If a reader in 1900 would have known how much money a *conto* and seventy *milreis* was, why should we not? I have the suspicion (witness Joyce and some of the editions of *Dubliners*, for instance) that a willingness to take seriously a writer's local roots is part of the process of recognizing his universality. In Machado's case, this process is still under way, and it is to be hoped that this new translation furthers the cause.

—*John Gledson*
University of Liverpool

Notes

1. "This afternoon, I reread a page of Flaubert's biography; I found the same loneliness and sadness and even the same illness, you know, the other one [*como sabe, o outro* . . .]" From a letter to Mário de Alencar, 29 August 1908, a month before Machado's death. *Obra Completa* (Rio de Janeiro: Aguilar, 1962), Vol. 3, p. 1094. Unless otherwise specified, all references to Machado's work are to this edition.

2. "Machado de Assis: A Biographical Sketch," included in Roberto Schwarz, *Misplaced Ideas* (London: Verso, 1992), pp. 78–83, is a useful summary of the author's life, concentrating on his early years.

3. This story, *Casa velha* [Old House] was published in *A Estação* in 1885–86. See my article, "*Casa velha*: A Contribution to a Better Understanding of Machado de Assis," in *Bulletin of Hispanic Studies* 60 (1983), pp. 31–48.

4. Interestingly, in the introduction to his multivolume study of the bourgeoisie in the nineteenth century, Peter Gay refers to these two decades as presenting a crucial contrast for judging "a broad band of far-reaching cultural shifts": *The Bourgeois Experience: Victoria to Freud*, Vol. 1: *Education of the Senses* (New York: Oxford University Press, 1984), p. 3.

5. See Antonio Candido, "The Brazilian Family," in T. L. Smith, *Brazil: Portrait of Half a Continent* (New York: Dryden, n.d.). We should note, however, that the early death of Bento's father is not in the least unrealistic in this tropical nineteenth-century setting; Machado's fiction is rife with young widows, most of them more available than Dona Gloria, Bento's mother.

6. See my *Deceptive Realism of Machado de Assis: A Dissenting Interpretation of* Dom Casmurro (Liverpool: Francis Cairns, 1984), p. 45.

7. For a list of the extensive and fascinating remains of Machado's library, see Jean-Michel Massa, "La Bibliothèque de Machado de Assis," in *Revista do Livro* 21–2 (March–April 1961), pp. 195–238.

8. An appreciation of the role of the *agregado/a* has been one of the fundamental insights of criticism of Machado de Assis in recent years. The most important book on the subject is Roberto Schwarz's *Ao Vencedor as Batatas* [The Winner Gets the Potatoes] (São Paulo: Duas Cidades, 1977). One of the essays in his *Misplaced Ideas*, "The Poor Old Woman and her Portraitist" (pp. 94–9) deals with one extremely poor *agregada*, Dona Plácida in the *Posthumous Memoirs of Brás Cubas*.

9. This chapter, "Um agregado (Capítulo de um livro inédito)" ["A Dependent (Chapter of an Unpublished Book)"] is published as an appendix to the critical edition of *Dom Casmurro* by the Comissão Machado de Assis (Rio de Janeiro: Instituto Nacional do Livro/Ministério da Educação e Cultura, 1969), pp. 251–5.

10. From "A nova geração" ["The new generation"] (1879) in *Obra Completa* Vol. 3, p. 836.

11. Perhaps the most moving of Machado's tributes to Renan are the essay "Henriqueta Renan" (*Obra Completa*, Vol. 2, pp. 626–36), and the *crônica* written on the occasion of his death in October 1892 (*Obra Completa*, Vol. 3, pp. 549–50).

12. Originally published in April 1904: see *Obra Completa*, Vol 3, pp 1021–3.

13. "Todas as crenças se confundem neste fim de século sem elas," see Machado de Assis, *A Semana (crônicas 1892–1893)* ed. John Gledson (São Paulo: Hucitec, 1996), p. 212 (*crônica* for 19 March 1993). For the previous quotation, see *crônica* for 26 February 1893, *ibid.*, p. 241.

14. One of the most famous is the "Devil's Sermon," published 4 September 1892, which contains the following advice: "Do not lay up for yourselves treasures on earth, where moth and rust doth corrupt, and where thieves may break in and steal. Rather, send your treasures to a bank in London, where neither moth nor rust doth corrupt, neither do thieves steal, and where you will go and see them on the Judgement Day." *A Semana, ed. cit., p. 114.*

15. Roberto Schwarz makes the comparison with Henry James in "A poesia envenenada de *Dom Casmurro*, in Duas meninas (São Paulo: Companhia das Letras, 1997), p. 12: "Like his contemporary Henry James, Machado invented *narrative situations*, or *narrators placed in a situation.*"

16. See "Variações sobre o mesmo tema," in Lúcia Miguel-Pereira, *Escritos da Maturidade* (Rio de Janeiro: Graphia, 1994), pp. 11–14.

17. This essay, along with Machado's reply to critics who came to Eça's defence, can be found in *Obra Completa*, Vol. 3, pp 903–13.

18. These novels are *Ressurreição* [Ressurrection], (1872), *A Mão e a Luva* [*The Hand and the Glove* (Lexington: University Press of Kentucky, 1970)], (1874), *Helena* [*Helena* (Berkeley: University of California Press, 1984)], (1876), and *Iaiá Garcia* [*Yayá Garcia* (London: Peter Owen, 1976) and *Yaya Garcia* (Lexington: University Press of Kentucky, 1977)], (1878).

19. See, e.g., the reference to "the painful or melancholy note, the pessimistic note, the note of Hartmann," "A nova geração" [The new generation] (1869) *Obra Completa* Vol. 3, p. 811. The influence of Schopenhauer—much the greater philosopher, of course—is much more pervasive. In one of his last surviving letters (*Obra Completa*, Vol. 3, p. 1093), Machado says he is rereading one of Schopenhauer's books.

DOM CASMURRO

I

The Title

One evening just lately, as I was coming back from town to Engenho Novo* on the Central line train, I met a young man from this neighborhood, whom I know by sight: enough to raise my hat to him. He greeted me, sat down next to me, started talking about the moon and ministerial comings and goings, and ended up reciting some of his verses. The journey was short, and it may be that the verses were not entirely bad. But it so happened that I was tired, and closed my eyes three or four times; enough for him to interrupt the reading and put his poems back in his pocket.

"Go on," I said waking up.

"I've finished," he murmured.

"They're very nice."

I saw him make a move to take them out again, but it was no more than a move: he was put out. Next day, he started calling me insulting names, and ended up nicknaming me *Dom Casmurro*. The neighbors, who dislike my quiet, reclusive habits, gave currency to the nickname, and in the end it stuck. Not that I got upset. I told the story to some of my friends in town, and they call me it too for fun, some in letters: "Dom Casmurro, I'm coming to dine with you on Sunday." "I'm going to Petrópolis,† Dom

---

* A recently developed suburb of Rio de Janeiro, some six miles from the center.

† Petrópolis is a city about twenty miles from Rio de Janeiro, situated in the mountains overlooking Guanabara Bay. Because of its relatively cool and healthy climate, away from the dangers of yellow-fever, it was a place of refuge for the rich during the summer months, and it was linked to the capital by the country's first railway. From the mid-century on, Pedro II encouraged German immigration to the city—thus the names of such areas as Renânia (literally, Rhineland).

Casmurro; it's the same house in Renânia; see if you can't drag yourself away from your lair in Engenho Novo, and come and spend a couple of weeks with me." "My dear Dom Casmurro, don't think I'm letting you off the theater tomorrow. Come and spend the night in town; I'll give you a box, tea, and a bed; the only thing I can't give you is a girl."

Don't look it up in dictionaries. In this case, *Casmurro* doesn't have the meaning they give, but the one the common people give it, of a quiet person who keeps himself to himself. The *Dom* was ironic, to accuse me of aristocratic pretensions. All because I nodded off! Still, I couldn't find a better title for my narrative; if I can't find another before I finish the book, I'll keep this one. My poet on the train will find out that I bear him no ill will. And with a little effort, since the title is his, he can think the whole work is. There are books that only owe that to their authors: some not even that much.

I I

The Book

Now I have explained the title, I can proceed to write the book. Before that, however, let me explain the motives that put the pen in my hand.

I live alone, with a servant. The house I live in is my own; I decided to have it built, prompted by a such a personal, private motive that I am embarrassed to put it in print, but here goes. One day, quite a few years ago, I had the notion of building in Engenho Novo a replica of the house I had been brought up in on the old Rua de Matacavalos,* and giving it the same aspect and layout as the other one, which has now disappeared. Builder and decorator understood my instructions perfectly: it is the same two-storey building, three windows at the front, a verandah at the back, the same bedrooms and living rooms. In the main room, the paintings on the ceiling and walls are more or less the same, with garlands of small flowers and large birds, at intervals, carrying them in their beaks. In the four corners of the ceiling, the figures of the seasons, and at the center of the walls, medallions of Caesar, Augustus, Nero and Massinissa,† with their names underneath ... Why these four characters I do not understand. When we moved into the Matacavalos house, it was already decorated in this way: it had been done in the previous decade. It must have been the taste of the time to put a classical flavor and ancient figures into paintings done in America. The rest is also analogous to this and similar to it. I have a small garden, flowers, vegetables, a casuarina tree,†† a well and a washing-stone. I use old china and old furniture. Finally, there is, now as in the old days, the same contrast between life inside the house, which is placid, and the noisy world outside.

Clearly my aim was to tie the two ends of life together, and bring back youth in old age. Well sir, I managed neither to reconstruct what was there, nor what I had been. Everywhere, though the surface may be the same, the character is different. If it was only others that were missing, all well and good: one gets over the loss of other people as best one can; but I myself am missing, and that lacuna is all-important. What is here, if I can put it this way, is like dye that you put on your beard and hair, and which only preserves the external habit, as they say in autopsies; the internal

---

* Now the Rua do Riachuelo in the center of Rio de Janeiro, it was then on the outskirts of the center, separate from the main commercial area.

† Massinissa: King of Numidia (c. 240–c. 149 BC). He collaborated with the Romans, and is most remembered for marrying Sophonisba, the wife of his enemy Siphax. When the Romans insisted she appear at the triumph to celebrate victory over her ex-husband, Massinissa sent her a cup of poison to drink, to spare her the humiliation.

†† A tree of Australian and Indian origin, similar to a long-needled pine in appearance.

parts will not take dye. A certificate saying I was twenty years old might fool others, like any false document, but not me. The friends I have left are all of recent date; all the older ones have gone to study geology in God's acre. As for female friends, I've known some for fifteen years, others for less, and they almost all believe in their own youth. Two or three might persuade others, but the language they use forces me to consult dictionaries, a tiresome occupation.

All the same, though life may have changed, that's not to say it's worse; just different, that's all. In certain respects, life in the old days now seems stripped of the charms I once thought it had; but it is also true that it has lost many of the thorns that made it painful, and I still have a few sweet, enchanting memories. Truth to tell, I go out little and seldom converse much when I do. I have few amusements. Most of the time is taken up with looking after the orchard and the garden, and reading. I eat well and don't sleep badly.

But everything palls in the long run, and this monotony ended up wearying me, too. I wanted a little variety, and had the idea of writing a book. Jurisprudence, philosophy and politics occurred to me; but I didn't have the necessary energy for such projects. Then I thought I might write a *History of the Suburbs*, less dry than the memoir Father Luís Gonçalves dos Santos wrote about the city of Rio itself;* a modest undertaking, but it required documents and dates as preliminaries, all of which would be boring and time-consuming. Then it was that the busts painted on the walls started to talk to me, and to tell me that, since they couldn't bring back times past, I should take a pen and recount some of them. Perhaps the narration would beguile me, and the old shades would pass lightly over me, as they passed over the poet—not the one on the train, but the author of *Faust*: *"Ah, come ye back once more, ye restless shades?"†*

---

* A reference to the *Memórias Para Servir à História do Reino do Brasil* (Memoirs to Contribute to the History of the Kingdom of Brazil), which recounts in great detail events in the country during the period when King John VI of Portugal had his court in Rio de Janeiro (1809–1821).

† The first line of Goethe's *Faust*, Part I.

This idea delighted me so much, that the pen is trembling in my hand even now. Yes, Nero, Augustus, Massinissa, and you, great Caesar, urging me on to write my own Commentaries, I'm grateful for the advice, and I'm going to put down on paper the reminiscences that come into my head. In this way, I will relive what I lived then, and strengthen my hand for some weightier work. To work then: let us begin by evoking a celebrated November afternoon that I have never forgotten. There were many others, better and worse, but that one has never been erased from my mind. Read on and you will understand what I mean.

I I I

The Accusation

I was about to enter the drawing room, when I heard my name spoken, and hid behind the door. This was in the Matacavalos house, in the month of November: the year is a trifle remote, but I have no intention of changing the dates of my life just to suit people who don't like old stories—it was in 1857.

"Dona Glória, madam, are you still set on the idea of sending our Bentinho to the seminary? It's past time he went, and there may be a difficulty in the way."

"What difficulty?"

"A great difficulty."

My mother wanted to know what it was. José Dias, after a few moments' careful thought, came to see if there was anyone in the corridor; he didn't notice me, went back and, subduing his voice, said that the difficulty lay in the house next door, the Páduas.

"The Páduas?"

"I've been going to tell you this for some time, but I didn't dare."

It doesn't seem right to me that our Bentinho should be hiding away in corners with *Turtleback*'s daughter: that's the difficulty, because if the two of them start flirting in earnest, you'll have a struggle to separate them."

"I don't think so. Hiding away in corners?"

"In a manner of speaking. Always whispering to one another, always together. Bentinho is never out of their house. The girl is a scatter-brain; the father pretends he doesn't see; wouldn't he be pleased if things went his way . . . I can understand your gesture; you don't believe people are so scheming, you think everyone is open and honest . . ."

"But, Senhor José Dias, I've seen the two children playing together, and I've never seen anything suspicious. Look at their ages: Bento's hardly fifteen. Capitu was fourteen last week; they're two children. Don't forget, they've been brought up together, after that great flood, ten years ago, when the Páduas lost so much; that's how we came to know one another. And now you expect me to believe. . . ? What do you think, brother Cosme?"

Uncle Cosme replied with a "Hmmph," which, translated into the vernacular, meant: "This is all in José Dias' imagination; the youngsters are having fun, I'm having fun. Where's the backgammon?"

"Yes, I think you are mistaken."

"It may be, madam. It is to be hoped you are right; but believe me that I only spoke after a great deal of careful thought . . ."

"In any case, time's getting on," interrupted my mother; "I'll go about putting him into the seminary straight away."

"Well, so long as the idea of making him a priest hasn't been abandoned, that's the main thing. Bentinho must do as his mother wishes. And in any event, the Brazilian church has a glorious destiny. Let us not forget that a bishop presided over the Constituent Assembly, and that Father Feijó governed the Empire . . ."*

---

* The first Constituent Assembly of Brazil after Independence in 1822 was held in 1823, and presided over by the Bishop of Rio de Janeiro, Dom José Caetano da Silva Coutinho. Father Diogo Antônio Feijó (1784–1843) was Regent of Brazil during the minority of the Emperor Pedro II.

"Governed with his ugly mug!" interrupted Uncle Cosme, giving rein to old political rancor.

"I'm sure I beg your pardon, Dr. Cosme: I'm not defending anyone, just stating facts. What I mean is that the clergy still have an important role to play in Brazil."

"What you want is a sound drubbing: go on, go and get the backgammon. As for the lad, if he's got to be a priest, it really would be a good idea if he didn't start saying mass behind doors. But look here, sister Glória, is it really necessary to make a priest of him?"

"It's a promise, it must be kept."

"I know you made a promise . . . but a promise like that . . . I don't know . . . When you think about it . . . What do you think, cousin Justina?"

"Me?"

"Well, I suppose everybody knows what's best for himself," went on Uncle Cosme, "Only God knows what's best for everyone. Still, a promise made so many years ago . . . What's this, sister Glória? Crying? Come now! Is this something to cry about?"

My mother blew her nose without answering. I think cousin Justina got up and went over to her. Then there was a profound silence, during which I was on tenterhooks to go into the room, but another stronger urge, another emotion . . . I couldn't hear the words that Uncle Cosme began to say. Cousin Justina tried to cheer her: "Cousin Glória, cousin Glória!" José Dias kept apologizing: "If I'd known, I wouldn't have spoken, but I did so out of veneration, out of esteem, out of affection, to fulfil a harsh duty, the harshest of duties. . . ."

I V

The Harshest of Duties!

José Dias loved superlatives. It was a way of giving an impressive aspect to his ideas; or, if these latter were lacking, they made the sentence longer. He got up to fetch the backgammon, which was in the back of the house. I flattened myself against the wall, and watched him go by with his starched white trousers, trouserstraps,* jacket, and cravat. He was one of the last people to use trouserstraps in Rio de Janeiro—perhaps in the whole world. He wore his trousers short so that they would be stretched very tightly. The black satin cravat, with a steel ring inside, immobilized his neck: it was the fashion at the time. His jacket, which was made of cheap cotton, lightweight and for indoor use, on him looked like a formal frock coat. He was thin, emaciated, and beginning to go bald; he must have been about fifty-five. He got up with his usual slow step: not the lethargic gait of a lazy man, but a logical, calculated slowness, a complete syllogism, the premise before the consequence, the consequence before the conclusion. The harshest of duties!

---

* Called *"presilhas,"* these were pieces of cloth that passed under the arch of the foot and thus stretched the trousers.

V

The Dependent

He didn't always proceed at that slow, stiff pace. He could also move in a flurry of gestures, agile and quick-moving, and he was as natural in one mode as in the other. Also, he laughed aloud, whenever necessary: it was a forced but somehow infectious laugh, in which his cheeks, teeth, eyes, his whole face, his whole person, the whole world seemed to laugh with him. At serious moments, he was extremely serious.

He had lived with us as a dependent for many years; my father was still at the old plantation at Itaguaí,* and I had just been born. One day he turned up there offering his services as a homeopathic doctor; he carried a *Manual* and a portable dispensary.† There were fever epidemics around: José Dias cured the overseer and a female slave, and would not accept any payment. So my father suggested he should stay and live there with us, with a small stipend. José Dias refused, saying that it was his duty to bring health to the poor man's hovel.

"Who's preventing you going elsewhere? Go where you like, but come and live with us."

"I'll come back in three months."

He came back in two weeks, accepted food and lodging with no other stipend, other than what they might be pleased to give him on festival days. When my father was elected deputy and came to Rio de Janeiro with the family, he came too, and had his room outside in the grounds. One day, when the fevers came back to Itaguaí, my father told him to go and attend to our slaves. José

---

* A town about forty miles west of Rio de Janeiro, on the low-lying land near the ocean. Bento's father would have been a sugar planter.

† Hahnemann's theories of homeopathic medicine appeared in Brazil in 1842, and it is probable that the *Manual* is the *Manuel de Médicine Homéopathique* by Gerhard Jahr, translated into Portuguese in 1846.

Dias at first said nothing; finally, with a sigh, he confessed that he was not a doctor. He had taken the title to help spread the new doctrine, and he hadn't done it without a great deal of hard study; but his conscience didn't allow him to take on any more patients.

"But you cured them the last time."

"I believe so; it would be better however to say that I followed the remedies prescribed in the books. There, there lies the real truth, in the sight of God. I was a charlatan ... No, don't deny it; my motives may have been worthy—they were. Homeopathy is the truth, and I lied in the service of truth. But it's time to set the record straight."

He was not dismissed, as he requested at the time: my father could no longer do without him. He had the gift of making himself amenable and indispensable; when we wasn't there, it was almost as if a member of the family were missing. When my father died, he was terribly distressed, so they told me: I don't myself remember. My mother was very grateful to him, and didn't allow him to leave his room in the garden. After the seventh-day mass, he went to take his leave of her.

"Stay with us, José Dias."

"Madam, I obey."

He had a small legacy in the will, a gilt-edged bond and a few words of praise. He copied these words out, framed them and hung them up in his room, above his bed. "This is the best bond," he would often say. As time went on, he acquired a certain authority in the family: or at least, people would listen to what he had to say; he didn't overdo it, and knew how to give his opinion submissively. When all's said and done, he was a friend: I won't say the best of friends, but then nothing's perfect in this world. And don't think he was naturally subservient; his respectful politeness was more the product of calculation than of his true character. His clothes lasted a long time; unlike people who soon wear out a new suit, he had his old ones brushed and smoothed, meticulously mended, buttoned, with the modest elegance of the poor. He was well-read, though in a disorganized fashion: enough to amuse us over dessert, or in the evenings, or to explain some strange phenomenon, talk of the effects of heat and cold, the poles and Robespierre. Often he would recount a journey he had made to Europe, and would confess that if it hadn't been for us, he would have gone back; he had friends in Lisbon, but our family, he said, under God, was everything to him.

"Under God or above Him?" Uncle Cosme asked him one day.

"Under Him," echoed José Dias, full of reverence.

And my mother, who was religious, was pleased to see that he put God in His proper place, and smiled her approval. José Dias nodded his head in thanks. My mother gave him small amounts of money from time to time. Uncle Cosme, who was a lawyer, entrusted him with the copying of legal documents.

VI

Uncle Cosme

Uncle Cosme had lived with my mother since she had been widowed. He was already widowed then, as was cousin Justina; it was the house of the three widows.

Fortune often plays strange tricks with nature. Brought up for a serene life living off capital, Uncle Cosme did not make money as a lawyer; he spent more than he earned. He had his office in the old Rua das Violas, near the law courts, which were in the Aljube, the old prison building. Uncle Cosme worked in criminal law. José Dias never missed a single one of his speeches for the defense. He would help Uncle Cosme on and off with his gown, complimenting him effusively at the end. At home, he would recount the arguments. Uncle Cosme, despite a pretense of modesty, gave a contented smile.

He was fat and heavy, short of breath and with sleepy eyes. One of my oldest memories is of seeing him every morning mounting the animal given him by my mother, and which took him to the office every morning. The slave who had gone to get it from the stable held the reins while he lifted his foot and placed it in the stirrup; after he had done this, there followed a moment for rest or reflection. Then, he gave the first shove—his body struggled to get up, but didn't manage it; a second shove produced the same effect. Finally, after a long interval, Uncle Cosme gathered all his physical and moral strength together, propelled himself one last time off the ground, and successfully landed in the saddle. Rarely did the animal fail to show by some gesture that it had received the world on its back. Uncle Cosme adjusted his ample form, and the mule went off at a trot.

Nor have I ever forgotten what he did to me one afternoon. Although I was born in the country (which I left when I was two) and in spite of the customs of the time, I didn't know how to ride, and was afraid of horses. Uncle Cosme lifted me up and sat me astride the mule. When I found myself so high up (I was nine), alone and unprotected, with the ground way below, I began to scream desperately: "Mamma!, Mamma!" She hurried to the scene, pale and trembling, thinking someone was killing me. She lifted me down and comforted me, while her brother asked:

"Sister Glória, how can a grown lad like him be afraid of a tame mule?"

"He's not used to it."

"Then he should get used to it. Even if he's to be a priest, if he has a country parish, he'll have to ride a horse; and, here in the city, until he's a priest, if he wants to cut a figure like the other lads, and doesn't know how to ride, he'll have good cause to complain of you, sister Glória."

"Let him, if he wants to; I'm afraid."

"Afraid! How absurd!"

The truth is that I only learned horsemanship later, less for the pleasure of it than because I was ashamed to say that I didn't know how to ride. "Now he'll really be chasing the girls," they said when I began the lessons. The same could not be said of Uncle Cosme. With him, it had been an old habit, and a necessity. Now, he was done with flirting. They say that when he was younger he was very popular with the ladies, and was a fervent political enthusiast; but the years had removed the greater part of his political and sexual ardor, and corpulence had dealt a final blow to his ambitions, both in the public arena and in more intimate spheres. Now, he only carried out his duties, without his old enthusiasm. In his leisure hours he would sit staring, or playing cards. From time to time he would tell jokes.

VII

Dona Glória

My mother was a good soul. When her husband, Pedro de Albuquerque Santiago, died, she was thirty-one, and she could have gone back to Itaguaí. She didn't want to; rather, she chose to live close to the church where my father had been buried. She sold the old plantation and the slaves, bought some more that she sent out to work or hired out, bought a dozen buildings and a quantity of government bonds, and settled down in the Matacavalos house, where she had lived for the last two years of her married life. She was the daughter of a lady from Minas Gerais, herself a descendent of a lady from São Paulo, of the Fernandes family.

So then, in the year of grace 1857, Dona Maria da Glória Fernandes Santiago was forty-two years old. She was still pretty and didn't look her age, but however much nature tried to preserve her from the ravages of time, she obstinately hid the remnants of her youthful looks. She wore an eternal dark dress, without ornaments, with a black shawl, folded in a triangle and fastened at the breast with a cameo. Her hair, which was plaited, was gathered at the nape of the neck by an old tortoiseshell comb; sometimes she wore a white frilled bonnet. She spent the whole day like this, from morning till night, in her flat leather shoes with their muffled sound, supervising all the household activities.

I have her portrait there on the wall, next to her husband's, just as they were in the other house. The paint has darkened with time, but it still gives a good idea of both. I don't remember anything about him, except vaguely that he was tall and wore his hair long; the portrait shows a round pair of eyes, which follow me everywhere, an effect of the painting that frightened me as a child. His neck emerges from a voluminous black necktie, and his face is clean shaven, except for a small patch just next to the ears. My mother's picture shows she was lovely. She was twenty, and she held a flower in her fingers. On the canvas, she seems to be offering the flower to her husband. What you can read on each of their faces is that, if conjugal bliss can be compared to winning the lottery, they've won it with a ticket they bought together.

My conclusion is that lotteries ought not to be abolished. No winner has ever yet accused them of immorality, as no one has ever called Pandora's box evil, since hope was left inside; it has to be left somewhere. Here I have them, then, the happily married couple of olden days, the contented lovers, the lucky ones, who have gone from this life to a better one, no doubt to continue the dream. When I grow weary of the lottery and Pandora, I lift my eyes to them, and forget unsuccessful tickets and the fateful box. The portraits are as good as the originals. My mother's, holding out the flower to her husband, seems to say: "I'm all yours, my handsome gentleman!" My father, looking at us, makes this comment: "See how the girl loves me. . . ." I don't know if they suffered from illnesses, just as I don't know if they had disappointments: I was a child, and at first I hadn't been born. After his death, I remember she wept a great deal. But here are the portraits of both, and the grime accumulated over time has not destroyed their original expressions. They are like snapshots of happiness.

VIII

It's Time

But it's time to return to that November afternoon, a clear, fresh afternoon, quiet as our house and the part of the street where we lived. Really, that was when my life began; everything that had happened before was like the putting-on of make-up and costumes by those who are about to go on stage, the lighting, the tuning of the fiddles, starting up the orchestra . . . Now I was about to begin my opera. "Life is an opera," as an old Italian tenor who lived and died here used to say to me . . . And he explained the definition to me one day, so convincingly that I ended up believing him. It might be worthwhile giving it here; it will only take a chapter.

IX

The Opera

His voice had gone, but he insisted that it had not. "I'm out of practice, that's the trouble," he would add. Whenever a new company arrived from Europe, he went to the impresario and revealed all the injustices under the sun; whereupon the impresario perpetrated another, and out he came railing against such iniquity. He still sported the moustaches of his stage roles. His gait, even though he was old, made it look as if he was paying court to a Babylonian princess. Sometimes, he hummed, without opening his mouth, a passage as old as himself or older: if you sing that way, you can still delude yourself you have a voice. He used to come here to dine with me sometimes. One night, after a lot of Chianti, he repeated the usual definition, and when I said to him that life might just as well be a sea voyage or a battle as an opera, he shook his head and replied:

"Life is an opera, and grand opera at that. The tenor and the baritone contend for the soprano, in the presence of the bass and the supporting cast, unless it's the soprano and the contralto contending for the tenor, in the presence of the same bass and the same supporting cast. There are numerous choruses and ballets, the orchestration is excellent. . . ."

"But, my dear Marcolini . . ."

"What . . . ?"

And, after taking a sip of liqueur, he set his glass down, and expounded the history of creation for me: here is a resumé of what he said.

God is the poet. The music is by Satan, a young and very promising composer, who was trained in the heavenly conservatory. A rival of Michael, Raphael and Gabriel, he resented the preference they enjoyed in the distribution of the prizes. It could also be that the over-sweet and mystical style of these other pupils was abhorrent to his essentially tragic genius. He plotted a rebellion which was discovered in time, and he was expelled from the conservatory. And that would have been that, if God had not written an opera libretto, which he had given up, being of the opinion that this type of recreation was inappropriate to His eternity. Satan took the manuscript with him to hell. With the aim of showing that he was better than the others—and perhaps of seeking a reconciliation with heaven—he composed the score, and as soon as he had finished it took it to the Heavenly Father.

"Lord, I have not forgotten the lessons I have learned," he said. "Here is the score, listen to it, have it played, and if you think it worthy of the heavenly heights, admit me with it to sit at your feet . . ."

"No," replied the Lord, "I don't want to hear a thing."

"But, Lord . . ."

"Not a thing, not a thing!"

Satan went on pleading, with no greater success, until God, tired and full of mercy, gave His consent for the opera to be performed, but outside heaven. He created a special theater, this planet, and invented a whole company, with all the principal and minor roles, the choruses and the dancers.

"Come and listen to some of the rehearsals!"

"No, I don't want to know about it. I've done enough, composing the libretto; I'll consent to sharing the royalties with you."

This refusal was perhaps unfortunate; the result was some awkward passages which a previous run-through and friendly collaboration might have avoided. And indeed, there are places where the words go one way, and the music another. There are people who maintain that that is precisely where the beauty of the composition lies, in its avoidance of monotony: such is the explanation of the Eden trio, Abel's aria, and the choruses of the guillotine and slavery. Not infrequently, the same situations occur more than once, without sufficient justification. Certain motifs, indeed, weary the listener by overmuch repetition. Also, there are passages that are obscure; the composer uses the massed choruses too much, causing confusion and concealing the true meaning. The orchestral parts, however, are treated with great skill. Such is the opinion of impartial observers.

The composer's friends assert that such a perfect work is not easily to be found. Some admit to a few blemishes and the odd thing missing, but it is probable that, as the opera proceeds, these latter will be filled in or explained, and the blemishes will disappear altogether: the composer has not discarded the idea of amending the work wherever he finds that it does not correspond completely to the poet's sublime conception. But the poet's friends do not agree. They maintain that the libretto has been sacrificed, that the music has distorted the meaning of the words, and though it may be beautiful in parts, and skilfully put together in others, it is completely different from the drama, even at variance with it. The element of the grotesque, for example, is not to be found in the poet's text: it is an excrescence, put there to imitate *The Merry Wives of Windsor*. This point is contested by the satanists, with every appearance of reason. They say that, at the time when the young Satan composed his opera, neither Shakespeare nor his farce had been born. They go as far as to affirm that the English poet's only genius was to transcribe the words of the opera, with such skill and so faithfully that he seems to be the author of the composition; but of course he is a plagiarist.

"This work," the old tenor concluded, "will last as long as the theater does, it being impossible to calculate when it will be destroyed as a matter of astronomic convenience. Its success is growing by the day. The poet and the composer get their royalties on time, though they are different, to accord with the words of the Scripture: 'Many are called, but few are chosen.' God is paid in gold, Satan in paper money."

"It's amusing . . ."

"Amusing?" he shouted furiously, but then he calmed down, and replied: "My dear Santiago, I am not amusing: I detest amusement. What I'm saying is the pure and absolute truth. One day, when all the books have become useless and been burnt, there will be someone, maybe a tenor—perhaps Italian—to teach this truth to mankind. Everything is music, my friend. In the beginning was *do*, then from *do* came *re*, etc. This glass—as he filled it once more—this glass is a tiny refrain. You can't hear it? Neither do you hear sticks or stones, but they all have their part in the opera . . ."

X

I Accept the Theory

No doubt this is a lot of metaphysics for a single tenor; but his loss of voice explains everything, and, in sum, there are philosophers who are nothing better than out-of-work tenors.

I, dearest reader, accept old Marcolini's theory, not only because it appears to be the truth—and appearance is often the whole of the truth—but because my life exactly fits the definition. I sang a very tender duet, then a trio, then a quartet ... But let's not get ahead of ourselves; let us proceed to that first afternoon, when I found out that I was already singing, because José Dias' revelation, dear reader, was principally directed at myself. He revealed me to myself.

X I

The Promise

As soon as I saw our dependent disappear down the corridor, I left my hiding place, and ran to the verandah at the back of the house. It was not the tears nor what made my mother shed them that concerned me. They were probably brought on by her ecclesiastical projects; I should explain them, for even then it was an old story—sixteen years old.

The projects dated from the time I was conceived. My mother's first child, a boy, had been born dead, and so she begged God that the second should live, and promised that, if it were male, she would destine him for the Church. Maybe she was hoping for a girl. She said nothing to my father, neither before nor after I was born; she intended to do it when I first went to school, but she was widowed before then. When she became a widow, she was terrified of being separated from me; but so devout was she, so God fearing, that she sought out witnesses to this obligation, and confided her promise to relatives and members of the family. Only, so that we should not be separated any sooner than necessary, she had me taught my first letters, Latin and doctrine, at home, with Father Cabral, an old friend of Uncle Cosme's who came round in the evening to play backgammon.

It is easy to promise things in the long term: the imagination stretches time out to infinity. My mother waited for the years to go by until the moment came. In the meantime, she tried to develop in me a liking for the idea of the Church; children's toys, books of devotion, images of saints, conversations at home, everything gravitated towards the altar. When we went to mass, she always told me that it was to learn to be a priest, that I should notice the priest, that I should keep my eyes on the priest. At home, I played at mass—somewhat in secret, because my mother said that mass was not a game. We set up an altar, Capitu and I. She acted the sacristan, and we changed the ritual so as to divide the host between us: the host was always a sweet. When we used to play in this way, it was very common to hear my neighbor say: "Is there mass today?" I knew what this meant, replied in the affirmative, and went to ask for the host by another name. I came back with it, we set up the altar, mumbled the Latin and hurried through the ceremonies. *Dominus, non sum dignus* . . . These words, which I should have said three times, I think I only said once, such was the greed of the priest and the sacristan. We drank neither wine nor water: the first because we had none, and the second so as not to spoil the taste of the sacrifice.

Lately, no one had mentioned the seminary, so that I thought the project had been dropped. At the age of fifteen, with no vocation, it would seem that the seminary of the world is what is required, not that of São José. My mother would often sit gazing at me, like a lost soul, or would take my hand in hers for no particular reason, just to squeeze it.

X I I

On the Verandah

I stopped on the verandah; I felt dizzy, stunned, my legs were trembling, and my heart seemed on the point of coming out of my mouth. I did not dare go down into our orchard, and through to the yard next door. I began to walk back and forth, stopping to lean against the wall, starting again and stopping. Confused voices kept repeating what José Dias had said:

"Always together . . ."

"Whispering . . ."

"If they start to flirt in earnest . . ."

Brick paving that I paced back and forth over that afternoon, yellowed columns that passed by to right and left as I came and went, you were imprinted with the better part of that crisis, the sensation of a new joy, which wrapped me up in myself, then dissolved, made me shudder, and poured out some unknown inner balsam. Sometimes I became aware of myself smiling, with a look of satisfied laughter about me which belied the abomination of my sin. And the jumbled voices went on repeating:

"Whispering . . ."

"Always together . . ."

"If they start to flirt in earnest . . ."

A palm tree, seeing me troubled and divining the cause, murmured in its branches that there was nothing wrong with fifteen-year-old boys getting into corners with girls of fourteen; quite the contrary, youths of that age had no other function, and corners were made for that very purpose. It was an old palm tree, and I believed in old palm trees even more than in old books. Birds, butterflies, a cricket trying out its summer song, all the living things of the air were of the same opinion.

So I loved Capitu, and she me? It was true that I did hang around her a great deal, but I could not think of anything between us that was really secret. Before she went to school, it was all just childish mischief; after she left school, it is true that we did not immediately return to the old intimacy, but little by little it came back, and in the last year had been complete again. Nevertheless, the subject of our conversations remained the same. Capitu at times called me handsome, a fine fellow, a real angel; at others, she took my hands to count my fingers. I began to remember these and other gestures and words, the pleasure I felt when she ran her hand through my hair, saying she thought it was very beautiful. Though I did not do the same thing to her, I said that hers was much more beautiful than mine. Then Capitu shook her head with a disappointed, melancholy look, the more astonishing in that she had really wonderful hair; I retorted by saying she was crazy. When she asked if I had dreamed of her the previous night, and I said no, she would tell me that she had dreamed of me. There were extraordinary adventures, in which we flew up to the Corcovado,* danced in the moonbeams, or the angels came to ask us our names, so that they could give them to other angels that had just been born. In all these dreams we were always together. The ones I had of her were not like this: they only reproduced incidents of our daily life together, and often they were no more than a simple repetition of the day, a phrase here, a gesture there. I also recounted mine. One day Capitu pointed out the difference, saying that hers were prettier than mine; I, after some hesitation, told her they were like the dreamer . . . She blushed bright red.

Well, quite frankly, only now did I understand the emotion that these confessions, and others like them, stirred in me. It was a novel emotion, and a delightful one, but its origin was a mystery to me—one I didn't even suspect the existence of. Her more recent silences, which had meant nothing to me, I now felt to be signs of something: the same was true of her half-spoken words, curious questions, vague replies, her thoughtful moments, the pleasure she took in remembering our childhood. I also noticed that it was a recent phenomenon for me to wake up thinking

* The high mountain to the south of the center of Rio de Janeiro, on which the famous statue of Christ the Redeemer now stands.

about Capitu, to remember her words, and tremble when I heard her steps. If they talked about her at home, I paid more attention than before, and depending on whether it was praise or criticism, the pleasure and pain this brought me were more intense than before, when we were only two mischievous children. I even thought of her during mass that month: not all the time, it is true, but at times I thought of her exclusively.

All of this had now been revealed to me by the mouth of José Dias, who had denounced me to myself, and whom I forgave everything, the evil he had spoken, the evil he had done, and anything that might come of these things. At that moment, eternal Truth itself, eternal Goodness, and all the other eternal Virtues were worth less to me than he was. I loved Capitu! Capitu loved me! And my legs strode back and forth, stopped still, tremulous, certain that they bestrode the whole world. That first throbbing of the sap, that revelation of consciousness to itself, is something I have never forgotten, nor have I ever had a comparable sensation. Naturally because it was mine. Naturally, too, because it was the first.

X I I I

Capitu

Suddenly, I heard a voice shout from inside the house next door:

"Capitu!"

And from the yard:

"Yes, Mamma!"

Again from the house:

"Come here!"

I couldn't stop myself. My legs took me down the three steps into the garden, and led me towards the neighboring yard. It was a habit they had in the afternoons, and in the mornings, too. For legs have personalities too, only inferior to the arms, and they can do things of their own accord when they are not directed by ideas from the head. Mine got almost as far as the wall. There was a connecting door there which my mother had had put in when Capitu and I were small. This door had no lock or latch; it was opened by pushing on one side or pulling on the other, and shut itself by the weight of a stone hanging on a rope. It was almost exclusively for our use. When we were children, we went visiting, knocking on one side, and being received on the other with many bows and curtsies. When Capitu's dolls fell ill, I was the doctor. I went into her garden with a stick under my arm, in imitation of Dr. João da Costa's walking stick: I took the patient's pulse, and asked her to show her tongue. "She's deaf, poor thing!" Capitu would exclaim. Then I stroked my chin, like the doctor, and finally prescribed leeches, or an emetic: this was the doctor's usual therapy.

"Capitu!"

"Yes, Mamma!"

"Stop making holes in the wall; come here."

Her mother's voice was nearer now, as if it came from the back door. I wanted to go through to their yard, but my legs, which had been so keen to move, now seemed stuck to the ground. Finally I made an effort, pushed the door and went in. Capitu was facing the opposite wall, and scratching on it with a nail. The noise of the door made her look round; when she saw me, she put her back to the wall, as if she wanted to hide something. I went towards her; I suppose I must have looked different, for she came over to me, and asked in a worried voice:

"What's the matter with you?"

"Me? Nothing's the matter."

"Yes there is; something's bothering you."

I wanted to insist that there was nothing wrong, but I couldn't say it. I was all eyes and heart, a heart which this time felt as if it really was coming out of my mouth. I couldn't keep my eyes off this fourteen-year-old girl, tall, strong and well built, in a tight fitting, somewhat faded cotton frock. Her thick hair hung down her back in two plaits tied together at the ends, as was the fashion at the time. She was of a dark complexion, with large, pale eyes, and a long, straight nose, a delicate mouth and a broad chin. Her hands, although used to hard household work, were well cared for; they were not scented with fine soaps or toilet water, but she kept them spotless with water from the well and ordinary soap. She wore strong cloth shoes, flat and old, which she herself kept mended.

"What's the matter with you?" she repeated.

"It's nothing," I finally stammered out.

Then I corrected myself.

"It's some news."

"News of what?"

I thought of telling her that I was going to enter the seminary, and see what impression it had on her. If it dismayed her, then she really cared for me; if not, then she didn't. But this was a brief, vague notion; I felt unable to speak clearly, somehow I couldn't see properly . . .

"Well?"

"You know . . ."

With that, I looked at the wall, at the place where she had been scratching, writing, or making holes as her mother had put it. I saw some marks there, and remembered the movement she had made to cover them up. I wanted to see them close to, and made a step in that direction. Capitu grabbed me, but, either because she feared I might get away from her, or to stop me by other means, she ran over and rubbed out what she had written. All this did was arouse my desire to read what was there.

XIV

The Inscription

Everything I recounted at the end of the last chapter happened in a moment. What happened next was even faster. I made a quick movement, and before she could rub them out, I read these two names, inscribed with the nail, and set out thus:

BENTO
CAPITOLINA

I turned to face her; Capitu had her eyes on the ground. She soon lifted them, slowly, and we stood there looking at one another . . . Childhood confession, I could give two or three pages over to you, but I must be economical. The truth is, we said nothing; the wall said it all for us. We did not move, but our hands stretched out little by little, all four of them, taking hold of each other, clasping each other, melting into one another. I didn't take down the exact time of the gesture. I should have done so; I regret not having a note written that same night, which I could reproduce here with all its spelling mistakes: though it would have none, such was the difference between the scholar and the adolescent. I knew all the rules of orthography, but had no suspicion of the rules of love; I had gone through orgies of Latin and was a virgin with women.

We did not unclasp our hands, nor did they drop of their own accord, out of weariness or inattention. Our eyes stared into one another, then looked away, strayed for a while, then came back to each other again . . . A future priest, I faced her as before an altar: one of her cheeks was the Epistle and the other the Gospel. Her mouth might have been the chalice, her lips the paten. All I needed to do was to say a new mass, according to a Latin that no one learns at school, and is the catholic language of mankind. Don't think me sacrilegious, devout lady reader; the purity of the intention cleanses anything unorthodox in the style. We stood there with heaven within us. Our hands, their nerve ends touching, made two creatures one: a single, seraphic being. Our eyes went on saying infinite things, and the words did not even try to pass our lips: they went back to the heart as silently as they had come. . .

XV

Another Sudden Voice

There came another sudden voice, this time a man's:
  "Are you playing at staring each other out?"
It was Capitu's father, who was at the back door, beside his wife. We quickly let go our hands, and stood there flustered. Capitu went to the wall, and furtively scratched out our names with the nail.
  "Capitu!"
  "Papa!"
  "You'll ruin the plaster."
Capitu was scratching over again, to be sure to efface what she had written completely. Pádua came out into the yard to see what it was, but his daughter had already begun something else, a profile, which she said was a portrait of him, and could equally well have been her mother's; it made him laugh, which was all that mattered. In any case, he was not angry, in fact quite affable, in spite of the suspect, or more than suspect attitude he had caught us in. He was a small, stocky man, with short arms and legs, and a rounded back, which is where the "Turtleback" nickname that José Dias had given him came from. No one else in the house called him that: only the dependent.

"Were you playing at staring one another out?" he asked.

I looked at a nearby elder tree; Capitu answered for both of us:

"Yes, that's what were doing, but Bento laughs in no time, he can't keep a straight face."

"He wasn't laughing when I came to the door."

"He'd laughed before; he can't help it. Do you want to see?"

With a serious face she stared at me, to make me join the game. A fright, however, makes one serious: I was still under the effect of the shock brought on by Pádua's entry on the scene, and I was incapable of laughing, however much I should have done so to corroborate Capitu. Tired of waiting, she turned her face away, saying that I couldn't laugh that time because he was there. Even then I didn't laugh. There are things which can only be learned late in life; to do them early on you have to be born with the talent. Even then, it is better to learn naturally early on, rather than late and artificially. Capitu, after two attempts, went to her mother, who was still at the back door, leaving me and her father full of admiration; looking at her and at me, he said, tenderly:

"Who would think she was only fourteen? She seems more like seventeen. Is Mamma well?" he went on turning round to face me.

"Yes."

"I haven't seen her for some days. I've been meaning to lick your uncle at cards, but I've not been able to: I've had to bring work home from the office; every night I'm there writing like a madman; a report I have to do. Have you seen my tanager? He's there at the back of the house. I was just going to get his cage; come and have a look."

There is no need for me to swear to it, for it to be believed that I had no desire to go. My desire was to go after Capitu, and tell her about the danger awaiting us, but her father was her father, and moreover he was particularly fond of birds. He had them of several species, colors, and sizes. The courtyard in the middle of the house was surrounded by cages with canaries in, and when they sang they made an infernal racket. He exchanged birds with other amateurs, bought some, and caught others in his own yard, setting traps for them. If they fell ill, he looked after them just as if they were human.

X V I

The Temporary Director

Pádua was an employee in a department of the Ministry of
War. He didn't earn much, but his wife spent little, and living
was cheap. Moreover, the house he lived in, of two storeys like
ours, though smaller, was his own property. He bought it when he
won the big prize with half a lottery ticket: ten contos.* Pádua's
first notion, when he won the prize, was to buy a thoroughbred
horse, a diamond necklace for his wife, a burial vault for the family, some birds from Europe, etc.; but his wife—this same Dona
Fortunata who is standing at the back door of the house, talking
to her daughter, and tall, strong, and well built like her, with the
same head and the same clear eyes—it was she who told him that
the best thing to do was to buy the house, and keep anything that
was left over to tide them through illnesses. Pádua hesitated a
good deal; in the end, he had to give way to advice from my
mother, to whom Dona Fortunata turned for help. Nor was that
the only occasion that my mother assisted them; one day, she even
saved Pádua's life. Listen; it's only a brief anecdote.

The director of the department where Pádua worked had to go
to the North of the country, on a special commission. Either
because of normal regulations, or by special appointment, Pádua
took the director's position, and with the appropriate honararia.
The change of fortune went to his head somewhat; it was before
the ten contos. He didn't stop at buying new clothes and improv-
ing the kitchen, he also spent money extravagantly, gave jewels to
his wife, killed a sucking pig on feast days, was seen at the theater,

* At that time (1857) ten contos would have been equivalent to $5,400 (£1100). One
thousand mil-réis made one conto. Based on the average sale price for male slaves
aged 20 to 25 in the coffee-rich town of Vassouras in the mid 1850s, ten contos would
have purchased seven slaves (at one conto, 400 mil-réis each), with something left
over.

even went as far as patent-leather shoes. And so he spent the twenty-two months supposing that the temporary directorship was eternal. One day he came to our house, distressed and half crazed; he was going to lose his position, for the permanent director had come back that morning. He asked my mother to look after his hapless wife and daughter; he could not bear the disgrace, and was going to kill himself. My mother spoke kindly to him, but he paid no attention.

"No, Madam, I cannot consent to such disgrace. To bring my family down in the world, to go back ... No, I'll kill myself! I can't admit this shame to my family. And the others? What will the neighbors say? And my friends? And public opinion?"

"What public opinion, Sr. Pádua? Stop this; be a man. Remember your wife has no one else ... what will she do? For a man to do such a thing ... Come, come, be a man."

Pádua dried his eyes and went home, where for some days he remained prostrate, silent, shut in the bedroom—or in the yard, next to the well, as if the idea of death wouldn't leave him. Dona Fortunata scolded him:

"Joãozinho, are you a child?"

But she heard him talk about death so much that she was frightened, and one day ran to ask my mother to do her the favor of seeing if she could save her husband from suicide. My mother went to the well where he was, and ordered him to live. What lunacy was this, thinking he was going to be disgraced, just because he was going to lose extra payments, and a temporary post? No, he should be a man, the father of a family, imitate his wife and daughter ... Pádua obeyed; he confessed that he would find the strength to comply with my mother's wishes.

"It's not my wishes that matter; it's your duty."

"Well, then, my duty; I know it's so."

On the next few days, he went in and out of the house, as if he were trying to hide, and with his eyes on the ground. He was not the same man who wore his hat out greeting the neighbors, smiling, looking straight ahead of him, even before the temporary directorship. As the weeks went by, the wound began to heal. Pádua began to take an interest in the home again, to look after his birds, to sleep well at night and during the siesta, to chat and retail local gossip. His serenity came back; and in its wake came happiness, in the form of two friends, who came round one Sunday to play a game of solo, with tokens instead of money. He laughed, he joked, he was his usual self; the wound had healed completely.

With time, an interesting phenomenon came about. Pádua began to talk about the temporary directorship, not only with no regrets for the lost honoraria, no shame at having lost the job, but even with a certain conceit and pride. The directorship became the hejira, from which he counted backwards and forwards.

"It was the time when I was director . . ."

Or:

"Oh, yes, I remember, it was before I became director, one or two months before . . . Wait a moment; my directorship began . . . That's it, it was a month and a half before, no more than that."

Or again:

"Exactly, I had been director for six months . . ."

Such is the posthumous taste of temporary glories. José Dias proclaimed that it was enduring vanity; but Father Cabral, who referred everything back to the Scriptures, said that neighbor Pádua's case could be summed up in the words of Eliphaz to Job: "Despise not thou the chastening of the Almighty: for He woundeth and His hands make whole."*

---

* Job 5: 17–18.

XVII

The Worms

"He woundeth and His hands make whole!" When I later found out that Achilles' lance also cured a wound it had inflicted, the fancy took me to write a dissertation on the topic. I went so far as to consult old books, dead books, buried books, opening them, comparing one with another, searching for the text and its meaning, to find the common origin of the pagan oracle and the Hebrew thought. I even consulted the worms in the books, to tell me what was in the texts they were chewing.

"Dear Sir," replied a long fat worm, "we know absolutely nothing about the texts we chew, neither do we decide what we chew, neither do we love or hate what we chew; we just chew."

I could get no more out of him. As if the word had been passed along, all the others told the same story. Perhaps this discreet silence about the texts they were chewing was another way of chewing what had already been chewed.

XVIII

A Plan

Neither her father nor mother came in to see us when Capitu and I talked about the seminary, in the drawing room. Looking right at me, Capitu wanted to know what the news was that was so upsetting me. When I told her what it was, she went as pale as wax.

"But I don't want to go," I added straight away, "I'm not going to any seminary; I don't want to, they can insist as much as they like, I'm not going."

Capitu at first said nothing. She withdrew her eyes, turned them inwards, and stayed that way, with her pupils vague and sightless, her mouth half open, stock still. Then, to back up what I had said, I began to swear that I would never be a priest. In those days I swore a great deal, each oath more extreme than the last, even by life and death. I swore by the hour of my death. Let the light be taken from me at the hour of my death if I went to the seminary. Capitu seemed neither to believe or disbelieve me: she seemed not even to hear me; it was as if she were made of wood. I wanted to speak to her, to shake her, but I hadn't the courage. This girl who had been my playmate, jumping around and dancing—I think she'd even slept in the same bed—now left me with my arms paralyzed and afraid. Finally, she came back from her trance, but her face was livid, and she broke out with these furious words:

"The sanctimonious so-and-so! Always at the altar rail. . .! Never away from mass!"

I was stunned. Capitu was so fond of my mother, and my mother of her, that I could not understand such a violent explosion. It is also true that she loved me, too, and naturally more, or better, or in another way, enough to explain her anger at the threat of a separation; but these offensive words—how could I understand her calling my mother such ugly things, the more so as she was defaming religious customs which she herself practised? For she also went to mass, and three or four times it was my mother who had taken her, in our old chaise. She had also given her a rosary, a gold cross and a Book of Hours ... I tried to defend her, but Capitu didn't let me, went on calling her sanctimonious and so on, in such a loud voice that I was afraid her parents would hear her. I have never seen her as angry as she was then; she seemed ready to tell everything to anyone who was listening. She clenched her teeth, shook her head ... Shocked, I didn't know what to do; I repeated my oaths, swore that I would return home that very night and tell them that nothing in the world would make me go to the seminary.

"You? You'll go."

"I'll not."

"You'll see if you go or not."

She went quiet again. When she spoke again, she had changed; she was not yet the Capitu I knew, but almost. She was thoughtful, calm, and spoke in a low voice. She wanted to know about the conversation at home; I recounted it all to her, except the part concerning her.

"And what's José Dias' interest in bringing this up?" she asked when I had finished.

"None, I think; it was just to create trouble. He's a mean person; but you wait, he'll pay me back. When I'm in charge here, you'll see, it'll be out in the street with him; I'll not have him my house a moment longer. Mamma's too good; she pays him too much attention: there were even tears . . ."

"Who cried? José Dias?"

"No, Mamma."

"What did she cry for?"

"I don't know. I only heard them telling her not to cry, that it was nothing to cry about . . . He even said he regretted what he'd said, and went out; that was when I left the corner and ran to the verandah, so as not to be seen. But you wait and see, he'll pay me for this!"

I said this clenching my fist, and uttered other threats. As I think back now, I don't think I was ridiculous; adolescence and childhood are not ridiculous when they do such things; it's one of their privileges. This fault or the danger of it begins in youth, grows with middle age and reaches its high point in old age. When one is fifteen, there is even a certain charm in threatening a great deal and carrying nothing out.

Capitu was reflecting. Reflection was not a rare occurrence with her, and you could tell it was happening by her eyes, which were shut tight. She asked me for a few more details, the actual words spoken by each person, and their tone. Since I did not want to tell her about the starting point of the conversation—that is, she herself—I could not give the whole meaning. Capitu concentrated particularly now on my mother's tears; she could not convince herself she understood them. In the middle of all this, she admitted that my mother certainly did not want to make me a priest out of malice; it was the old promise, which she, God fearing as she was, dared not break. I was so pleased to see that she made up for the insults that had sprung from her a short time before that I took her hand and squeezed it. Capitu let herself go, laughing; then the conversation began to nod off and finally went to sleep. We had gone over to the window; a black who for some time had been hawking coconut sweets, stopped in the street opposite and asked:

"Missy want coconut today?"

"No," said Capitu.

"Coconut good."

"Go away," she replied, but not harshly.

"Give some here!" said I, putting my hand down to take two.

I bought them, but I had to eat both of them on my own; Capitu refused hers. I noticed that, in the middle of the crisis, I still had time for sweets. It is not the moment to discuss whether this was a virtue or a defect; let's just note that my friend, though she was calm and lucid, wanted nothing to do with sweets, though she liked them very much. However, the refrain that the black went away singing, the refrain of afternoons long ago, so familiar in our neighborhood when we were children:

> Cry, little girl, cry,
> Got no money to buy . . .

—it seemed as if the refrain had annoyed her. It wasn't the tune; she knew it by heart, from a long way back, and used to repeat it in our childhood games, laughing, jumping, exchanging roles with me, first buying then selling a nonexistent sweet. I think that the words, intended to needle children's vanity, were what irritated her now, for soon after she said to me:

"If I were rich, you'd run away, get on a steamer and go to Europe."

As she said this, she was watching my eyes, but I think they must not have told her anything, or simply showed that I was grateful for her kind intentions: it's true that it was such a well-meaning thought that I could overlook the fantastic nature of the adventure.

As you see, Capitu, at the age of fourteen, already had some daring ideas, though much less daring than others she had later. But they were only daring in themselves: in practice they became clever, insinuating, stealthy, and reached the required end, not with a single bound, but with lots of little jumps. I don't know if I make myself plain. Imagine a grand conception carried out with small means. Thus, staying with the vague, hypothetical desire to send me to Europe: Capitu, if it were in her power, would not have me embark on the steamer and flee; she would stretch a line of canoes from here to there, by means of which I, seeming to go to the Laje fortress* on a floating bridge, would actually go to Bordeaux, leaving my mother waiting for me on the beach. This was the peculiar nature of my friend's character; so it is not surprising that, opposing my plans for open resistance, she went by milder means, persevering, with words, by slow, daily persuasion, and giving consideration first to the people we could count on. She rejected Uncle Cosme; he was all for an easy life, and even if he didn't approve of my being ordained he would not stir himself to prevent it. Cousin Justina was better than he, and better than either would be Father Cabral, who carried great authority. But the priest would do nothing against the interests of the Church; only if I confessed to him that I felt no vocation. . .

"Can I admit that in confession?"

"Yes, I suppose so, but that would be to come out in the open, and there is a better way. José Dias . . ."

"What about José Dias?"

"He could be really useful."

"But it was him that brought the subject up . . ."

"It doesn't matter," Capitu went on, "now he'll say something else. He's very fond of you. Don't be apologetic with him. It all

---

* On a small island in the mouth of the bay on which Rio de Janeiro stands.

depends on you not being afraid: show that you'll be master one day, show him what you want and what you can do. Make sure he understands that it's not a favor you're asking. Sing his praises, too: he loves to be praised. Dona Glória pays a good deal of attention to him, but that's not what's most important; the main thing is that, if he has to serve your interests, he'll speak much more warmly than anyone else."

"I don't think so, Capitu."

"Then go to the seminary."

"Never."

"What can you lose by trying? Let's try it out: do what I say. Maybe Dona Glória will change her mind; if she doesn't, we'll do something else—we'll use Father Cabral. Don't you remember how you went to the theater for the first time, two months ago? Dona Glória didn't want you to go, and that was enough for José Dias not to insist; but he wanted to go, and he made a speech, remember?"

"I remember; he said that the theater was a school of manners."

"That's it; he insisted so much that your mother ended up agreeing, and paid for both your tickets . . . Go on, ask, demand it. Look—say that you're willing to go to São Paulo to study law."*

I quivered with pleasure. São Paulo was a fragile screen, destined to be pushed aside one day, instead of the solid, eternal spiritual wall. I promised to speak to José Dias in the terms she had suggested. Capitu repeated them, stressing some as more important than others, and questioned me about them afterwards, to make sure I had understood, and had mixed nothing up. She insisted that I should ask politely, but like asking for a glass of water from someone who has the obligation to bring it. I recount these niceties, so that the morning freshness of my young friend may be understood; later comes the evening, and there was morning and there was evening the first day, as in Genesis, where there were seven days in succession.

---

* In the nineteenth century there were no universities in Brazil. Many of the elite sent their sons to complete their education at either of the two law schools, in São Paulo or Recife.

X I X

Without Fail

When I came back home night had fallen. I hurried, but not so fast that I did not have time to ponder the terms I would use when speaking to José Dias. I formulated the request in my head, choosing the words, along with their tone, half way between dry and friendly. In the garden, before going into the house, I repeated them under my breath, then out loud, to see if they were right, and complied with Capitu's instructions: "I need to speak to you tomorrow, *without fail*, choose the place and let me know." I said them slowly, and the words *without fail* more slowly still, as if to underline them. I then repeated them over again, and found them too dry, almost brusque, and, to be frank, not suitable for a young lad addressing a mature man. I tried to find others, and came to a stop.

In the end I said to myself that the words would do: the essential thing was to say them in a tone that would not give offence. The proof is that when I repeated them over again, they came out as almost pleading. All I had to do was not be too assertive, nor too amiable, but somewhere between the two. "And Capitu's right, I thought, the house is mine, and he's no more than a dependent . . . But he's clever, he can quite well work for me, and upset Mamma's plan."

X X

A Thousand Paternosters
and a Thousand Ave Marias

I raised my eyes to the heavens, which were getting overcast, but it was not to see whether they were cloudy or clear. It was to another heaven that I lifted up my soul: to my refuge, my friend. Then I said to myself:

"I promise to say a thousand paternosters and a thousand ave marias, if José Dias sees to it that I don't have to go to the seminary."

It was an enormous quantity. The reason was that I was loaded down with unfulfilled promises. The last one had been two hundred paternosters and two hundred ave marias, if it didn't rain one afternoon on an outing to Santa Teresa. It didn't rain, but I didn't say the prayers. Ever since I was small I had become used to asking favors of heaven, promising prayers if they were granted. I said the first ones, the next were put off, and as they piled up they were gradually forgotten. In this way I got to twenty, thirty, fifty. I got into the hundreds, and now it was a thousand. It was a way of bribing the divine will by the number of prayers; furthermore, each new promise was made and sworn on the basis that the outstanding debt would be paid. But what can you do, when your soul has been marked by sloth from the cradle, and life has done nothing to change this? Heaven would do me the favor, and I would put off the payment. In the end, I got lost in the accounts.

"A thousand, a thousand," I repeated to myself.

In truth, the favor that I was asking was now immense, nothing less than the salvation or wreck of my whole existence. A thousand, a thousand, a thousand. I needed a sum that would pay off all the arrears. If He were irritated at my forgetfulness, God might very well refuse to hear me without a great deal of money ... Serious reader, it's possible these childish worries bore you, that is if you don't think them ridiculous. Sublime they certainly were not. I thought for a long time how to redeem the spiritual debt. I could find no other currency in which, at least in intention, everything could be paid off, and the books of my moral conscience closed without a deficit. To have a hundred masses said, or climb the steps to Glória Church* on my knees to hear another, to go to the Holy Land, everything that the old slave women told me about famous promises—all these things came to mind, but they did not carry conviction. It was hard to climb a hill on one's knees: I was bound to bruise them. The Holy Land was a long way off. It was a lot of masses, and I might find my soul was in pawn again . . .

X X I

Cousin Justina

On the verandah I found cousin Justina, walking back and forth. She came to the top of the steps and asked where I had been:

"I've been next door, chatting to Dona Fortunata, and forgot the time. It's late, isn't it? Did mamma ask where I was?"

"She did, but I told her you'd already come in."

The lie amazed me, no less than the open admission of it. Not that cousin Justina was a one for hiding her opinions: on the contrary, she frankly told Peter the evil she thought of Paul, and Paul the evil she thought of Peter; but to confess that she had lied was

---

*A small baroque church, situated at the top of a hill, and a well-known landmark not more than a mile or two from Bento's house.

a novelty to me. She was in her forties, lean and pale, with a thin mouth and inquisitive eyes. My mother had her to live with us as a favor, and also for her own ends: she wanted to have a companion in the house, and preferred a relative to an outsider.

We walked for some minutes on the verandah, which was lit by a large lamp. She wanted to know if I had forgotten my mother's ecclesiastical plans, and when I told her I hadn't, she inquired how much I was looking forward to being a priest. I replied evasively:

"A priest's life is very nice."

"Yes, it's very nice; but what I'm asking is whether you would like to be a priest," she explained with a laugh.

"I like whatever mamma wants."

"Cousin Glória very much wants you to be ordained, but even if she didn't, there's someone here at home who keeps putting the idea into her head."

"Who is it?"

"Who, indeed! Who do you think? It's not cousin Cosme, who couldn't care about it; nor me."

"José Dias?" I concluded.

"Naturally."

I wrinkled my forehead questioningly, as if I knew nothing. Cousin Justina finished by saying that that very afternoon José Dias had reminded my mother of her old promise.

"It may be that, as the days go by, cousin Glória may gradually forget her promise; but how can she forget it if a certain person is for ever harping on about the seminary? And the speeches he makes, extolling the Church, saying that a priest's life is this and it's that, all with those words only he understands, and with that affected air ... And mind you it's only to cause mischief, because he's as religious as this lamp here. Yes, it's true, this very day. Don't pretend you don't understand. You can't imagine what he was like this afternoon."

"But did he just speak for no special reason?" I asked, to see if she would talk about his revelation of my dalliance with our nextdoor neighbor.

She said nothing—only made a gesture as if to indicate that there was something else she couldn't say. Again she told me not to play the innocent, and restated all the evil she thought of José Dias, which was not a little—a designing, calculating, snooping toady, and for all his polite veneer, a boor. After a few moments, I said:

"Cousin Justina, would you be willing to do something?"

"What?"

"Would you ... Suppose I didn't want to be a priest ... you could ask Mamma ..."

"Certainly not," she quickly cut in, "Cousin Glória is fixed on this business, and nothing in the world will make her change her mind—only time. When you were still small, she told this story to all our friends, and even our acquaintances. I certainly won't refresh her memory: I'm not one to do anyone a bad turn; but ask her to do something else—that I can't do. If she should consult me, very well; if she said to me: "Cousin Justina, what do you think?," my reply would be: "Cousin Glória, I think that, if he wants to be a priest, he can go to the seminary; but, if he doesn't, it would be better if he stayed here." That's what I would say, and will say if some day she asks my opinion. But go and speak to her without being asked—that I won't do."

XXII

Other People's Sensations

I found out nothing more, and later regretted that I had asked; I should have followed Capitu's advice. Then, as I was going inside, cousin Justina held me back for a few minutes, talking of the heat and the forthcoming festival of the Conception, of my old oratories, and finally of Capitu. She spoke no ill of her; on the contrary, she hinted that she might grow into a pretty girl. I, who already thought her very beautiful, would have proclaimed that she was the loveliest creature in the world, if caution had not given me a measure of discretion. Even so, as cousin Justina began to praise her manner, her seriousness, her habits, the way she helped in the home, the affection she had for my mother, all this aroused me to praise her, too. Even when I didn't do it directly in words, I did so in the gestures of approval with which I accompanied her every assertion, and certainly in the happiness that must have lit up my face. I did not see that I was confirming José Dias' accusations, which she had heard that afternoon in the living room: that is, if she didn't already suspect something. I only thought of that later in bed. Only then did I feel that, as I was speaking, cousin Justina's eyes seemed to touch me, hear me, smell me, taste me: they seemed to stand in for all the other senses. It couldn't have been jealousy; there was no place for jealousy for a youngster of my age in a forty-year-old widow. It is true that, after some time, she modified her praise, and even made a few critical remarks about Capitu, telling me that she was mischievous and always looking at the ground; but even then, I don't think it was jealousy. Rather I think ... yes ... this is what I think: cousin Justina found a vague reawakening of her own sensations from watching those of others. Lips can give pleasure merely by narrating.

X X I I I

The Time is Fixed

"I must speak to you tomorrow, without fail; choose the place and let me know."

I think José Dias was unused to my speaking in this way.

The tone had not come out as peremptory as I had feared it would, but the words were, and my not inquiring, asking or hesitating, as was a child's place and was my habit, surely gave him the notion that here was a new person and a new situation. It happened in the corridor, as we were going in for tea; José Dias came out full of the reading of Walter Scott that he had been doing for my mother and cousin Justina. He read in a slow, singsong voice. In his mouth, the castles and parks were larger, the lakes had more water in them, and the "celestial vault" was furnished with a few more thousand sparkling stars. In the dialogues, he alternated the sounds of the voices, making them slightly harsher or softer according to the sex of the person speaking: with moderation, too, he conveyed tenderness and anger.

When he left me on the verandah, he said:

"Tomorrow, in the street. I have some purchases to make, and you can come with me, I'll ask Mamma. Have you got a lesson?"

"The lesson was today."

"Quite so. I won't ask you what it is; I am sure it is something serious and proper."

"Oh, yes."

"Till tomorrow, then."

Everything worked out as it should. There was only one change: my mother thought the weather too hot and would not allow me to go on foot; we got into the bus* outside the house.

"It doesn't matter," José Dias said to me, "we can get off at the entrance to the Promenade."†

---

* In the 1850s, the "ônibus," as it was called, was a horse-drawn carriage, with seats for about a dozen passengers.

† The Passeio Público, part of which still exists, was a formal garden on the edge of the water, commanding an extensive view of Guanabara Bay.

X X I V

Like a Mother and a Servant

José Dias treated me with a mother's affection and a servant's attentiveness. The first thing that he arranged as soon as I was old enough to go out, was to dispense with the page boy; he became my page, and accompanied me in the street. He looked after my affairs at home, my books, my shoes, my cleanliness and my grammar. When I was eight, my plurals sometimes carried the wrong endings, and he would correct them, half seriously to give the requisite authority to the lesson, half laughing to ask pardon for correcting me. In this way he helped my primary teacher. Later, when Father Cabral taught me Latin, doctrine, and sacred history, he sat in on the lessons and made ecclesiastical comments. At the end, he would ask the priest: "Our young friend is making admirable progress, is he not?" He called me "a prodigy"; told my mother that he had known very intelligent boys in years gone by, but that I surpassed them all, not to mention the fact that, for my age, I already possessed a number of solid moral qualities. Even though I could hardly appreciate the value of these words of praise, I took pleasure in them; it was praise, after all.

X X V

At the Promenade

We went into the Promenade. There were some old faces: others, sick or merely idle, were dismally spread out along the path from the gate to the terrace overlooking the bay. We went up towards the terrace. As we went, to work up my courage, I talked about the garden:

"I haven't been here for a long time, a year maybe."

"Pardon me," he cut in, "not three months ago you came here with our neighbor Pádua; don't you remember?"

"That's true, but it was only a brief visit . . ."

"He asked your mother to let him bring you with him, and she permitted it—she's as good as the blessed Virgin; but listen to me, since we're on the subject, it's not right for you to be seen in the streets with Pádua."

"But I've been a few times . . ."

"When you were younger; when you were a child, it was natural; he could pass for a servant. But you're getting to be a young man, and he's becoming more and more familiar. Dona Glória surely can't approve of that. The Páduas are not all bad. Capitu, in spite of those eyes the devil gave her . . . Have you noticed her eyes? They're a bit like a gypsy's, oblique and sly. Well, in spite of them, she could get by, if it weren't for her airs, and her flattery. Oh, her flattery! Dona Fortunata deserves respect, and as for him, I don't deny that he's honest, he's got a good job, owns the house he lives in. But honesty and respect aren't enough, and the other qualities are outweighed by the bad company he keeps. He has a real penchant for vulgar people. No sooner sniff someone common—that's your man. I don't say this because I dislike him, or because he speaks ill of me, and mocks my down-at-heel shoes, as he did the other day . . ."

"I beg your pardon," I interrupted stopping in my tracks, "I've never heard of him speaking ill of you; on the contrary, one day not long ago, he said to someone, in my presence, that you were 'a very capable man and that you spoke like a deputy in Parliament'."

José Dias smiled delightedly, but he made a great effort and composed his face again; then he replied:

"I owe him no thanks for that. Others, of greater merit, have favored me with their high opinion. And nothing of this prevents him being what I say."

We had gone on again: we went up to the terrace, and looked out towards the sea.

"I see that you only want what's best for me," I said after a few moments.

"But what else could I want, Bentinho?"

"In that case, I want to ask you a favor."

"A favor? Ask me, order me. What is it?"

"Mamma . . ."

For some time I could not say the rest, though it wasn't much, and I had it by heart. José Dias asked again what it was, gently shook me, lifted my chin, and gazed at me anxiously, like cousin Justina the evening before.

"Mamma what? What about Mamma?"

"Mamma wants me to be a priest, but I can't be a priest," I finally said.

José Dias straightened up, thunderstruck.

"I can't," I went on, no less thunderstruck than he, "I'm not cut out for it, I don't want a priest's life. I'm ready to do anything she wants; mamma knows I'll do anything she says; I'm willing to be whatever she likes, even a bus driver. But not a priest; I can't be a priest. It's a fine profession; but it's not for me."

This speech didn't come out all at once, of a piece, connected naturally, and decisive, as it looks on the printed page, but in bits, chewed up, and in a low, timid voice. Nonetheless, José Dias had heard it in astonishment. He had certainly not counted on any resistance, however feeble; but what surprised him even more was my conclusion:

"I'm counting on you to save me."

The dependent's eyes opened wide, his eyebrows arched, and the pleasure that I expected to give him by choosing him as protector did not show in any of his features. There was hardly room in his face for his stupefaction. It was true that the subject of my speech had revealed a new person; I did not recognize myself. But my final words gave this a wholly new force. José Dias was stunned. When his eyes came back to their original dimensions:

"But what can I do?" he asked.

"A great deal. You know that at home everyone thinks highly of you. Mamma often asks your advice, doesn't she? Uncle Cosme says you are a talented person ..."

"It's good of them," he replied, flattered. "These are the favors of worthy people, deserving of all manner of ... There you are! No one will ever hear me speak ill of such people; and why? because they are illustrious and virtuous. Your mother is a saint, your uncle a most perfect gentleman. I have known distinguished families; none can compare with yours in nobility of sentiments. As for the talent your uncle sees in me, it is only one: the ability to see what is good and worthy of admiration and esteem."

"You also know how to help your friends, such as me."

"My dear boy, how can I be of help to you? I can't dissuade your mother from a project which is not just a promise: it's been her dream and her ambition for many years. Even if I could, it's too late. Just yesterday she did me the honor of saying to me: 'José Dias, I must put Bentinho into the seminary'."

Timidity is not the bad coinage it might seem to be. If I had been bolder it is probable that I would have burst out and called him a liar, so indignant did I feel. But then it would have been necessary to confess to him that I had been eavesdropping, and one action balanced out the other. I contented myself with replying that it was not too late.

"It's not too late, there's still time, if you want."

"If I want? But what else do I want, but to be of service to you? What can I desire but for you to be happy, as you deserve?"

"There still is time. Believe me, it's not that I'm an idler. I'm ready for anything; if she wants me to study law, I'll go to São Paulo ..."

X X V I

Law is Wonderful

Over José Dias' face there passed something like the flash of an idea—an idea that made him extraordinarily happy. He went silent for a few moments; my eyes were fixed on him, and his had turned towards the entrance to the bay. When I pressed the point:

"It is late," he said, "but to prove there's no lack of willing on my part, I'll go and speak to your mother. I don't promise you I'll succeed, but I will try; I'll put my heart and soul into it. You really don't want to be a priest? Law is a wonderful thing, dear boy . . . You could go to São Paulo, Pernambuco, or even farther afield. There are good universities out there in the great world. Go into law, if you've the calling. I'll speak to Dona Glória, but don't just count on me; speak to your Uncle too."

"I shall."

"And make your prayers to God—God and the Holy Virgin," he concluded, pointing up to the sky.

The sky was somewhat overcast. Near the beach, large black birds were circling in the air, flapping their wings or hovering, then coming down to dip their feet in the water, only to soar up and swoop down again. But neither the shadows in the sky nor the birds' fantastic dances took my mind away from my companion. After I had said yes, I corrected myself:

"God will do what you want Him to."

"Don't blaspheme. God is the Lord of all; He is, in Himself, the earth and the heavens, the past, present and future. Pray to Him for happiness, and I will do the same . . . Since you can't be a priest, and prefer the law . . . Law is a wonderful thing, and that is not to belittle theology, which is better than all the others, just as the priest's life is the holiest . . . Why not study law abroad? It would be better to go straight to some university, and at the same time as you study, you could travel. We can go together; we'll see foreign countries, we'll hear English, French, Italian, Spanish, Russian, even Swedish. Dona Glória probably won't be able to go with you; even if she can and does go, she'll not want to deal with business matters, papers, registration forms, arranging lodgings, going here and there with you . . . Oh, the law is most wonderful!"

"That's agreed then: you'll ask Mamma not to send me to the seminary?"

"I will certainly ask, but to ask is not to receive. My dearest boy, if wishes were commands, we've made it, we're on board. You can't imagine what Europe is like: oh, Europe . . ."

He raised a leg and pirouetted. One of his ambitions was to go back to Europe, and he often spoke of it, without tempting my mother or Uncle Cosme, however much he commended the climate and the sights . . . He had not considered the possibility of going with me, and staying there for the eternity of my studies.

"We're on board, Bentinho, we're on board!"

X X V I I

At the Gateway

At the gateway to the Promenade, a beggar held his hand out to us. José Dias went on ahead, but I thought about Capitu and the seminary, took a couple of small coins out of my pocket and gave them to the beggar. He kissed them; I asked him to pray to God for me, that I might satisfy all my desires.

"Yes, my angel."

"My name is Bento," I added, so that he knew.

XXVIII

In the Street

José Dias was so happy that the gravity which was his usual manner in the street gave way to his elastic, restless demeanor. Gesticulating and talking a great deal, he made me stop over and over again at shop windows or theater bills. He recounted the plot of some of the plays and recited monologues in verse. He did all his errands, paid bills, collected rents; for himself he bought a cheap lottery ticket. Then finally, formality carried the day over flexibility, and he began to talk with deliberation again, using his usual superlatives. I didn't see that this was a natural change; I was afraid that he might have changed his mind, and began to treat him with affectionate words and gestures, until we got back in the bus.

XXIX

The Emperor

On the way, we met the Emperor,* who was coming from the School of Medicine. The bus we were in stopped, as did all

---

* The Emperor Pedro II (1825–92), was 32 at the time. The Brazilian Empire was a constitutional monarchy, in which, however, the Emperor wielded considerable power. Part of this was symbolic, as this scene demonstrates: in a real sense, he commanded the allegiance of his subjects. Dom Pedro had the reputation of being a patient, studious man, and was a great admirer of modern science and progress—a fact also in evidence in this chapter.

the other vehicles; the passengers got out and removed their hats until the Imperial coach had passed. When I went back to my seat, I had a fantasy, nothing less than the idea of going to see the Emperor, telling him everything and asking him to intervene. I wouldn't confide this idea to Capitu. "If His Majesty asks, Mamma will give way," I thought to myself.

Then I saw the Emperor listening to me, reflecting and in the end saying yes, he would go and speak to my mother; and I kissed his hand, with tears in my eyes. Next thing, I was at home waiting, until I heard the outriders and the cavalry escort: It's the Emperor! It's the Emperor! Everybody came to the window to see him pass by, but he didn't pass by. The coach stopped at our door, and the Emperor got out and came in. Great excitement in the neighborhood: "The Emperor has gone into Dona Glória's house! What on earth can be happening?" Our family came out to receive him; my mother was the first to kiss his hand. Then the Emperor, all smiles, whether he came into the living room or not—I don't remember, dreams are often confused—asked my mother not to make me a priest, and she, flattered and obedient, promised she would not.

"Medicine—why don't you send him to study medicine?"

"If such is Your Majesty's pleasure . . ."

"Send him to study medicine; it's a fine career, and we've got good teachers here. Haven't you ever been to our School? It's splendid. We've got first-class doctors, who can match the best in other countries. Medicine is a great science; the mere fact that it gives health, identifies diseases, combats them, defeats them . . . You yourself must have seen miracles. True, your husband died, but the illness was fatal, and he didn't take sufficient care of himself . . . It's a fine career; send him to our School. Do it for me, will you? Is that what you want, Bentinho?"

"If Mamma wants."

"I do, my son. It is His Majesty's command."

Then the Emperor held out his hand to be kissed, and went out, accompanied by all of us, with the street full of people and the windows crammed. There was an astonished silence. The Emperor entered the coach, bowed, and said goodbye with his hand, still repeating: "Medicine, our School." And the coach left, amid envy and humble thanks.

All this I saw and heard. For Ariosto's imagination was no more fertile than that of children and lovers; and the corner of a bus is enough space to see the impossible. For some moments— minutes, even—I consoled myself with this vision, until the plan collapsed and I returned to the dreamless faces of my fellow passengers.

X X X

The Blessed Sacrament

You will have gathered that the Emperor's suggestion about medicine was the simple product of my lack of desire to leave Rio de Janeiro. Daydreams are like other dreams: they are woven according to the patterns of our wishes and memories. It was one thing to go to São Paulo, but Europe ... It was a long way off, a lot of sea to cross and a long time to spend. Long live medicine! I would tell Capitu of these hopes.

"It seems the Sacrament is coming out," said someone on the bus. "I can hear a bell; yes, I think it's in Santo Antônio dos Pobres. Stop, conductor!"

The conductor pulled the cord which was connected to the driver's arm, the bus stopped, and the man got off. José Dias jerked his head round twice, grabbed me by the arm and made me get off with him. We too were going to accompany the Sacrament. The bell was indeed calling the faithful to the service of extreme unction. There were already some people in the sacristy. It was the first time I had ever been present at such a solemn occasion; I obeyed, somewhat embarrassed at first, but soon pleased with myself, less because of the charity being performed than because I was taking a man's position. When the sacristan began to hand out the surplices, someone came in out of breath; it was my neighbor Pádua, who had also come to accompany the Sacrament. He saw us and came over to greet us. José Dias gave an irritated gesture, and barely replied with one brief word: he was looking at the priest, who was washing his hands. Then, as Pádua was talking to the sacristan in a low voice, he went nearer; I did the same thing. Pádua was asking the sacristan if he could carry one of the poles of the canopy. José Dias asked for one for himself:

"There's only one available," said the sacristan.

"That one then," said José Dias.

"But I'd asked first," ventured Pádua.

"You asked first, but you came in late," retorted José Dias, "I was already here. You carry a candle."

Pádua, for all he was afraid of José Dias, insisted that he wanted the pole, all this in a low, muted voice. The sacristan found a way of contenting both rivals, taking it on himself to ask one of the other carriers of the poles to give up his to Pádua, who was well known in the parish, as was José Dias. He did so, but José Dias upset this arrangement too. No, since there was another pole available, he asked for it to be given to me, a "young seminarist," who had a better right to this honor. Pádua went as pale as the candles. It was a severe trial for a father's heart. The sacristan, who recognized me from seeing me there with my mother on Sundays, asked out of curiosity if I really was a seminarist.

"Not yet, but he will be," replied José Dias winking at me with his left eye: in spite of this, I was furious.

"Very well, I give way to our Bentinho," sighed Capitu's father.

For my part, I wanted to give him the pole; I remembered that he was accustomed to accompanying the Blessed Sacrament to the dying, carrying a candle, but that the last time he had got one of the canopy poles. The special distinction attaching to the canopy came from the fact that it covered the priest and the Sacrament; anyone could carry a candle. He himself had told me this, full of smiles and pious pride. So one can understand the excitement with which he had come into the church; for the second time he was going to get the canopy, so much so that he decided to go straight away and ask for it. No such luck! He went back to the common candle: it was the temporary administration all over again; he was going back to his old role ... I wanted to give him the pole; but José Dias prevented this act of generosity, and asked the sacristan to give us, him and me, the two front poles, so that we led the procession.

With our surplices on, the candles distributed and lit, the priest and the ciborium ready, the sacristan with the aspersorium and the bell in his hands, the procession went out into the street. When I saw myself carrying one of the poles, passing through the kneeling ranks of the faithful, I was filled with emotion. Pádua had to gnaw his candle with bitterness. A metaphor, no doubt, but I can think of no better way of conveying our neighbor's pain and humiliation. In any case, I couldn't look at him for long, nor at the dependent who, parallel with me, held his head high as if he himself were the Lord God of Hosts. In a short while, I felt tired; my arms were dropping, but luckily the house was close by, in the Rua do Senado.

The sick person was a widow, a consumptive with a daughter of fifteen or sixteen, who was crying at the door to the room. She was not a pretty girl, perhaps not even agreeable; her hair hung down uncombed, and her tears wrinkled her eyes. All the same, the whole scene spoke to my heart and moved me. The priest confessed the sick woman, gave her communion and extreme unction. The girl began to weep so much that I felt the tears coming to my eyes and fled. I went over to a window. Poor creature! The pain itself was catching; wound up with memories of my mother, it hurt me more, and when I finally thought of Capitu I felt the urge to cry. I ran into the corridor, and heard someone say to me:

"Don't cry like that!"

The image of Capitu was in my mind, and just as I had imagined her crying a little before, now I saw her brimful of laughter; I saw her write on the wall, speak to me, turn around with her arms in the air; I distinctly heard my name, with an intoxicating sweetness, and it was her voice that uttered it. The burning candles, which before had seemed so gloomy, now had the look of nuptial lustre ... What was nuptial lustre? I don't know; it was the opposite of death, and nothing fits that description better than weddings. This new feeling so took hold of me that José Dias came over to me, and whispered in my ear:

"Don't laugh like that!"

I quickly composed myself. Now it was the moment to leave. I took hold of my pole; and, as I already knew how far it was and we were now going back to the church, the distance seemed less—the pole hardly weighed at all. Moreover, the sun outside, the stir in the street, the boys of my age who gazed enviously at me, the women who came to the windows and alley ways and piously knelt down as we passed, all of this made me feel quite sprightly again.

Pádua, on the other hand, looked even more humiliated. Although it was I who had taken his place, he could not console himself with that candle, that miserable candle. All the same, there were others who were also carrying candles, and whose demeanor suited their position; they were not delighted, but neither were they sad. One could see that they walked with honor.

X X X I

Capitu's Curiosity

Capitu preferred anything to the seminary. Instead of being downcast at the threat of the long separation should the European idea come to fruition, she was pleased. When I told her of my Imperial dream:

"No, Bentinho, let's leave the Emperor in peace," she replied, "for the time being, let's stick with José Dias' promise. When did he say he'd speak to your mother?"

"He didn't fix a day; he promised that he'd see, that he'd speak as soon as he could, and said that I should pray to God."

Capitu asked me to repeat all the dependent's replies, the alterations in his gestures and even the pirouette, which I had hardly mentioned. She asked for the tone of all his words. She gave it all her minute attention. She seemed to ruminate on everything, the story itself and the dialogue. Or you could say that she was comparing, labelling and, as it were, pinning my account up in her memory. Perhaps this image is better than the preceding one, but best of all would be none. Capitu was Capitu, that is, a very particular person, more of a woman than I was a man. If I've not said it already, there you have it. And if I have, there you have it anyway. There are things which must be impressed on the reader's mind by dint of repetition.

She was also more curious than I. Capitu's curiosity is a subject for a whole chapter. It came in all guises, explicable and inexplicable, useful and useless, some serious, others frivolous; she liked to know everything. At the school where from the age of seven she had learned reading, writing, and arithmetic, French, religious doctrine, and needlework, she did not, for example, learn lace-making: for that very reason, she asked cousin Justina to teach it her. The only reason she didn't study Latin with Father Cabral was because the priest, after suggesting it to her in fun, ended up saying that Latin was not a language for girls. One day Capitu admitted to me that this very argument fired her desire to learn it. On the other hand, she decided to learn English with an old teacher friend of her father's, his partner at solo, but she didn't persevere. Uncle Cosme taught her backgammon.

"Come and get a drubbing, Capitu," he would say to her.

Capitu obeyed and played with skill and care, you could almost say lovingly. One day I came across her doing a pencil portrait; she was putting the finishing touches to it, and asked me to wait and see if it was a good likeness. It was of my father, copied from the canvas my mother kept in the drawing room, and which I still have. It certainly wasn't perfect; quite the contrary, he looked popeyed, and the hair consisted of small circles one on top of the other. But given that she had no rudiments of the art of drawing, and had done it from memory in a short space of time, I thought it was a work of great merit; make allowances for my age and my feelings for the portraitist. Even so, I am sure that she could easily have learned painting, as she learned music later. She was already looking longingly at the piano in our house, a useless old piece of furniture with nothing but sentimental value. She read our novels, leafed through our books of engravings, wanting to know all about the ruins, the people, the military campaigns, the name, the place, the story behind everything. José Dias gave her this information with a certain pride in his erudition, which did not go much deeper than his plantation homeopathy.

One day, Capitu wanted to know who the busts in the drawing room were. The dependent told her briefly, dwelling somewhat more on Caesar, with exclamations and Latin sayings:

"Caesar! Julius Caesar! A great man! *Tu quoque, Brute?*"

Capitu did not think Caesar's profile handsome, but the deeds recounted by José Dias elicited gestures of admiration from her. She stood for a long while staring at the bust. A man who could do anything, and did! A man who gave a lady a pearl worth six million sesterces!

"How much was each sesterce worth?"

José Dias, who couldn't quite remember the value of a sesterce, answered enthusiastically: "He's the greatest man in history!"

Caesar's pearl lit up Capitu's eyes. That was the occasion on which she asked my mother why she no longer wore the jewels in the portrait. She was referring to the one in the drawing room, next to my father's; in it, she had a large necklace, a diadem, and earrings.

"They're widowed jewels, like me, Capitu."

"When did you put them on?"

"For the Coronation."

"Oh, tell me about the Coronation!"

She already knew what her parents had told her, but naturally thought that they would hardly know anything beyond what had happened in the streets. She wanted to know about the privileged seats in the Imperial Chapel and the ballrooms. She had been born long after these famous festivities. Often hearing talk of the Emperor's Majority,* she insisted one day on knowing about this event; they told her, and she thought the Emperor had been quite right to want to ascend to the throne at fifteen. Everything was a subject for Capitu's curiosity: old furniture, old furnishings, customs, stories about Itaguaí, my mother's childhood and adolescence, something said here, a memory there, an old proverb she'd heard ...

XXXII

Undertow Eyes

Nothing escaped Capitu's curiosity. There was one occasion, though, when I do not know if she was the teacher or the pupil, or both at the same time: the same was true of me. I'll tell the story in the next chapter. In this one I will only say that, some days after the agreement with the dependent, I went to see my young friend; it was ten in the morning. Dona Fortunata, who was in the yard, didn't even wait for me to ask where her daughter was.

"She's in the parlor combing her hair," she said, "go in on tiptoes to give her a fright."

---

* Pedro II should have reached his Majority at the age of 18, in December 1843. However, in the midst of a political crisis in May 1840, the Liberal party decided for its own purposes to anticipate his coming of age, which then took place in December of that year, on his fifteenth birthday. Convenient myth—later denied by the Emperor himself—had it that the supporters of this move had asked the Emperor when he wanted to rule, and that he replied "Quero já" ("I want to now").

I did as I was told, but either my footsteps or the mirror gave me away. It may not have been the latter; it was a twopenny mirror (with apologies for the cheapness), bought from an Italian pedlar, with a rough frame, hanging by a brass ring between the two windows. If it wasn't that, it was my footsteps. Whichever it was, hardly had I entered the room when comb, hair, all of her flew up in the air, and all I heard was this question:

"Has something happened?"

"Nothing new," I replied, "I came to see you before Father Cabral comes for my lesson. Did you have a good night?"

"Fine. Has José Dias not spoken yet?"

"It doesn't seem like it."

"When is he going to?"

"He says that today or tomorrow he intends to touch on the question. He won't go straight to the point; he'll just allude to the topic casually first, no more than a hint. Later, he'll get to the nub of the matter. First he wants to see if Mamma has her mind made up . . ."

"Of course she has," Capitu interrupted, "if there was no need for someone to win this battle now, once and for all, we wouldn't be bringing the subject up. I don't know if José Dias can have that much influence any more; I think he'll do everything in his power, if he feels that you really don't want to be a priest, but will be get his way. . . ? She does usually listen to him. But if . . . Oh, this is murder! Keep on at him, Bentinho."

"I will; he must speak to her today."

"Do you swear?"

"I swear! Let me see your eyes, Capitu."

I had remembered the definition José Dias had given them; "a gypsy's eyes, oblique and sly." I didn't know what oblique was, but I did know what sly was, and I wanted to see if they could be called that. Capitu let herself be stared at and examined. She only asked me what the matter was—had I never seen her eyes before? I found nothing out of the ordinary: just the color and the soft sweetness I knew of old. When I took so long over this contemplation, I think she got another notion of what I wanted; she thought it was a pretext to look at them more closely, with my eyes longingly fixed on hers: and to this I attribute the fact that they began to get larger, larger still and darker, with an expression. . .

Lovers' language, give me an exact and poetic comparison to say what those eyes of Capitu were like. No image comes to mind that doesn't offend against the rules of good style, to say what they were and what they did to me. Undertow eyes? Why not? Undertow. That's the notion that the new expression put in my head. They held some kind of mysterious, active fluid, a force that dragged one in, like the undertow of a wave retreating from the shore on stormy days. So as not to be dragged in, I held on to anything around them, her ears, her arms, her hair spread about her shoulders; but as soon as I returned to the pupils of her eyes again, the wave emerging from them grew towards me, deep and dark, threatening to envelop me, draw me in and swallow me up. How many minutes did this game last? Only the clocks of heaven could have registered that space of time which was infinite, yet brief. Eternity has its pendula; just because it never ends does not mean it takes no cognizance of the duration of bliss and damnation. The joy of the blessed in heaven must be doubled by knowing the sum of torments their enemies have already suffered in hell; so too the quantity of delights their foes enjoy in heaven must increase the agony of the damned. This particular torture escaped the divine Dante's notice; but I am not here to correct poets. I am simply about to recount that, after an unspecified time, I finally grasped Capitu's hair, but this time with my hands, and said—so as to say something—that I would comb it for her, if she wanted.

"You?"

"Yes, me."

"All you'll do is get my hair tangled up."

"If I do, you can untangle it afterwards."

"We'll see."

X X X I I I

Combing

Capitu turned her back to me and faced the mirror. I took hold of her hair, gathered it all together, and began to smooth it out with the comb, from her forehead to the tips: it stretched down to her waist. It was no good with her standing up; you won't have forgotten that she was a shade taller than I was, but even if we have been the same height it would have been impossible. I asked her to sit down.

"It'll be better if you sit here."

She sat down. "Let's see the great hairdresser," she said with a laugh. I went on smoothing out her hair, very carefully, and divided it into two equal parts, to make the two plaits. I didn't make them straight away, or as fast as a professional hairdresser might imagine: slowly, very slowly, I enjoyed the feel of those thick strands, which were a part of her. I did the work clumsily, sometimes out of sheer ineptitude, at others deliberately, so as to undo what I had done and do it again. My fingers brushed her neck, or her back with its cotton dress: it was a delicious sensation. But in the end, however interminable I wanted this to be, I ran out of hair. I didn't ask the heavens for the strands to be as long as Aurora's, because I was as yet unfamiliar with this goddess who was later introduced to me by the poets; but I did want to comb them for ever and ever, weaving two braids that would envelop infinity an unnamable number of times. If all this seems a little emphatic, irritating reader, it's because you have never combed a girl's hair, you've never put your adolescent hands on the young head of a nymph ... A nymph! I've become all mythological. A little while ago, talking about her undertow eyes, I even wrote "Thetis"*; I crossed out Thetis, let's cross out nymph; let's

---

* Greek goddess of the sea, mother of Achilles.

say only a beloved creature, which is a word which embraces all the powers, pagan and Christian. In the end, I finished the two braids. Where was the ribbon to tie their ends together? On the table, a miserable little piece of crumpled material. I tied the ends of the braids, joined them with a bow, gave the work some final touches, stretching it out here, smoothing it there. Then I exclaimed:

"Ready!"

"Let's see if it's all right."

"Look in the mirror."

Instead of going to the mirror, what do you think Capitu did? Don't forget that she was seated, with her back to me. Capitu leaned her head backwards, coming so far that I had to hold it in my hands; the chair had a low back. Then I bent over her, face to face, but inversely, the eyes of one in line with the mouth of the other. I asked her to lift her head: she might get dizzy or hurt her neck. I even said she looked ugly; but not even that affected her.

"Get up, Capitu!"

She would not. She didn't lift her head, and so we remained, staring at each other, until she pursed her lips, I lowered mine, and. . .

The kiss had an extraordinary effect; Capitu got up quickly, and I recoiled to the wall with a kind of vertigo, speechless, my eyes darkened over. When vision returned, I saw that Capitu had her eyes on the ground. I dared not say anything; even if I had wanted to, I was tongue-tied. I was caught, stunned: no gesture or impulse could pry me from the wall and make me rush towards her with a thousand warm and endearing words . . . Don't make fun of my fifteen years, precocious reader. At seventeen, Des Grieux—Des Grieux, what's more—had not yet thought about the difference between the sexes.*

---

* The hero of *Manon Lescaut* (1733), by the Abbé Prévost, one of the most famous and influential novels of the eighteenth century. Des Grieux is an innocent young seminarist who falls in love with Manon, a girl of lower-class origins, and ruins himself for her, finally following her into exile in America, where she dies in his arms.

X X X I V

I Am a Man!

We heard footsteps in the corridor; it was Dona Fortunata. Capitu quickly composed herself, so quickly that when her mother put her head round the door she was shaking her head and laughing. There was not a trace of embarrassment, nor was she in the least discomfited: it was a clear, spontaneous laugh, which she explained with these cheery words:

"Mamma, look at the way this gentleman has done my hair; he asked me if he could finish combing it, and this is the result. Look at these plaits!"

"What's the matter with that?" replied her mother, overflowing with kindness. "It's very good; nobody could say it was done by someone who doesn't know how to comb."

"What, Mamma? This?" retorted Capitu undoing the plaits. "Oh, Mamma!"

And with a gesture of wilful, amused irritation she sometimes displayed, she picked up the comb and smoothed out the hair to do it again. Dona Fortunata called her foolish, and told me to pay no attention to her, it was nothing, nothing but her daughter's crazy notions. She looked tenderly at me and then at her. Then, I think she suspected something. Seeing me silent, abashed, glued to the wall, she may have thought that we had been doing more than just combing, and smiled, pretending she had seen nothing. . .

I, too, wanted to speak to cover up my emotions, so I called some words up from here inside, and they promptly appeared, but tumbling over one another, and filling my mouth up in such a way that none of them could get out. Capitu's kiss kept my lips sealed. However much they tried, not a single word, not the smallest particle was able to burst forth. So they all went back to the heart whence they had come, mumbling: "Here's someone who'll never make his mark in the world, if his emotions rule him like that . . ."

So, surprised by her mother, we were opposites, she hiding with words what I betrayed by my silence. Dona Fortunata relieved me of my hesitation by saying that my mother had sent for me for my Latin lesson: Father Cabral was waiting for me. It was a way out; I said goodbye and hurried down the corridor. As I went, I heard the mother scolding her daughter's manners, but the daughter said nothing.

I ran to my room and picked up my books, but I did not go on to the schoolroom; I sat down on the bed, remembering the combing of the hair and the rest. I shuddered, I had moments when my mind went blank, and I lost consciousness of myself and of the things around me: I had no idea where or how I was living. Then I came to and saw the bed, the walls, the books, the floor: I heard some sound from outside, vague, whether near or far off— then I lost it all again and only felt Capitu's lips ... I felt them stretched out below mine, which in turn reached towards hers, and then they joined together. Suddenly, involuntarily, without thinking, my mouth uttered these proud words:

"I am a man!"

I thought they might have heard me, because the words came out in a loud voice, and I ran to the bedroom door. There was no one outside. I went back in and, under my breath, said again that I was a man. I can still hear the echo of those words in my ears. The pleasure I felt was enormous. Columbus, when he discovered America, had no greater thrill. I hope that the banality of the comparison is made up for by its aptness: for it is true that in every adolescent there is a hidden world, an admiral and an October sun. I made other discoveries later; none dazzled me as much. José Dias' accusation had excited me, the old palm tree's lesson too; the sight of our names which she had scratched on the garden wall gave me a shock, as you have seen; nothing compared to the sensation of the kiss. These things might have been lies or illusions: even if they were true, they were the bare bones of the truth, not its flesh and blood. Even the hands touching, holding, almost melting into each other, could not say everything:

"I am a man!"

When I repeated this for the third time, I thought of the seminary, but as of a danger that is past, an evil averted, a vanished nightmare. All my nerves told me that men are not priests. My blood was of the same opinion. Again I felt Capitu's lips. Perhaps I am making too much of these oscular recollections; but it is of the essence of nostalgia to go over old memories again and again. Well, of all the memories of those days I think this is the sweetest, the freshest, the most all-embracing, the one which completely revealed me to myself. I have had others, vast and numerous, and sweet too, of several kinds, many of them intellectual, and just as intense. Even if I were a great man, the memory of them would not be as powerful as this.

X X X V

The Protonotary Apostolic

Finally I picked up my books and ran to my lesson. I didn't exactly run; half way, I stopped, realizing that it must be very late and that they might see something in my face. I thought of lying, of saying that I had had a turn and fallen to the ground; but the fright this would give my mother made me reject the idea. I thought of promising a few dozen paternosters; but I still had another promise owing and a favor pending . . . No, let's wait and see; I went on, and heard cheerful voices in loud conversation. When I entered the room, no one scolded me.

Father Cabral had received a message the previous day from the internuncio; he went to see him, and was told that, by pontifical decree, he had just been named protonotary apostolic. He and our whole household were delighted by this honor from the Pope. Uncle Cosme and cousin Justina kept repeating the title admiringly; it was the first time it had sounded in our ears, which were used to canons, monsignors, bishops, nuncios, and internuncios; but what was an protonotary apostolic? Father Cabral explained that while it was not exactly an appointment to the Curia, it was its equivalent in terms of the honor. Uncle Cosme, seeing himself exalted in his partner at cards, repeated:

"Protonotary apostolic!"

And turning to me: "Prepare yourself, Bentinho; one day you might be a protonotary apostolic."

Cabral listened to the repetition of the title with pleasure. He would stop and then take a few steps, smiling or drumming his fingers on his snuffbox. The length of the title somehow doubled its magnificence, though it made it too long to attach to his name: it was Uncle Cosme who made this second observation. Father Cabral replied that there was no need to say it all; he could just be called Protonotary Cabral. The apostolic could be taken as read.

"Protonotary Cabral."

"Yes, you're right; Protonotary Cabral."

"But, Protonotary," said cousin Justina so that she could get used to title, "does this mean you have to go to Rome?"

"No, Dona Justina."

"No, it's just the honors," observed my mother.

"However, there's no reason," said Cabral, who was still thinking, "there's no reason why on more formal occasions, at public events, in formal letters, etc., the full title should not be used: protonotary apostolic. For everyday use, protonotary is sufficient."

"Of course," everyone agreed.

José Dias, who came in a little after me, applauded the distinction, and recalled, apropos, the first political acts of Pius IX, which had given such great hopes to Italy; but no one took the subject up.* The man of the hour and the place was my old Latin teacher. I, recovering from my fears, realized that I should congratulate him, too, and this praise touched him no less than that of the oth-

---

* Pius IX (Giovanni Mastai), Pope from 1846 to 1878, began his reign with a series of liberal acts (amnesty to political prisoners and reduction of censorship on books), but in the wake of the 1848 revolutions, drew back from this liberal stance, later becoming famous for the *Syllabus*, an attack on "modern heresies," and for promulgating papal infallibility (1871).

ers. He gave me a fatherly pat on the cheek, and ended up by giving me a holiday. It was almost too much happiness for me to take in. A kiss and a holiday! I think my face must have shown just that, because Uncle Cosme, his belly shaking with laughter, called me a scoundrel; but José Dias put a check on my happiness:

"One should never be happy to be idle; he will always need Latin, *even if he doesn't become a priest.*"

I knew my man. It was the first word, the seed sown in the ground, just in passing, as if to accustom the family to their sound. My mother gave me a loving, sad smile, but she immediately replied:

"He'll be a priest, and a fine priest."

"Don't forget, sister Glória, and a protonotary, too. A protonotary apostolic."

"Protonotary Santiago," Cabral underlined.

I don't know if my Latin master merely intended to get used to joining the title with someone's name; what I do know is that when I heard my name tied to that title, I had an urge to say something rude. But this urge was just an idea, an idea without expression, which kept itself to itself, just like some other ideas a little later . . . But they demand a chapter to themselves. Let us complete this one by saying that the Latin master spoke for a time about my ordination as a priest, though without showing much interest. He was looking for a different subject to pretend he had forgotten his own glory, but it was this that dazzled him. He was a thin old man, serene, and with good qualities. He had some defects; the most notable being that he liked his food, without being exactly gluttonous; he ate little, but was fond of good quality, choice dishes, and our cuisine, while simple, was less monotonous than his. So, when my mother asked him to stay to dinner so that we could drink his health, the eyes he accepted with might have been protonotarian, but they were not apostolic. And to thank my mother he again used me, describing my ecclesiastical future, and wanted to know if I was going to the seminary soon, in the following year, and offered himself to speak to "my Lord Bishop," peppering everything he said with "Protonotary Santiago."

XXXVI

Idea without Legs,
Idea without Arms

I left them, saying that I was going to play, and went to think again about the morning's adventure. It was the best thing I could do, without the aid of Latin—or even with its aid. After five minutes, it occurred to me to go running to the house next door, take hold of Capitu, undo her plaits, make them up again and them finish them off in that same particular way, mouth to mouth. That's it, come on, that's it . . . Just an idea! An idea without legs! My other legs had no desire to run or walk. Much later, they went out slowly and took me to Capitu's house. When I got there, I saw her in the parlor, the same parlor, sitting on the settee, with a pillow on her lap, peacefully sewing. She didn't look me in the face, but hesitantly, out of the corner of her eye, or, if you prefer the dependent's terminology, obliquely and slyly. She stuck the needle in the cloth, and was still. I was on the other side of the table, and didn't know what to do; the words I had formulated slipped from me again. We spent a few minutes like this: then she abandoned her sewing, got up and stood there expectantly. I went over to her, and asked if her mother had said anything; she said no. She replied with a gesture of her mouth, that I think encouraged me to come closer. What is certain is that Capitu drew back a little.

This was an opportunity to take hold of her, pull her towards me and kiss her. Just an idea! An idea without arms. Mine hung by my side, lifeless. I knew nothing of the Scriptures. If I had, it is probable that the spirit of Satan would have made me give a direct, natural meaning to the mystical language of the Song of Songs. And so, I would have obeyed the first verse: "Let him kiss me with the kisses of his mouth." And as for the arms, inert as they were, I merely had to obey the sixth verse of the second chapter: "His left hand is under my head, and his right hand doth embrace me." You can see how the gestures are timed. All I had to do was carry it out; but even if I had known these texts, Capitu's demeanor was now so reserved, that I think I might well have stayed still. However, it was she who released me from this situation.

XXXVII

The Soul is Full of Mysteries

"Had Father Cabral been waiting long?"
     "I didn't have a lesson today; I got a holiday."
I explained the reason for the holiday. I also told her that Father Cabral had spoken of my going to the seminary, backing up my mother's resolve, and I said some nasty, harsh things about him. Capitu thought for some time, and ended up asking me if she could go and pay her compliments to the priest that evening, at our house.
     "You can, but what for?"
     "Papa will naturally want to go too, but it would be better if he went to Father Cabral's house; it's more polite. Not me, I'm nearly a woman," she concluded, with a laugh.
     Her laughter cheered me. The words seemed to be a joke at her own expense, the more so since, after the events of the morning, she was as much a woman as I was a man. I thought her charming, and to tell the truth, I wanted to prove to her that she was a complete woman. I took her gently by the right hand, then the left, and stopped at that point, astonished at myself and trembling. This time it was an idea with hands. I wanted to pull Capitu's towards me, so as to force her to come with them, but

the action still did not correspond to the intention. Even so, I thought myself bold and daring. I wasn't imitating anyone; I didn't have the company of other boys to tell me of their exploits. I had never read about the rape of Lucretia. All I knew about the Romans was that they spoke like the people in Padre Pereira's grammar, and that they were compatriots of Pontius Pilate.* I don't deny that the conclusion of the morning's combing was a great step down the road of amorous expertise, but her gestures then were the exact opposite of what she did now. In the morning, she leaned her head back: now she avoided me. Nor was that the only way that the situations differed. On another point, where there seemed to be repetition, there was a contrast.

I think I went as if to pull her towards me. I don't swear to it, for I was so excited that I could not be completely conscious of my acts; but I must have done, for she drew back and tried to free her hands from mine; then, perhaps because she could not go any further back, she put one of her feet forward and the other back, and turned her chest away from me. It was this gesture that made me hold onto her hands tightly. Her chest finally tired of this and gave in, but her head would not do so too, and, hanging back, rendered all my efforts useless—because, dear reader, I was now making a considerable effort. Not being acquainted with the Song of Songs, it never occured to me to place my left hand under her head; in any case, such a gesture presupposes a meeting of wills, and Capitu, who was now resisting me, would take advantage of it to remove the other hand and get away from me completely. We continued to struggle in this way, noiselessly, because in spite of the movements of attack and defense, we were cautious enough to be sure that no one in the house could hear us; the soul is full of mysteries. Now I know I was pulling her: her head was still drawn back, until it got tired; but then it was the turn of the mouth. Capitu's mouth began a inverse movement in relation to mine, going to one side while I went to the other. And we were at this point of stalemate, I not daring to go any further, when a little was all that was needed . . .

* Padre Pereira's grammar was a popular Latin primer.

At which point we heard knocking at the door, and people talking in the corridor. It was Capitu's father, who had come back from the office a little early, as he sometimes did. "Open the door, Nanata! Capitu, open the door!" In appearance it was the same situation as in the morning, when her mother came across us, but only in appearance; in reality, it was different. Consider that in the morning everything was over, and Dona Fortunata's footsteps were a warning for us to compose ourselves. Now we were struggling with our hands entwined, and nothing had even started.

We heard the bolt on the door that led into the hallway; it was Capitu's mother opening it. Since I am confessing everything, I hereby affirm that I did not have time to let my friend's hands go: I thought of doing so and got as far as trying to, but Capitu, before her father came right in the door, made an unexpected movement, put her mouth to mine, and gave of her own accord what she had been determinedly refusing. I repeat, the soul is full of mysteries.

X X X V I I I

Goodness, What a Fright!

When Pádua came through the hall and into the parlor, Capitu was standing with her back to me and bending over her sewing as if to gather it together. In a loud voice she asked:

"But, Bentinho, what is a protonotary apostolic?"

"Well, hello!" exclaimed her father.

"Goodness, what a fright!"

Now the scene is the same as the previous one; but if I recount here, after forty years, the twin situations just as they happened, it is to show that Capitu was not only able to control herself in her mother's presence; she was no more afraid of her father. In the midst of a crisis which left me tongue-tied, she expressed herself as innocently as could be. I am persuaded that her heart beat no faster or slower. She said she had been startled, and put on a rather annoyed look; but I, who knew what had happened, saw it was a pretence and felt envious. She went to greet her father, who shook my hand and wanted to know why his daughter was talking about protonotaries apostolic. Capitu repeated to him what she had heard from me, and immediately expressed the opinion that he ought to go and congratulate the priest at his house; she would go to mine. And so, gathering her sewing things, she ran down the corridor, shouting like a child:

"Mamma, dinner, Papa's home!"

X X X I X

My Vocation

Father Cabral was in the first flush of glory, when the slightest congratulations seem like laudatory odes. The time comes when those who have been honored take this praise for granted, and accept it without acknowledgement, blankfaced. The excitement of the first moment is the best; that state of mind which sees the bending of a tree in the wind as a personal homage from the world's flora brings more delicate, more intimate sensations than any other. Cabral listened to Capitu's words with infinite pleasure.

"Thank you, Capitu, thank you very much; I am delighted you are pleased. Is Papa well? And Mamma? No need to ask you: your face is the picture of health. Are we keeping up with our prayers?"

To all these questions, Capitu had ready, appropriate answers. She had a better dress on, and her most formal shoes. She did not come in with her usual familiarity, but stopped at the living-room door, before going to kiss my mother's hand, then the priest's. As she gave him the title of protonotary twice in five minutes, José Dias, to get even with the competition, made a little speech in honor of the "paternal heart of the most august Pius IX."

"You're a great speechifier," said Uncle Cosme, when he finished.

José Dias smiled without being offended. Father Cabral endorsed the dependent's praises, though without his superlatives; José Dias added that Cardinal Mastai had plainly been cut out for the papal tiara from the beginning of time. And, winking at me, he concluded:

"Vocation is everything. The ecclesiastical state is most perfect, so long as the priest has been destined from the cradle. If there is no vocation—I speak of real, sincere vocation—a young man can quite well study humanities, which are also useful and honorable."

Father Cabral replied:

"Vocation stands for a great deal, but the sovereign power belongs to God. A man may well have no liking for the Church, and even persecute it: one day, God speaks to him, and he becomes an apostle: look at St. Paul."

"I don't contest that, but what I am saying is something else. What I am saying is that one can well serve God without being a priest, in this world; is that not so?"

"It is."

"Well then!" exclaimed José Dias triumphantly, looking around him. "Without a vocation one cannot have a good priest, and in any liberal profession one may serve God, as is our duty."

"Quite so, but vocations do not only come from the cradle."

"But it is the best way."

"A boy with no taste for the life of the church may well end up by being a very good priest; all is as God determines. I don't want to set myself up as an example, but look at me: I was born with a vocation for medicine; my godfather, who was curate at the church of Santa Rita, kept on at my father to send me to the seminary, and my father gave way. Well, sir, I enjoyed the lessons and the company of the priests so much that I ended up taking orders. But suppose things had not happened that way, and that I had not changed my vocation, what would have happened? I would have studied some subjects it is useful to know, and which are always better taught in such places."

Cousin Justina intervened:

"What? Can one go to a seminary and not come out a priest?"

Father Cabral said yes, that one could, and turning to me, spoke of my vocation, which was manifest; my toys had always had to do with the Church, and I loved divine service. This was no proof: all the children in my time were devout. Cabral added that the rector of São José, whom he had recently told of my mother's promise, held that my birth was a miracle; he himself was of the same opinion. Capitu, who stayed close to my mother, paid no attention to the anxious looks I directed at her; she did not even seem to be listening to the conversation about the seminary and its consequences, though she had its main points by heart, as I found out afterwards. Twice I went to the window, hoping that she would go too, and that we would be free and alone till the end of the world, if it should ever end, but Capitu did not come. She didn't leave my mother's side, until she went home. It was time for her ave marias, and she said goodbye.

"Go with her, Bentinho," said my mother.

"There's no need, Dona Glória," she said with a laugh, "I know the way. Goodbye, Senhor protonotary . . ."

"Goodbye, Capitu."

I had already taken a step across the room, and of course my duty, my desire, all the impulses of my youth and of the moment were to cross it completely, follow my neighbor down the corridor, go down through our garden into her yard, give her a third kiss and say goodbye. I took no notice of her refusal, which I thought was a pretence, and went down the corridor: but Capitu, who was hurrying, stopped and signalled to me to go back. I did not obey; I went up to her.

"Don't come with me; we'll talk tomorrow."

"But I wanted to tell you . . ."

"Tomorrow."

"Listen!"

"Stay here!"

She was speaking low; she took my hand, and put a finger to my lips. A slave woman, who came from inside the house to light the lamp in the corridor, seeing us like that, almost in the dark, laughed sympathetically and murmured, loud enough for us to hear it, something that I did and didn't understand. Capitu whispered to me that she had suspected us, and might well tell the others. Again she insisted that I stay, and went out; I stayed there motionless, glued to the spot.

X L

A Mare

Left on my own, I sat thinking for a while, and had a fantasy. You're already familiar with my fantasies. I've recounted the Emperor's visit; I've told you about the house here in Engenho Novo, which reproduces the Matacavalos house ... My imagination has been the companion of my whole existence, lively, quick, restless, sometimes timid and inclined to stop short, but more often capable of covering huge areas in its flight. I think it was in Tacitus that I read that Iberian mares conceive from the wind; if it wasn't there, it was in some other ancient author, who decided to record this superstition in his books.* In this respect, my imagination was a great Iberian mare; the least breeze brought forth a

* Latin authors who record this myth about Iberian mares do not include Tacitus, but Varro, in *De re rustica*, and Columela, in his *Treatise on Agriculture*, mention it.

foal, and that foal soon turned into Alexander's horse; but enough of daring metaphors, unsuitable for a fifteen-year-old. Let me tell the story simply. The fantasy at that moment was to confess my love to my mother, so as to tell her that I had no vocation for the Church. The discussion about vocation all came back to me now, and, while it alarmed me, it also offered me a way out. "Yes, that's it," I thought, "I'll tell Mamma I have no vocation, and confess our loves; if she has any doubts, I'll tell her what happened the other day, the combing of the hair and the rest . . ."

X L I

The Private Audience

The rest made me stop a little longer in the corridor, thinking. I saw Dr João da Costa come in, and the usual game of ombre was set up. My mother came out of the room, and seeing me, asked me if I had seen Capitu home.

"No, Mamma, she went on her own."

And, almost throwing myself at her, I said:

"Mamma, I've got something to say to you."

"What is it?"

Alarmed, she wanted to know where the pain was—my head, my chest, my stomach?—and she felt my forehead to see if I had a fever.

"No, no, I'm fine."

"What is it then?"

"It's something, Mamma . . . But listen, look, it's better after we've had tea; a little later . . . There's nothing wrong; you get frightened at everything; there's nothing to worry about."

"You're not sick?"

"No, Mamma."

"It's that cold coming back. You're pretending because you don't want to take your medicine and sweat it off, but you've got a cold; I can tell by your voice."

I tried to laugh, to prove that there was nothing wrong. But even so she would not let me put off what I had to say to her; she took me by the hand, led me to her room, lit a candle, and ordered me to tell her everything. So, to begin somewhere, I asked her when I was going to the seminary.

"Only in the new year, after the holidays."

"Am I going . . . to stay?"

"How do you mean, to stay?"

"Will I come back home?"

"You'll come back on Saturdays and for holidays: that's the best way. When you're ordained, you'll come and live with me."

I wiped my eyes and nose. She caressed me, then tried to reproach me, but I think her voice was trembling, and her eyes looked moist. Then I said that I, too, was sad about our separation. She said that it was not a separation; just a little absence, for the sake of my studies. After the first few days, I would be fine: in no time I would get used to my classmates and teachers, and I would come to love my life with them.

"I only love you, Mamma."

There was no cunning behind these words, but I was glad I had said them, to make her believe that she was the only object of my affections; it diverted suspicion from Capitu. How many wicked intentions there are that take advantage of a half-truth like this, expressed in an innocent, pure phrase! It makes one think that lying is, at times, as involuntary as perspiration. Notice, however, dear reader, that I was trying to divert suspicions from Capitu, when I had gone to my mother precisely in order to confirm them; but the world is full of contradictions. The truth is that my mother was as innocent as the world's first dawn, before the first sin; and certainly she was not capable even intuitively of seeing the connection between one thing and another—that is, she would not deduce from my sudden opposition that I was hiding away in corners with Capitu, as José Dias had said to her. She was silent for a few moments; then she replied without imposing her authority, which encouraged my own resistance. So I spoke to her of my vocation, which had been discussed that afternoon, and which I confessed I did not feel within me.

"But you loved the idea of being a priest so much," she said, "don't you remember how you used to beg to go and see the seminarists coming out of São José, in their cassocks? At home, when José Dias called you most Reverend sir, you enjoyed the joke so much. How can it be that now. . . ? I don't believe it, Bentinho. And anyhow . . . vocation? But vocation comes with habit," she went on, repeating what she had heard from my Latin teacher.

When I tried to respond, she reproved me, not harshly but somewhat firmly, and I went back to being the submissive son I was. Then, she spoke at length, and seriously about the promise she had made; she didn't tell me of the circumstances, or the occasion or motives for it, which I only came to know about later. She did reaffirm the most important thing, that is, that she had to fulfil the promise, in payment to God.

"Our Lord came to my aid, and saved your life, and I cannot lie to Him or fail Him, Bentinho; these things cannot be done without sinning, and God, who is great and powerful, would not allow me to do it; no, Bentinho; I know I should be punished, and severely punished. It's good and holy to be a priest; you know lots of them, like Father Cabral, who lives so happily with his sister; an uncle of mine was a priest too, and they say he was nearly made a bishop . . . Stop playacting, Bentinho."

I think the look I gave her was so reproachful, that she straight away took the word back; no, not playacting, she knew quite well that I loved her, and I was incapable of feigning a feeling I didn't have. Weakness was what she meant, that I shouldn't be so weak, that I should be a man and do as I ought, for her sake and for the good of my soul. All these things and others were said a little hurriedly, and her voice was not clear, but veiled and choked. I saw that her emotions were again taking hold of her, but she would not go back on her plans, so I ventured to ask her:

"What if you asked God to release you from your promise?"

"No, I can't ask that. Are you crazy, Bentinho? And how would I know that God was releasing me?"

"Maybe in a dream; I sometimes dream of angels and saints."

"So do I, my son; but it's useless ... Come on, it's late; let's go down to the living room. That's understood then: sometime in the first two months of next year, you'll go to the seminary. And I want you to get to know the books you're studying really well; it'll look good, not only for you, but for Father Cabral. They're eager to get to know you at the seminary because Father Cabral speaks so enthusiastically about you."

She went to the door and we both came out. But before she did, she turned around to me, and I saw her on the point of clasping me to her bosom and telling me that I wouldn't be a priest. This was already what she wanted in her heart, as the time got closer. She wanted some way to pay the debt she had contracted, some other coinage worth as much or more, and she could find none.

X L I I

Capitu Reflects

The next day I went next door as soon as I could. Capitu was saying goodbye to two friends from school who had come to visit her, Paula and Sancha, the former fifteen, the latter seventeen. The first was a doctor's daughter; Sancha's father was a dealer in American goods. Capitu was downcast, and had a kerchief tied round her head; her mother told me she had read too much the previous evening, before and after tea, in the parlor and in bed, until long after midnight, with a nightlamp. . .

"If I'd lit a candle you'd have been angry, Mamma. I'm fine now."

She began to untie her kerchief: her mother hesitantly told her it was better to keep it on, but Capitu replied that it wasn't necessary, she was fine.

We remained alone in the living room; Capitu confirmed her mother's story, adding that she had had a bad night because of what she had heard at our house. I also told her what had happened to me, the talk with my mother, my entreaties, her tears, and in the end the final decisive answer: in two or three months I would go to the seminary. What could we do now? Capitu listened to me with eager attention, then gloomily; when I finished, she could hardly breathe, as if about to burst with anger, but she controlled herself.

This took place so long ago that I cannot say with certainty whether she really cried or if she just wiped her eyes; I think she just wiped them. Seeing the gesture, I took her by the hand to cheer her up, but I, too, needed cheering. We slumped onto the sofa, and sat there staring into space. I'm lying: she was staring at the floor. I did the same thing, as soon as I saw her doing so ... But I think that Capitu was looking inside herself, while I really was looking at the floor, the worm-eaten cracks, two flies crawling around, and a chipped chair-leg. It wasn't much, but it took my mind off our troubles. When I looked at Capitu again, I saw that she was completely still, and became so frightened that I shook her gently. She came back to the surface and asked me to tell her again what had happened with my mother. I did as she asked, toning the story down this time, so as not to upset her. Don't call me a dissembler, call me compassionate; it is true that I was afraid of losing Capitu, if all her hopes were ended, but it was painful to see her suffer. But the whole truth is that I already repented of having spoken to my mother, before any effective work on José Dias' part; thinking about it, I wished I had not had the disappointment, even though I thought it inevitable: it might have been delayed. Capitu was reflecting, reflecting, reflecting...

XLIII

Are you Afraid?

Suddenly she stopped reflecting, fixed me with her undertow eyes, and asked me if I was afraid.

"Afraid?"

"Yes, I'm asking if you're afraid?"

"Afraid of what?"

"Afraid of being beaten, being locked up, of fighting, walking, working . . ."

I didn't understand. If she had simply said to me: "Let's run away!" I might have obeyed her or I might not; but in any case I would have understood. But a question like that, vague and out of context; I had no idea what it meant.

"But . . . I don't understand. Being beaten?"

"Yes."

"Beaten who by? Who's going to beat me?"

Capitu made a gesture of impatience. The undertow eyes were motionless, and seemed to grow. I didn't know what to do with myself, and not wanting to ask her again, I began to think about who was going to beat me, and why, and why I was going to be locked up, and who was going to arrest me. God help me! In my imagination I saw the city jail, a dark, evil-smelling place. I saw the prison ships, too, and the Barbonos barracks, and the reformatory. All these wonderful social institutions enveloped me in their mystery, but Capitu's undertow eyes went on looking at me and growing, so much so that they drove these things completely from my mind. Capitu's mistake was that she did not let them grow to infinity: rather they went back to their normal dimensions, and she moved them in her usual way. Capitu came back to her usual self, said that she had been joking, that I shouldn't get upset, and, with a charming gesture, she patted me on the cheek with a smile, and said:

"You're scared!"

"Me? But . . ."

"It's nothing, Bentinho. Who on earth's going to beat you or arrest you? I'm sorry, I'm feeling a bit crazy today; I felt like playing games, and . . ."

"No, Capitu; you're not playing games; just now, neither of us feels like playing games."

"You're right, it was just me being crazy; see you later."

"What do you mean, see you later?"

"My headache's coming back; I'm going to put a slice of lemon on my temples."

She did as she said, and tied the kerchief round her forehead again. Then, she went with me to the yard to say goodbye; but even there we lingered for some minutes, sitting on the edge of the well. There was a strong wind, and the sky was overcast. Capitu spoke again of our separation, as of something certain and definite, however much I, fearing just that, tried to find arguments to cheer her up. Capitu, when she was not talking, was sketching noses and profiles on the ground with a bamboo stick. Since she had begun to draw, this was one of her amusements: anything could serve as paper and pencil. I was reminded of how she had scratched our names on the wall, and decided to do the same thing on the ground. I asked for the stick. Either she didn't hear me, or she paid no attention.

X L I V

The First Child

"Give it here, let me write something."

Capitu looked at me, but in a way that reminded me of

José Dias' definition, oblique and sly; she raised her gaze without raising her eyes. Her voice a little subdued, she asked me:

"Tell me something, but tell me the truth, I want no pretence; tell me, hand on heart."

"What is it? Go on."

"If you had to choose between me and your mother, who would you choose?"

"Me?"

She nodded.

"I'd choose . . . but why choose? Mamma would never ask me that."

"Perhaps not, but I am asking. Suppose that you're in the seminary and you get news that I'm going to die . . ."

"Don't say that!"

". . . or that I'll kill myself out of longing for you if you don't come straight away, and your mother doesn't want you to come; tell me, would you come?"

"I'd come."

"Against your mother's orders?"

"Against Mamma's orders."

"You'd leave the seminary, leave your mother, leave everything, to come to see me when I'm dying?"

"Don't talk about dying, Capitu!"

Capitu gave a colorless, incredulous little laugh, and with the stick she wrote a word on the ground. I bent over and read: *liar*.

It was all so strange, that I didn't know what to do in reply. I couldn't fathom the reasons for what she had written, any more than for what she had said. If I could have thought of an insult, great or small, I might have written one, too, with the same stick, but I couldn't think of any. My mind was blank. At the same time I became alarmed lest anyone heard us or saw what was written. Who could have, since we were alone? Dona Fortunata had come to the back door once, but had gone in soon after. We were all alone. I remember that some swallows passed over the yard and flew towards Santa Teresa hill; nothing more. The vague, confused sound of voices in the distance, a clatter of hooves in the street, the twittering of Pádua's birds coming from the house itself. Nothing else, or only this curious phenomenon, that the word she had written not only looked at me from the ground as if in mockery: it even seemed as if it were echoing in the air. Then I had a cruel notion; I said that a priest's life was not so bad after all, and that I could accept it without too much trouble. As revenge, it was puerile; but I nursed the secret hope of seeing her fling herself at me bathed in tears. Capitu only opened her eyes wide, and finally said:

"Being a priest is a good thing, no doubt of it; the only thing better is being a canon, because of the purple stockings. Purple is a lovely color. The more I think about it, you'd better be a canon."

"But you can't be a canon without being a priest first," I said to her, biting my lip.

"Well, start with the black stockings, and the purple ones will come later. What I wouldn't miss for anything is your first mass; tell me in time so that I can make a fashionable dress, with a hoop skirt and big flounces ... But by that time fashion may have changed. It'll have to be a big church, the Carmo or São Francisco."

"Or the Candelária."

"Candelária, too. Any one will do, so long as I can come to your first mass. I'll really make an impression. Lots of people will say: "Who's that charming young woman there in such a pretty dress?" "That's Dona Capitolina, a girl that used to live in the Rua de Matacavalos ..."

"Used to live? Are you going to move?"

"Who knows where he'll be living tomorrow?" she said, with a slightly melancholy tone to her voice; but, coming straight back to her sarcasm; "And you up at the altar, with your alb, and a golden cape over it, chanting ... *Pater noster* ..."

Ah, how I regret not being a romantic poet, to recount this duel of ironies! I would tell of my sallies and hers, the humor of one and the quick-wittedness of the other, the blood flowing, and the fury in my soul, right up to my final thrust, which was as follows:

"All right, Capitu, you can come to my first mass, but on one condition."

To which she replied:

"Name it, your Reverence."

"Promise me something?"

"What is it?"

"Say you promise."

"I'll not promise till I know what it is."

"Well, it's really two things," I went on, for something else had occurred to me.

"Two? Tell me what they are."

"The first is that you must make confession with me, so that I can administer penance and absolution. The second is that ..."

"I promise the first," she said, seeing me hesitate, and added that she was waiting for the second.

On my word it was a struggle, and I wish it had never come out of my mouth; I would not have heard what I did hear, and I would not have to write something here which some might not believe.

"The second thing ... yes ... it's that ... Promise me that I'll be the priest that marries you?"

"That marries me?" she said, somewhat taken aback.

Then she dropped the corners of her mouth, and shook her head.

"No, Bentinho," she said, "that would mean waiting a long time; you won't be a priest for a while, it takes many years ... Look, I'll promise something else; I'll promise that you will baptize my first child."

X L V

Shake your Head, Reader

Shake your head, reader; make all the incredulous gestures you like. Throw the book out, even, if boredom hasn't made you do it already; anything is possible. But, if you haven't done so and only now do you feel like it, I trust that you will pick the book up again and open it at the same page, without believing that the author is telling the truth. However, nothing is more true. That was the way that Capitu spoke, with just those words and in that manner. She spoke of her first child, as if it were her first doll.

As for my shock, great as it was, a strange sensation was mixed in with it. A fluid went through me. That threat of a first child, Capitu's first child, her marriage to someone else, and so our complete separation, the loss, the annihilation, all this produced such an effect that I was at a loss for words or gestures: I was struck dumb. Capitu was smiling; I saw her first child playing on the floor...

X L V I

Peace

We made peace just as we had made war—quickly. If I was seeking my own glory in this book, I would say that I began the negotiations; but no, it was she who started them. Some moments later, as I sat there hanging my head, she lowered her head too, but turned her eyes up so that she could look into mine. I played hard to get; then I made as if to get up and go away, but I didn't get up, nor do I know if I had the strength to go. Capitu looked at me with such tender eyes, and her position itself made them so supplicating, that I let myself be, put my arm around her waist, she took hold of my fingertips, and ...

Once more, Dona Fortunata appeared in the doorway; I don't know what for: she didn't even give me time to pull my arm away, and disappeared immediately. She may only have been doing her duty by her conscience, carrying out a ceremony, like obligatory prayers said in a hurry, with no real devotion; unless it was to ascertain with her own eyes the reality that her heart told her was there . . .

Whatever it was, my arm continued holding her daughter's waist, and that was how we made up. Best of all was that each of us now wanted to take the blame for what had been said, and we begged forgiveness of each other. Capitu put the blame on her insomnia, on her headache, her low spirits, and finally, "on the sulks." I, who was very prone to tears in those days, felt my eyes go moist . . . It was pure love, it was the effect of my darling's sufferings, it was the tenderness of reconciliation.

X L V I I

Madam's Gone Out

"All right, it's over," I said finally; "but explain one thing to me—why did you ask me if I was afraid of being beaten?"

"No reason at all," Capitu replied, after some hesitation. "Why bring that up again?"

"Tell me though. Was it because of the seminary?"

"Yes; I've heard they beat the boys there . . . No? I don't believe it either."

I was satisfied with the explanation; there could be no other. If, as I think, Capitu was not telling the truth, one has to admit that she could not tell it; lying is like one of those maids who are quick to reply to visitors that "Madam's gone out," when madam doesn't wish to speak to anyone. Such complicity gives a peculiar pleasure; sharing the sin makes people more equal, to say nothing of the pleasure of seeing the faces of those who have been deceived, and their backs as they go down the steps . . . Truth had not gone out, it was at home, in Capitu's heart, half asleep over its own repentance. And I didn't leave sad or angry; I thought the maid delightful, alluring, better than the mistress.

The swallows now flew by in the opposite direction, or perhaps they weren't the same ones. We, however, were the same; there we were, sharing our illusions and our fears, and already beginning to share our memories.

X L V I I I

The Oath at the Well

"No," I exclaimed suddenly.

"No what?"

We had been silent for a few minutes, during which time I thought a great deal and finally had an idea; my exclamation, however, was so loud that my neighbor got a fright.

"I'm not having it," I went on. "They say that we're not old enough to marry, that we're children, youngsters—that's what I've heard them say, youngsters. Fine: but two or three years will soon be over. Will you swear something? Swear that you'll marry no one but me?"

Capitu had no hesitation in swearing: I even saw that her cheeks were flushed with pleasure. She swore twice and then a third time:

"Even if you marry someone else, I'll keep my oath, and never marry."

"If I marry someone else?"

"Anything can happen, Bentinho. You might find another girl who loves you, you could fall in love with her and marry her. Who am I for you to think of me if that happened?"

"But I'm swearing, too! I swear, I swear by Almighty God that I will marry no one but you. Is that enough?"

"It should be enough," she said, "I don't dare ask any more. Yes, you swear ... But let's swear another way; let's swear that we'll marry one another, come what may."

You can see the difference; it was more than the choice of the spouse, it was the affirmation that we were going to be married. My young friend was able to think clearly and fast. It was true, the previous formula was limited, as it was merely exclusive. We could end up unmarried, like the sun and moon, without going back on the oath at the well. This formula was better, and had the advantage of strengthening my will against my ordination. We swore by the second formula, and were so happy that all fear of danger vanished. We were religious, and heaven was our witness. I no longer feared even the seminary.

"If they really insist, I'll go; but I'll pretend it's just any school; I'm not going to be ordained."

Capitu feared our separation, but ended up accepting this scheme as best. We would not upset my mother, and time would fly until the moment when the marriage could take place. Any resistance to the seminary, on the other hand, would confirm José Dias' accusation. It was Capitu, not I, who made this reflection.

X L I X

A Candle on Saturdays

And that is how, after so much struggle, we finally approached the safe haven where we should have sheltered from the first.

Don't be too critical, if you think you could have been a better pilot; hearts cannot be navigated as easily as the oceans of this world. We were happy, and began to talk of the future. I promised my future wife a quiet, delightful life, in the country or just outside the city. We would come here once a year. If it was in the suburbs, it would be far off, where no one would come to disturb us. In my opinion, the house should be neither large nor small, but in between; I planted flowers, chose furniture, a chaise, and an oratory. Yes, we would have a beautiful oratory, tall, in jacaranda wood, with an image of Our Lady of the Conception. I lingered over this longer than over the rest, partly because we were religious, and partly to make up for the cassock that I was going to throw by the wayside; but there was still something there that I attribute to the unconscious secret desire to ensure the protection of heaven. We would light a candle on Saturdays . . .

L

A Compromise

Some months later I went to the São José seminary. If I could count the tears I wept the day before and on the morning of my departure, they would add up to more than all those shed since Adam and Eve. This is somewhat of an exaggeration; but it is good to be emphatic from time to time, to make up for this obsession with accuracy that plagues me. However, if I were to rely on the memory of the sensation, I would not be far from the truth; at fifteen, everything is infinite. The truth is that however prepared I was, I suffered a great deal. My mother suffered too, but inwardly, in her heart and soul; moreover, Father Cabral had found a compromise, to try out my vocation; if at the end of two years, I revealed no ecclesiastical vocation, I would pursue another career.

"Promises should be fulfilled as God wills it. Suppose that Our Lord refuses to incline your son to the Church, and that he does not get the pleasure from the habits of seminary life that God gave me, then it must be that God's will is otherwise. You could not have given your son, before he was born, a vocation that Our Lord has refused him . . ."

It was a concession from the priest. It gave my mother an advance pardon, making the remission of the debt come from the creditor. Her eyes shone, but her lips said no. José Dias, having failed to go to Europe with me, took the next best thing, and backed up "the Protonotary's proposal"; it merely seemed to him that one year was enough.

"I am certain," he said, winking at me, "that in a year our Bentinho's ecclesiastical vocation will manifest itself clearly and decisively. He'll make a first-rate priest, no doubt of that. But if it doesn't come in a year . . ."

Later, he said to me in private:

"Go for a year: a year will soon be gone. If you still don't like it, it's because God doesn't will it, as the Father says, and in that case, my young friend, the best solution is Europe."

Capitu gave me the same advice when my mother told her that I was definitively going to the seminary:

"My daughter, you're going to lose your playmate . . ."

She was so pleased at being addressed as "my daughter" (it was the first time my mother had done so), that she didn't even have time to be sad: she kissed my mother's hand, and said that she had been told about it already, by me. Privately, she encouraged me to endure everything patiently; after a year everything would have changed, and a year would go quickly by. We were not yet saying farewell; that happened the day before I went, in a manner that requires a chapter to itself. All I'll say here is that, just as we were becoming more attached to one another, she attached herself to my mother, became more attentive and affectionate, was always in her company, with eyes only for her. My mother was by nature as affectionate as she was sensitive; every little thing gave her joy or anguish. She began to discover a number of new charms in Capitu: fine, rare gifts. She gave her a ring of hers, and some other trinkets. She refused to be photographed when Capitu asked for her picture; but she had a miniature, done when she was twenty-five and, after some hesitation, resolved to give it her. Capitu's eyes, when she got this present, cannot be described; they were not oblique,nor were they undertow eyes: they were direct, clear, and bright. She passionately kissed the portrait, and my mother did the same to her. All this reminds me of our farewells.

L I

In the Half-Light

In the half-light, all must be brief as that moment. Our farewells did not take long, though they were as long as we could make them, in her house, in the parlor, before the candles were lit; that was where we finally said goodbye. We swore once more that we would marry each other, and it was not only the squeeze of our hands that sealed the contract, as in the yard: it was the meeting of our loving lips ... I might take this out when the book is printed, unless I change my mind before then. In fact, it can stay, because in all truth it is our defense. What the holy commandment says is that we should not take the Lord's name *in vain*. I was not entering the seminary under false pretenses, since I had a contract signed and registered in heaven itself. As for the seal, God made clean lips as He made clean hands, and the evil intent is rather in your perverse mind than in that pair of adolescents ... Oh, sweet companion of my childhood, I was pure, and pure I remained, and entered the portals of São José pure, in appearance to seek priestly investiture, and before that, a vocation. But you were my vocation, you my true investiture.

L I I

Old Pádua

Now I will recount old Pádua's goodbyes. Early in the morning he came to our house. My mother told him to go and speak to me in my room.

"May I?" he asked, putting his head round the door.

I went to shake his hand; he embraced me tenderly.

"May you be happy!" he said to me, "You will be greatly missed by me and all my family, believe me. We all have a great regard for you, as you deserve. If anyone says anything different, don't believe him. It's wicked intrigues. When I married I, too, was the victim of intrigues; they were soon undone. God is great and knows the truth. If some day you were to lose your mother and uncle—something which, by the light of heaven, I hope never happens, for they are good people, excellent people, and I am grateful for the kindnesses they have shown me ... No, I'm not like others, certain parasites, outsiders who sow dissension in families, vulgar flatterers, no, not me; I'm not like that; I don't gorge myself on other people's food, or live in other people's houses ... Still, they're the lucky ones!"

"Why does he talk like this?" I thought. "He must know that José Dias speaks ill of him."

"But, as I was saying, if some day you should lose your family, you can count on our company. Of course it's not enough, but our affection is enormous, believe me. Priest or not, our house is at your disposal. I only ask that you don't forget me, don't forget old Pádua . . ."

He sighed and went on:

"Don't forget your old Pádua: if you've some trifle you could leave me as a souvenir, a Latin exercise book, anything, a waist-coat button, any little thing that's of no use to you. The memories are what matter."

I gave a start. I had wrapped in paper a long and beautiful lock of my hair, that I had cut the previous day. My intention was to take it to Capitu when I left; but I had the idea of giving it to the father—the daughter would know to keep it safe. I took the packet and gave it him.

"Here: keep this."

"A lock of your hair!" exclaimed Pádua opening and shutting the packet. "Oh, thank you! Thank you from me and my family! I'll give it to the old woman for safekeeping, or to the youngster: she's more careful than her mother. Aren't they lovely? How could you have cut such beautiful hair? Give me an embrace! Another! And another! Goodbye!"

His eyes were really moist; his face had a disillusioned look, like someone who has saved up all his hopes, and put them on a single lottery ticket, only for the accursed number to draw a blank—such a lovely number, too!

L I I I

On My Way

I left for the seminary. Spare me the other farewells. My mother clasped me to her breast. Cousin Justina sighed. I think she hardly cried, if at all. There are people to whom tears come slowly, or never come at all; it's said they suffer more than the others. Cousin Justina was probably hiding her intimate sufferings, while she corrected my mother's oversights, gave advice and issued orders. Uncle Cosme, when I kissed his hand to say goodbye, said to me with a laugh:

"Off you go, lad; come back Pope!"

José Dias, composed and grave, said nothing at first; we had spoken the previous day, in his room, where I went to see if it might still be possible to avoid the seminary. Nothing could now be done, but he gave me hopes, and above all he cheered me up. Before the year was out we'd be on board. As I thought this too short a time, he explained:

"They say it's not a good time to cross the Atlantic: I'll make inquiries. If it's not, we'll go in March or April."

"I can study medicine right here."

José Dias ran his fingers up and down his braces with an impatient gesture, pursed his lips, and then formally rejected the notion.

"I would not hesitate to approve the idea," he said, "if it weren't for the fact that in the School of Medicine they teach, exclusively, that allopathic filth. Allopathy is the error of the ages, and will perish; it's murder, a lie, an illusion. If they tell you that in the School of Medicine you can learn that part of the sciences which is common to all systems, that is true; allopathy errs in the realm of therapeutics. Physiology, anatomy, pathology, are neither allopathic nor homeopathic, but it is best to learn everything from the beginning, from the books and the lips of men who cultivate the truth . . ."

Thus he had spoken the previous day in his room. Now, he said nothing, or proffered some aphorism about religion and the family. I remember this one: "To divide a thing with God is still to possess it." When my mother gave me her last kiss: "A most loving scene," he sighed. It was the morning of a beautiful day. The slave-children were whispering to each other; the women came to take their blessing: "Your blessing, massa Bentinho! Don't forget your old Joana! Miquelina pray for your worship!" In the street, José Dias still insisted on hope for the future:

"Put up with it for a year; by then it'll all be arranged."

L I V

The Panegyric of Saint Monica

In the seminary . . . Oh, no! I'm not going to tell the story of my life at the seminary: nor would a single chapter be enough. No, dear sir; it is possible that some day I may compose a brief account of what I saw and experienced there, of the people I lived with, of the customs of the place, and everything else. This itch to write, when you catch it in your fifties, never goes away. One may be cured of it in one's youth; to go no further, right here in the seminary there was a fellow student who wrote verses, in the manner of Junqueira Freire, poet and monk, whose book had recently appeared.* He took orders; years later I encountered him in the choir of the church of São Pedro, and asked him to show me his latest verses.

---

* Luís José Junqueira Freire (1832–1855) was a Benedictine monk who abandoned the order in the year before his death. His *Inspirações do claustro* (1855), very popular when it first appeared, and one of the most characteristic products of the second generation of Brazilian Romantic poets, is full of the conflicts—sexual and religious—that led to his renunciation of his vows.

"What verses?" he asked, somewhat startled.

"Yours. Don't you remember, at the seminary . . ."

"Ah!" he smiled.

He smiled, and while he carried on looking in an open book for the time he had to say mass the following day, he confessed to me that he not had written any more poetry since being ordained. It had tickled him when he was young: now he'd scratched himself, it was over, and he was fine. And he spoke to me in prose of an infinite number of events of the day, the high cost of living, Father X's sermon . . . a vicar's post in Minas. . .

The opposite of this was a seminarist who did not enter the Church. He was called . . . There's no need to give his name; his story is enough. He had written a *Panegyric of Saint Monica*, which had earned praise from some quarters, and at that time was read by the seminarists.* He got permission to print it, and dedicated it to St. Augustine. All this is ancient history; what is more recent is that one day, in 1882, when I was attending to some business in the Navy Department, I came across this ex-colleague of mine, who was now head of an administrative section. He had left the seminary, abandoned letters, married, and forgotten everything except the *Panegyric of Saint Monica*, some twenty-nine pages, which he went on handing out in later life. As I needed some information, I went to ask him for it, and one couldn't have asked for more courtesy and efficiency; he gave me everything, clearly, correctly, and copiously. Naturally we talked of the past, personal memories, things that happened in class, trivial incidents, a book, a word, a saying, all the old rubbish spilled out, and we laughed and sighed together. We spent a while recalling our memories of the seminary. Whether because of their associations with the place, or because we were young then, the memories had such power to bring happiness that if there had been any shadow over it in the past, it did not appear now. He confessed that he had lost contact with all his friends from the seminary.

"Me too, or almost all; no doubt they all went back to their

---

* Saint Monica was the mother of St. Augustine, to whom he attributed his conversion to Christianity.

provinces when they were ordained, and the ones from here must have taken posts elsewhere."

"Happy times!" he sighed.

Then, after some reflection, fixing me with faded, insistent eyes, he asked me:

"Have you kept my *Panegyric*?"

I didn't know what to say; I tried to move my lips, but not a word would come out; finally, I asked:

"Panegyric? What panegyric?"

"My *Panegyric of Saint Monica.*"

I didn't remember straight away, but the explanation should have been enough; and after some moments of mental investigation, I answered that I had kept it for a long time, but what with moving house, travels. . .

"I'll bring you a copy."

Before twenty-four hours were up, he was in my house, with the pamphlet, a twenty-six-year-old pamphlet, soiled, marked by time, but with no missing pages, and a respectful, hand-written dedication.

"It's the second-last copy," he said to me, "now I've only got one left, and that I cannot give to anyone."

And, seeing me leafing through the little book:

"See if you remember any passages," he said.

A twenty-six-year interval can put an end to closer, more constant friendships than this, but it was a matter of courtesy, charity even, to remember some page or other; I read one of them, stressing certain phrases to give him the impression that they had found an echo in my memory. He agreed that they were beautiful, but he preferred others, and pointed them out.

"Do you remember?"

"Yes, of course. *The Panegyric of Saint Monica*! How it takes me back to my youth! I've never forgotten the seminary, believe me. The years go by, one thing happens after another, new sensations, new friendships that go the way of all flesh, too; such is life . . . Well, dear colleague, nothing has obscured the memory of that time we spent together, the priests, the lessons, our games . . . you remember the games we used to play? Father Lopes, oh, Father Lopes ..."

Staring into space, he must have been listening, and of course heard what I had said, but he only said one thing, and even that after staying silent for a while: he brought his eyes back into focus and sighed:

"It's certainly been a success, my *Panegyric!*"

L V

A Sonnet

This said, he shook my hands with all the force of his enormous gratitude, said goodbye and left. I was left alone, with the *Panegyric*, and what its pages brought back to me is worth a chapter or more. Before that, however—and because I too had my *Panegyric*—I will tell the story of a sonnet that I never wrote; it was when I was at the seminary, and the first line is as follows:

"Oh, flower of heaven! Oh! flower chaste and pure!"

How and why this line came into my head, I do not know; it came just like that, as I lay in bed, like an isolated exclamation, and, when I realized that it scanned like a line of poetry, it occurred to me to compose something with it, a sonnet. Insomnia, that muse with staring eyes, stopped me sleeping for an hour or two; it was an itch that needed scratching, and I scratched enthusiastically. I didn't make up my mind on a sonnet right away; at first I thought of other forms, whether in blank verse or rhyme, but in the end I stuck to the sonnet. It was a short, serviceable poem. As for the idea to be expressed, this first line wasn't yet an idea, merely an exclamation; the idea would come later. So in my bed, wrapped in my sheets, I tried to compose a poem. I was as excited as a mother who feels her child, her first child about to be born. I was going to be a poet, and compete with that monk from Bahia who had only recently been discovered, and was then in fashion; I, a seminarist, would tell of my woes in verse, as he had spoken of his sufferings in the cloister. I got the line by heart, and repeated it to the sheets, under my breath; frankly, I thought it was beautiful, and still now I don't think it's bad:

"Oh, flower of heaven! Oh! flower chaste and pure!"

Who was the flower? Capitu, of course; but it could be virtue, poetry, religion, any other concept that would fit the metaphor of flower, and flower of heaven. I waited for the rest, reciting the line over and over, lying now on my left side, now on my right; finally, I lay on my back, with my eyes on the ceiling; even so, nothing more came. Then I remarked that the most lauded sonnets were those that ended with a "golden key," that is, with one of those lines that sum everything up, in their meaning and their form. I thought of inventing one of these lines, thinking that the final line, if it were composed in order, after the thirteen previous ones, would be unlikely to display such perfection; I imagined that such keys were made before the lock. Thus it was that I decided to compose the last line of the sonnet, and after a great deal of sweating, out came this:

"Though life be lost, the battle still is won!"

Without boasting, and speaking as if someone else had composed it, it was a magnificent line. Sonorous, without a doubt. And there was an idea behind it—victory won at the cost of life itself—which was exalted and noble. It may be that it was not very original, but neither was it commonplace; and still today I cannot explain by what mysterious means it entered into such a young head. At that moment I thought it sublime. I recited the golden key over and over again; then I repeated the two lines consecutively, and set about linking them by the twelve central ones. In the light of the last line, I thought it better that the subject should not be Capitu; it would be justice. It was more appropriate to say that, in the struggle for justice, one might lose one's life, but the battle was still won. It also occurred to me to take "battle" in the literal sense, and turn it into the battle for one's country, for example; in that case, the flower of heaven would be freedom. This meaning, however, since the poet was a seminarist, might not be as suitable as the first, and I spent some minutes hesitating between them. I thought that justice was better, but in the end finally chose another idea, that of charity. I then recited the two lines, each in the manner suited to them, the first languorously:

"Oh, flower of heaven! Oh! flower chaste and pure!"

and the second with vigor:

"Though life be lost, the battle still is won!"

The sensation I had was that a perfect sonnet was going to emerge. It was no small thing to have a good beginning and end. To give myself a bath of inspiration, I thought of some famous sonnets, and noticed that most of them had a great ease about them; the lines emanated from each other, like the idea itself, so that you couldn't work out if the idea had created the verses, or the verses had generated the idea. Then I went back to my sonnet and once more repeated the first line and waited for the second; the second didn't come, nor the third, nor the fourth: none came. Rage swelled up in me, and more than once I thought of getting out of bed and getting ink and paper. Maybe if I wrote things down, the lines would come, but. . .

Tired of waiting, I thought of altering the meaning of the last line by turning it round, in the following manner:

"The battle may be lost, but life is won!"

The sense was exactly the opposite, but perhaps this might just bring the inspiration. In this case, the meaning would be ironic: if you do not practise charity, you may win in life, but lose the battle for heaven. I summoned up more strength and waited. I had no window: if I had, I might have gone to ask for an idea from the night sky. Who knows if the fireflies, shining here below, might not have acted as echoes of the stars, and this living metaphor might have given me the elusive lines, with the appropriate rhymes and meanings?

I toiled in vain, searched, scoured, waited, but the lines did not come. Later on in life I wrote some pages in prose, and now I am composing this narrative: I find that there is nothing as difficult as writing, well or ill. Well, gentlemen, nothing consoles me for the loss of that sonnet I never wrote. But, since I believe that sonnets exist ready made, like odes and dramas and other works of art, for such are the laws of metaphysics, I give these two lines to the first person with time on his hands who comes along. Some Sunday, if it's raining, out in the country, or at any moment of leisure, he can try and see if the sonnet comes out. The whole point is to provide it with an idea and fill the missing middle.

L V I

A Seminarist

All this the mischievous little book kept on repeating, with its old print and its Latin quotations. I saw the outlines of many seminarists arise from its pages—the Albuquerque brothers, for instance, one of whom is a canon in Bahia, while the other pursued medicine as a career and, so they say, has discovered a specific against yellow fever.* I saw Bastos, a skinny lad, who's a vicar in Meia-Ponte, if he's not already dead; Luís Borges, though a priest, became a politician, and ended up a Senator of the Empire ... How many other faces stared at me from the cold pages of the *Panegyric*! No, they weren't cold; they had the warmth of budding youth, of the past, my own warmth. I wanted to read them again, and managed to understand parts of the text, just as if I had been reading it for the first time, though it seemed shorter. It was delightful to wander through it; at times, unconsciously, I turned the page over as if I were really reading; I think it was when my eyes went to the bottom of the page, and the hand, so used to helping out, did its usual job ...

Here is another seminarist. His name was Ezequiel de Sousa Escobar. He was a slim youth, with pale eyes, a little elusive, like his hands, like his feet, like his speech, like everything about him. If you weren't used to him, he could make you feel dizzy, not knowing where to take a hold on him. He didn't look you in the eye, and didn't speak clearly and continuously; his hand didn't grip yours, nor let itself be gripped, because, when you thought you had hold of his fingers, they were so slender and short you found there was nothing there. The same can be said of the feet, here one moment, gone the next. This difficulty in settling was the greatest obstacle he found in adapting to seminary ways. He had a instant smile, but also a hearty, relaxed laugh. One thing, perhaps, was not elusive as the rest, and that was his habit of reflecting; often we would find him, with his eyes turned inwards, thinking. He always told us he was meditating on some spiritual matter, either that or committing yesterday's lesson to memory. When he became an intimate of mine, he frequently asked me for explanations and detailed repetitions, and had the capacity to memorize them all, every last word. It may be that this faculty got in the way of some other.

He was three years older than I, the son of a lawyer from Curitiba who was related to a businessman in Rio de Janeiro who

---

* Yellow fever epidemics still killed thousands every summer, especially in Rio de Janeiro.

acted as his agent.* The father was a strongly devout Catholic. Escobar had a sister, who was an angel, he said.

"It's not only her beauty that's angelic—it's her goodness, too. You can't imagine what a good creature she is. She writes to me a lot: I must show you her letters."

Indeed they were simple and affectionate, full of endearments and advice. Escobar told me interesting stories about her, all of which came down to illustrating the goodness and the intelligence of this sweet creature; such were her virtues that they might have made me marry her, had it not been for Capitu. She died not long after. Seduced by his words, I was on the point of telling him my story then and there. At first I was shy, but he found his way into my confidence. Those elusive ways ceased when he wanted them to, and time and the new environment made them settle down, too. Escobar opened up his whole soul, from the front door to the bottom of the garden. Our souls, as you know, are laid out like houses, often with windows on every side, lots of light and fresh air. There are also houses that are closed and dark, with no windows at all, or with a few barred windows, like convents or prisons. In the same way, there are chapels and bazaars, simple lean-tos and sumptuous palaces.

I don't know what mine was. I was not yet *Casmurro*, nor *Dom Casmurro*. Shyness prevented me being open, but since the doors had neither keys nor locks, all that was needed was to push them, and Escobar pushed and entered. I found him inside, and here he stayed, until. . .

* Curitiba is the capital of the southern state of Paraná.

LVII

In Preparation

A h!, but it wasn't only the seminarists who arose from the old pages of the *Panegyric*. They also brought back old sensations to me, so many and varied that I couldn't recount them all without taking space from the rest of what I have to tell. One of these sensations, and one of the first, I would have preferred to tell in Latin. It's not that the subject hasn't got good honest words in our language, which is chaste for the chaste, as it is foul for the foul. Yes, "most chaste" lady reader, as my late-lamented José Dias would have said, you can read the chapter to the end, without fear of being shocked or embarrassed.

In fact, now I'll put the story into another chapter. However respectable it may turn out, there's still something less than austere about the subject, which demands a few lines of rest and preparation. This chapter can serve that purpose. And that is already a great deal, dear reader and friend; the heart, when it anticipates what is to come—the importance and number of the events themselves—is strengthened and forearmed, and the evil is much the less for it. It is also true if this doesn't happen now, then it never will. You can even see a degree of ingenuity on my part here; for, as you read what you are about to read, it is probable that you will find it much less crude than you expected.

L V I I I

The Treaty

It happened that, one Monday, as I was going back to the seminary, I saw a lady fall down in the street. My first reaction, in such a case, ought to have been of pity or laughter; it was neither one thing or the other, because—and this is what I would have liked to have said in Latin—because the lady was wearing very well-washed stockings, and she didn't dirty them, and had silk garters, and didn't lose them. Several people went to help her, but they had no opportunity to lift her from the ground; she got up very annoyed, dusted herself off, thanked them, and disappeared down the next street.

"This fashion for imitating the French girls on the Rua do Ouvidor," said José Dias to me, as he walked along and commented on the fall, "is obviously wrong.* Our girls should walk as they always did, slowly and leisurely, not with this Frenchified tick-tack, tick-tack . . ."

I hardly heard him. The lady's stockings and garters whitened and curled around in front of me, then walked on, fell, got up, and went away. When we got to the corner, I looked down the street, and saw our unfortunate lady in the distance, going at the same pace, tick-tack, tick-tack . . .

"It doesn't look as if she hurt herself," I said.

"So much the better for her, but she must have scratched her knees; it's nothing more than a fad, scurrying around like that . . ."

I think he said "fad"; I stopped at the "scratched knees." From that moment, until I got to the seminary, I didn't see a woman in the street that I didn't want to fall; some I guessed were wearing their stockings well stretched, with tight garters . . . Maybe there

---

* The Rua do Ouvidor was the central shopping street of downtown Rio de Janeiro; most of the fashion shops were French.

were some who weren't even wearing stockings . . . But I saw them with them on . . . Or . . . It's also possible. . .

I intersperse this with ellipses, to give an idea of my thoughts, which were diffuse and confused in just this manner; but I am probably not conveying what I mean. My head was hot, and I felt unsteady on my feet. In the seminary, the first hour was unbearable. The cassocks began to look like skirts, and brought back the lady's fall. It was no longer just one that fell; every one I met in the street now showed me her blue garters in a flash: they were blue. At night, I dreamt of them. A multitude of abominable creatures started walking round me, tick-tack, tick-tack . . . They were beautiful, some slim, others plump, and all of them as agile as the devil. I woke up, and tried to drive them away with curses and other methods, but as soon as I went back to sleep they came back, and hand in hand around me, they made a vast circle of skirts, or, mounted in the air, rained legs and feet on my head. It went on like this till dawn. I could sleep no longer, and prayed paternosters, ave marias and credos. Since this book is the unvarnished truth, I have to confess that I had to interrupt my prayers to accompany a faraway figure, tick-tack, tick-tack . . . I hurriedly went back to my prayer, always picking it up in the middle to get it right, as if there had been no interruption, but no doubt I didn't start where I had left off.

Since the evil continued into the early morning, I tried to defeat it, but in such a way that I wouldn't lose it altogether. Wise men of the Scriptures, divine what I did. This was the answer: since I could not turn these images away from me, I had recourse to a treaty between my conscience and my imagination. These female visions would from now on be thought of as simple incarnations of the vices, and for that very reason susceptible of contemplation, as the best way of tempering the character and of arming it for the harsh struggles of life. I didn't formulate this in words, nor was it necessary to do so; the contract was made tacitly, with some repugnance, but it was made. And for some days, it was I myself who called up these visions to strengthen myself, and did not reject them until they themselves went away exhausted.

L I X

Companions with Good Memories

There are reminiscences which will not lie down until the pen or the tongue has published them. An ancient author said that he cursed companions with good memories. Life is full of such companions, and it may be that I am one of them, although the proof that my memory is fallible can be found precisely in the fact that I cannot think of the name of that same author: but he was one of the ancients, and that's enough.*

No, no, my memory is not good. On the contrary, it can be compared to someone who has lived in numerous lodgings, without remembering either faces or names, and only a few of their circumstances. For someone who passes his whole life in the same family house, with the same old furniture and clothes, people and affections, everything is engraved on his mind through continuity and repetition. How I envy those who have not forgotten the color of the first trousers they wore! I can't recall the color of those I put on yesterday. I can only swear that they were not yellow because I detest that color; but even that may be forgetfulness and confusion.

Let us hope it is forgetfulness rather than confusion; let me explain myself. There is no way of emending a confused book, but everything can be put into books with omissions. I never get upset when I read one of this latter type. What I do, when I get to the end, is shut my eyes and think of all the things I didn't find in it. How many delightful ideas occur to me then! What profound reflections! The rivers, mountains, churches that I didn't see in the pages I have read, all appear to me now with their waters,

* The author in question is Lucian of Samosata (c. 125–c. 190 A.D.), a Greek satirist notable for his dialogues, and very influential on later writers such as Erasmus and Swift. Machado was very familiar with his work. The phrase cited is from *Lapithes or The Banquet.*

their trees, their altars, and the generals draw the swords that had stayed in their scabbards, and the trumpets sound out the notes that were sleeping in the metal, and everything proceeds in the most unpredictably lively way.

For everything can be found outside a book with gaps in it, dear reader. Thus I fill in others' lacunae: in this way too you can fill in mine.

L X

Dear Panegyric!

This is the way that I wrote my *Panegyric*, and I did more: I put in it not only what was missing of the saint herself, but also things that had nothing to do with her. You have seen the sonnet, the stockings, the garters, the seminarist Escobar and several others. Now you will see what more came out of the yellowed pages of the little book.

Dear little book, you were of no use at all, but then what use is an old pair of slippers? However, often in such slippers there is, as it were, the aroma and the warmth of two feet. Worn out and tattered, nonetheless they still remind us that someone put them on in the morning, when they got up, or took them off at night, when they went to bed again. And if this is not an apt comparison, because slippers are a part of the person, and had contact with the feet, here are other memories, like the stone in the street, the door to the house, a particular whistle, a street-seller's refrain, like the one for coconut sweets that I told you of in Chapter XVIII. In fact, at the moment when I reproduced that cry, I was so overcome with nostalgia that I had the idea of having it written out by a friend of mine, a music teacher, and stuck on at the bottom of the chapter. If afterwards I deprived the chapter of this privilege, it was because another musician I showed it to naively confessed to me that he could find nothing in the transcription that made him feel nostalgic. So that the same thing doesn't happen to other professionals who might read me, it's best to save the book's publisher the work and expense of the illustration. You've seen that I didn't put anything in, nor will I. Now I believe that it is not enough for street cries, or pamphlets written in seminaries, to contain within them circumstances, people, and sensations; people must have known them and suffered them in reality: without that everything is silent and colorless.

But let's go on to what else came out of these faded pages.

L X I

Homer's Cow

There was a great deal else. I saw the first days of separation, hard and oppressive, in spite of the words of comfort given me by the priests and seminarists, and those of my mother and Uncle Cosme, brought to the seminary by José Dias.

"They're all missing you," he said, "but of course the one who misses you most is naturally the one with the tenderest heart; and whose is that?" he said writing the reply in his eyes.

"Mamma's," I immediately replied.

José Dias grasped my hands with feeling, and immediately gave a picture of my mother's unhappiness: she spoke of me every day, almost every hour. He always approved of what she did; and since he put in some word about the gifts which God had given me, my mother's dejection on these occasions was indescribable; and he told me all this with tears of admiration. Uncle Cosme also got very upset.

"Just yesterday an interesting thing happened. I having said to your most excellent mother that God had given her, not a son, but an angel from heaven, the doctor was so moved that he found no other way of overcoming his tears than praising me in that mocking way, as only he knows how. Needless to say, Dona Glória wiped away a furtive tear. That's a mother for you! What a most loving heart!"

"But, Sr. José Dias, when am I to get out of here?"

"Leave that to me. The trip to Europe is what we need, but it can be done one or two years from now, in 1859 or 1860 . . ."

"No sooner than that!"

"This year would be better, but give it time. Be patient, carry on studying, nothing's lost in leaving here with some learning; and what's more, even if you don't become a priest, the experience of the seminary is useful, and it's no bad thing to enter the world anointed with the holy oils of theology . . ."

At this point—I remember as if it were today—José Dias' eyes flashed so intensely that I was amazed. His lids then shut, and stayed thus for a few moments, until they lifted again, and his eyes fixed on the patio wall, as if absorbed in something: unless they were absorbed in themselves. Then they dragged themselves away from the wall and began to wander round the whole patio. I might compare him to Homer's cow; it wandered and moaned around the calf which it had just given birth to.* I did not ask him what the matter was, either out of shyness, or because two lecturers, one of whom taught theology, were coming in our direction. As they passed us, the dependent, who knew them, greeted them with appropriately deferential words, and asked how I was getting on.

"We can't promise anything yet," said one of them, "but it seems he'll do well."

"That's what I was saying just now," José Dias replied. "I hope to be present at his first mass; but even if he doesn't take orders,

* *Iliad,* Canto xvii, ll. 1–10.

he couldn't have a better course of instruction than here. For the journey of life," he concluded lingering over his words, "he will be anointed with the holy oils of theology . . ."

This time the flash in his eyes was not so bright, his eyelids didn't close, nor did his pupils make their former movements. On the contrary, he was all attentiveness and enquiry: at most, a bright, friendly smile played around his lips. The theology teacher liked his metaphor, and told him so; he thanked him, and told him they were ideas that came out in the course of conversation; he was neither a writer nor an orator. I on the other hand didn't like it at all; and as soon as the lecturers were gone, I shook my head:

"I don't want to know about the holy oils of theology; I want to get out of here as soon as possible, right now . . ."

"Now is impossible, my angel; but it might happen much sooner than we think. Who knows, perhaps this very year, in '58? I have a plan set up, and I'm already thinking of the words I'll use to lay it before Dona Glória; I'm certain she'll give way and come with us."

"I doubt Mamma will go abroad."

"We'll see. Mothers are capable of anything; but, with her or without her, I'm certain we'll be going, and I'll make every effort I can, be sure of that. Patience is what's required. And do nothing here that might give rise to criticism or complaints; be as docile as you can and give every appearance of being contented. Didn't you hear the teacher's praise? You've been behaving yourself. Keep it up, then."

"But 1859 or 1860 is a long time off."

"It will be this year," José Dias replied.

"Three months from now?"

"Or six."

"No; three months."

"Very well then. Now I've got a plan that seems better than any other. It is to combine the absence of vocation for the Church and the need for a change of climate. Why don't you cough?"

"Why don't I cough?"

"Not right away, but I'll tell you when to start coughing, as necessary, gradually, a little, dry cough, and some loss of appetite; I'll prepare your most excellent mother . . . Oh! all this is for her sake. Since her son can't serve the Church as it should be served, the best way of fulfilling God's will is to dedicate him to something else. This world too is a church for the righteous . . ."

I thought it was Homer's cow again, as if this "world too is a church for the righteous" was going to be another calf, a brother for the "holy oils of theology." But I allowed him no time for maternal affection, and replied:

"Ah! I understand! Put on a show of illness so that I have to go away, is that it?"

José Dias hesitated a little, and then explained:

"You'll be showing nothing but the truth, because, frankly, Bentinho, I've been somewhat concerned about your chest for some months now. Your chest is not right. When you were small, you had some fever and wheezing . . . It all went away, but there are days when you look pale. I'm not saying it's an illness, but illness can come on fast. A house can fall down in a second. So, if the dear, saintly lady doesn't want to come with us—or so that she will come sooner, I think that a good cough . . . If the cough is to come sooner or later, it's better to hurry it along . . . Leave it to me, I'll tell you when . . ."

"Yes, but when I come out of here it won't be to take passage straight away. First I'll come out, and then we'll arrange the journey; we can go next year. Don't they say that the best time to go is April or May? May, then. First I leave the seminary, two months from now . . ."

And because the words were itching in my throat, I quickly turned around and asked him pointblank:

"How's Capitu?"

LXII

A Touch of Iago

It was a tactless question to ask, at the very moment when I was attempting to put the journey off. It amounted to a confession that the principal or only motive for my aversion of the seminary was Capitu, and it would make him think that the journey was unlikely. I realized this as soon as I had spoken; I wanted to correct myself, but I didn't know how, nor did he give me time.

"She's been as happy as ever; she's a giddy little thing. Just waiting to find some local beau to marry her . . ."

I'm sure I went pale; at least, I felt a cold shiver running through my whole body. The news that she was happy while I cried every night produced that effect, and it was accompanied by such a violent beating of the heart that even now I seem to hear it. There might be some exaggeration in this; but that's the way with human discourse, a mixture of the overblown and the undersized, which make up for each other, and in the end level out. On the other hand, if we take it that I hear it not in my ears but in my memory, we will come at the real truth. My memory still now hears my heart thumping at that moment. Don't forget that these were the emotions of first love. I almost asked José Dias to explain Capitu's happiness to me, what she was doing, if she was laughing, singing or jumping up and down, but I stopped myself in time, and then another idea. . .

Not another idea—a cruel, unknown feeling, pure jealousy, dearly beloved reader. That was what bit into me, as I repeated to myself José Dias' words: "some local beau." The truth is that I had never thought of such a calamity. I lived so much in her, of her and for her, that the intervention of some beau was almost a notion lacking in reality; it had never occurred to me that there were local beaux, of varying ages and types, who always went out for rides of an afternoon. Now I remembered that some of them looked at Capitu—and I felt myself so much her master that it was as if they were looking at me, as if they were fulfilling a simple duty of admiration and envy. Separated one from the other by space and destiny, the evil seemed not only possible, but certain. And Capitu's happiness confirmed the suspicion; if she was continually happy it was because she was already flirting with someone else, following him with her eyes in the street, talking to him at the window in the evening, exchanging flowers and...

And ... what? You know what else they would exchange; if you can't work it out for yourself, there's no point in reading the rest of the chapter and the book, you'll find nothing more, even if I lay it out as explicitly as possible, complete with etymologies. But if you have worked it out, you'll understand that after shuddering, I had an impulse to rush out through the gate, run down the hill, get to Pádua's house, grab Capitu and order her to confess how many, how many, how many the local beau had already given her. I did nothing. Even the dreams I'm telling you of did not have, in those three or four minutes, as much logic in their movements and thoughts. They were fragmentary, patched, botched, like a twisted, unfinished drawing, a confusion, a whirlwind, blinding and deafening me. When I came to again, José Dias was finishing a sentence, whose beginning I didn't hear, and whose end was vague also: "the account she'll give of herself." What account, who to? I naturally thought he was still speaking of Capitu, and I wanted to ask him if he was, but the impulse was no sooner born than it died, like so many other generations of thoughts. I limited myself to asking the dependent when I would go home to see my mother.

"I'm missing Mamma. Can I go this week?"

"On Saturday."

"Saturday? Oh, yes, yes! Ask Mamma to send for me on Saturday! Saturday! This Saturday, right? Ask her to send for me without fail."

LXIII

Halves of a Dream

Ibecame anxious for Saturday to come. Until then I was perse-cuted by dreams, even when I was awake; I'll not recount them here so as not to lengthen this part of the book. I'll just tell one, and in as few words as I can; or rather I'll put two in, because one had its origin in the other, unless the two are halves of a single whole. All this is obscure, lady reader, but the fault lies with your sex, perturbing the adolescence of a poor seminarist in this way. If it wasn't for you, this book would perhaps be no more than a parish sermon, if I'd become a priest, or a pastoral letter, if a bishop, or an encyclical, if I'd become Pope, as Uncle Cosme had recommended: "Off you go lad; come back Pope!" Ah, why didn't I fulfil this desire? After Napoleon, lieutenant and Emperor, in this century all destinies are possible.

As for the dream, it was this. As I was spying on the local beaux, I saw one of them chatting with my young friend next to the window. I ran to the place, and he fled; I came up to Capitu, but she was not alone, she had her father next to her, drying his eyes and looking at a miserable lottery ticket. Since all this was unclear to me, I was going to ask for an explanation, when he gave it of his own accord; the beau had come to give him the list of the lottery prizes, and the ticket had come out blank. Its number was 4004. He told me that this symmetry in the figures was mysterious and beautiful, and that probably the wheel had gone wrong; it was impossible that he hadn't got the big prize. While he was talking, Capitu was giving me all the big and little prizes in the world with her eyes. The biggest of all would be given with the mouth. And here the second part of the dream comes in. Pádua disappeared, along with his hopes for the ticket. Capitu leaned out, I quickly glanced up and down the street: it was deserted. I took her hands, mumbled something or other, and woke up alone in the dormitory.

The interest of what you have just read lies not in the matter of the dream, but in the efforts I made to see if I could go back to sleep and follow it up. Never in the world can you imagine with what energy and obstinacy I tried to shut my eyes as tightly as possible, to forget everything and go to sleep, but I couldn't. The very effort of doing so made me unable to sleep until dawn. About that time, I managed to doze off, but then neither beaux, nor lottery tickets, nor big or small prizes—nothing at all came to visit me. I dreamed no more that night, and I was no good at lessons the next day.

L X I V

An Idea and a Scruple

Rereading the last chapter, and idea and a scruple come to mind. The scruple has to do precisely with writing the idea down, since there is nothing more banal on earth, even if its banality is that of the sun and moon, which the heavens give us every day and every month. I turned from my manuscript, and looked at the walls. You know that this house in Engenho Novo, in its dimensions, arrangement and wall paintings, is the replica of my old house on the Rua de Matacavalos. Furthermore, as I told you in Chapter II, my aim in imitating the other house was to tie the two ends of life together—something, by the way, which I have not achieved. Well, the same thing happened to that dream in the seminary, however much I tried to sleep and did sleep. From which I conclude that one of the roles of man is to shut his eyes and keep them tight shut, to see if he can continue into the night of his old age the dream curtailed in the night of his youth. Such is the new and banal idea that I hadn't wanted to put here, and I am only writing it down provisionally.

Before finishing this chapter, I went to the window to inquire of Night why dreams should be so tenuous that they dissolve at the slightest opening of an eye or turn of the body, and do not continue. She did not reply straight away. She was deliciously beautiful, the hills were pale in the moonlight, and there was a dead hush in the air. As I insisted, Night declared that dreams no longer belong to her jurisdiction. When they lived on the island that Lucian gave them, where Night had her palace, and whence she brought them forth with their several aspects, she could have given me a possible explanation.* But time had changed everything. The ancient dreams had been pensioned off, and the modern ones are inside people's brains. Even if the latter wanted to imitate the former, they would be unable to; the isle of dreams, like the isle of love, like all the islands in all the seas, is now the object of rivalry between Europe and the United States.

It was an allusion to the Philippines.† Since I have no love of politics, and even less of international politics, I shut the window and came in to finish this chapter before going to bed. I no longer ask for Lucian's dreams, nor the others, children of memory or digestion. I am contented with a quiet, undisturbed sleep. In the cool morning air, I will carry on recounting the rest of my story and its characters.

---

* For Lucian of Samosata, see the previous note. The quotation is from *True History*, which describes several imaginary countries, among them the Isle of Dreams.

† In 1899, when Bento is writing the book, the U.S. took control of the Philippines from Spain in the course of the Spanish-American War.

L X V

Dissembling

That Saturday came, other Saturdays came, and I ended up developing a liking for my new life. I alternated between home and the seminary. The priests liked me, the boys too, and Escobar more than the boys or the priests. At the end of five weeks, I was on the point of telling him of my troubles and hopes; Capitu held me back.

"Escobar is my very good friend, Capitu!"

"By he's not my friend."

"He may be in time; he's already said to me that he wants to come here to meet Mamma."

"It doesn't matter; you have no right to tell a secret that is not only yours, but mine too, and I give you permission to tell no one."

She was right; I kept quiet and obeyed. Another matter in which I complied with her ideas was on the first Saturday, when I went to her house, and, after some minutes of conversation, she advised me to leave.

"Don't stay any longer today; go home, and I'll come over soon. It's only natural that Dona Glória will want to be with you for a long time, or for the whole time if she can."

In all this my companion gave evidence of such clear thinking that there is almost no need for me to cite a third example, but what are examples for but citing, and this is such a good one that it would be a crime to omit it. It was on my third or fourth visit home. My mother, after I had replied to a thousand questions about the way I was treated, my studies, my friendships, the discipline, and if anything was hurting, if I was sleeping well, everything that a mother's tenderness can invent to try the patience of her son, ended by turning to José Dias:

"Sr. José Dias, can you still doubt that a good priest will come out of this?"

"My dearest lady...."

"And you, Capitu," interrupted my mother, turning to Pádua's daughter, who was in the room with her, "don't you think that our Bentinho will make a good priest?"

"I think so, madam," replied Capitu, full of conviction.

I did not approve of her conviction. I told her so, the next morning, in her yard, reminding her of the words of the previous day, and confronting her for the first time with the happiness she had shown since my going to the seminary, while I was tormented with longing. Capitu became very serious, and asked how I would have her act, seeing they suspected us; she too had had disconsolate nights, and the days in her house were as sad as mine; I could go and ask her father and mother. Her mother had gone as far as to tell her, indirectly, that she should give up all thought of me.

"With Dona Glória and Dona Justina of course I put on a happy face, so that José Dias' accusation doesn't seem true. If it did seem true, they would try to separate us more, and maybe would even go so far as exclude me from the house ... For me, the oath we swore that we will marry one another is enough."

That was it; we had to dissemble, so as to kill off any suspicions, and at the same time enjoy all our former liberty, to build our future with confidence. But the example is completed by what I heard the next day, at lunch; my mother, when Uncle Cosme said that he wanted to see what kind of figure I would make blessing the people at mass, recounted that some days before, speaking about girls marrying young, Capitu had said to her: "Well, the one who'll marry me will be Father Bentinho; I'll wait till he's ordained!" Uncle Cosme laughed, José Dias consented to smile, and only cousin Justina raised her eyebrows, and looked at me questioningly. Though I had looked at them all, I could not withstand cousin Justina's look, and tried to eat. But I could hardly swallow; I was so contented with Capitu's great deceit that I could think of nothing else, and as soon as I had eaten, ran to tell her about the conversation and praise her guile. Capitu smiled gratefully.

"You're right, Capitu," I concluded; "we're going to hoodwink them all."

"Won't we just?" she said ingenuously.

L X V I

Intimacy

Capitu was finding her way into my mother's heart. They spent most of the time together, talking about me apropos of the sun and the rain, or apropos of nothing at all; Capitu went there to sew in the mornings; sometimes she stayed for dinner.

Cousin Justina did not go along with my mother where such kindnesses were concerned, but she did not treat my young friend entirely badly. She was honest enough to tell you what a low opinion she had of anyone, and she had a high opinion of no one. Maybe of her husband, but her husband was dead; in any case, there had never been anyone to compete with him for affection, industry, and honesty, for manners and wit. This opinion, according to Uncle Cosme, was posthumous, since when he was alive they were always quarreling, and for the last six months they lived apart. All the more honor to her sense of justice; praising the dead is a way of praying for them. She was probably also fond of my mother, or if she thought any ill of her it was kept a secret between her and her pillow. Naturally, on the surface Justina gave her all due respect. I don't think she aspired to a legacy; people who think that way become more solicitous than is natural, more cheerful, more assiduous, multiplying their attentions and out-shining the servants. All this was against cousin Justina's nature, which was a mixture of bitterness and rancor. As she lived with us as a favor, it can be understood that she would show no disrespect for the lady of the house, and would keep her resentment quiet, or would only speak ill of her to God and the devil.

If she felt resentful of my mother, this was not another reason to detest Capitu, for she had no need of extra reasons. However, Capitu's intimacy made her all the more annoying to my cousin. If at first she did not treat Capitu badly, with time she changed her manner and ended up avoiding her. Capitu, attentive as always, when she noticed she was not there, asked after her and went to look for her. Cousin Justina put up with this concern. Life is full of obligations that we fulfil, however much we may want to flout them. Moreover, Capitu was able to deploy a certain captivating magic; cousin Justina ended up smiling, however sourly, but when she was alone with my mother she would find a bad word to say about the girl.

When my mother fell ill of a fever which put her at death's door, she wanted Capitu to be her nurse. Cousin Justina, even though this relieved her of troublesome chores, never forgave my young friend for her intervention. One day, she asked her if she had nothing to do at home; on another occasion, laughing, she unleashed this witticism on her: "You've no need to be in such a hurry; you'll get what you want in the fullness of time."

LXVII

A Sin

I won't take the patient out of bed now without recounting what happened to me. After five days, my mother awoke one morning so disturbed that she ordered them to send for me at the seminary. In vain Uncle Cosme said:

"Sister Glória, you're becoming alarmed for no reason, the fever will pass . . ."

"No! no! send for him! I might die, and my soul will not be saved if Bentinho isn't by my side."

"We'll alarm him."

"Don't tell him anything then, but go and get him now, this minute, without delay."

They thought it was delirium; but since it was no trouble to send for me, José Dias was entrusted with the message. He came in so bewildered that he alarmed me. He told the rector privately what had happened, and I received permission to go home. In the street, we walked along silently, without him altering his usual step—the premise before the consequence, the consequence before the conclusion—but his head was bowed, and from time to time he gave a sigh. I was afraid of reading in his face some shocking, irrevocable piece of news. He had only spoken to me of the illness as a simple matter; but the fact that they had sent for me, the silence, the sighs might mean something more. My heart was pounding, my legs were giving way under me, more than once I thought I was falling down. . .

My anxious desire to hear the truth was complicated by the fear of knowing it. It was the first time that death had appeared so close to me, surrounding me, and staring at me with its dark, hollow eyes. The further I went along the Rua dos Barbonos, the more I was terrified by the idea of getting home, going in, hearing the sobs, seeing a dead body . . . Oh! I could never set down here everything that I felt in those terrible moments. However superlatively slowly José Dias walked along the street, it seemed to slide beneath my feet, the houses flew past me on each side, and a bugle that at that moment sounded in the Municipal Guard barracks echoed in my ears like the last trumpet.

I went on, got to the arches of the Lapa aqueduct, and turned into the Rua de Matacavalos. The house was not there, but a long way past the Rua dos Inválidos, near the Rua do Senado. Three or four times, I had wanted to question my companion, without daring to open my mouth; but now, I didn't even want to do that. I only walked on, accepting the worst, as a stroke of destiny, as a necessary part of the human condition, and it was then that Hope, to combat Terror, whispered into my ear—not these words, for nothing reached expression in words, but an idea which could be translated by them: "If Mamma's dead, it's the end of the seminary."

Reader, it was a lightning flash. No sooner had it lit up the night that it went, and the darkness became all the deeper, from the remorse it left behind. It was the prompting of my lust and egotism. Filial piety fainted away for an instant, with the prospect of certain freedom, through the disappearance of the debt and the debtor; it was an instant, less than an instant, the hundredth part of an instant, and even so it was enough to complicate my distress with remorse.

José Dias was sighing. Once he looked at me with such pity that I thought he had seen what had happened, and I almost asked him not to say anything to anybody, that I would punish myself, etc. But in the pity there was so much love that it could not be sorrow at my sin; but then it was still my mother's death ... I felt a great anguish, a knot in my throat, and I could help it no longer, and burst out crying.

"What is it, Bentinho?"

"Mamma ... ?"

"No! No! What an idea! Her condition is of the gravest, but the illness is not fatal: God can do all things. Dry your eyes: it's not right for a boy of your age to be crying in the street. It's nothing, a fever ... The stronger they come, the sooner they go ... No, not with your hands; where's your handkerchief?"

I dried my eyes, although the only word that had remained in my heart from what José Dias had said was *gravest*. Afterwards, I saw that he had only wanted to say *grave*, but the use of the superlative stretches things out, and for the love of a phrase, José Dias increased my misery. If you find anything similar in this book, dear reader, let me know, so that I can correct it in the second edition: there's nothing worse than giving the longest of legs to the shortest of ideas. I dried my eyes, as I say, and went on, anxious now to get home, and ask my mother's pardon for the wicked thought I had had. Finally, we arrived, went in, I went trembling up the six steps, and soon, leaning over the bed, I heard my mother's tender words as she clasped my hands, calling me her son. She seemed to be on fire, and her eyes burned in mine; her whole being seemed consumed by a volcano inside her. I knelt by the bed, but as it was high, I was far from her caresses:

"No, my son, get up, get up!"

Capitu, who was in the bedroom, approved of my entrance, my

gestures, words, and tears, as she told me afterwards; but naturally she did not suspect all the reasons for my distress. Going to my room, I thought of telling my mother everything, as soon as she was better, but this idea soon lost its hold over me. It was nothing more than a whim, an action I would never carry out, however much the sin weighed on me. So, moved by remorse, once more I used the old expedient of spiritual promises, and asked God to pardon me and save my mother's life, and I would say two thousand paternosters. If any priest is reading me, may he forgive this device; it was the last time I had recourse to it. The crisis I found myself in, no less than my habits and my faith, explains everything. It was two thousand more; and where had the old ones gone? I paid neither the latter nor the former, but if such promises come from pure, true souls, they are like fiduciary money—even though the debtor does not redeem them, they are worth their face value.

L X V I I I

Let's Postpone Virtue

Few would have the courage to confess that thought I had in the Rua de Matacavalos. I will confess everything of importance to my story. Montaigne wrote of himself: *ce ne sont pas mes gestes que j'escris; c'est moi, c'est mon essence.** Well, there is only one way of putting one's essence onto paper, and that is by telling it all, the good and the bad. That is what I am doing, as I remember it and as it fits into the construction or reconstruction of my self. For example, now that I have recounted a sin, I would happily tell

* A quotation from Book II, Chapter 6 of Montaigne's *Essais*: "De l'exercitation" ("Of exercise"): "It is not my gestures that I describe: it is I, it is my essence."

the story of some good deed done at that time, if I could remember one, but I can't; it can wait for a better opportunity.

You'll lose nothing by waiting, my friend; on the contrary, now it occurs to me that ... Not only are good deeds good on any occasion, but they are also possible or probable, according to a theory I have about sins and virtues, which is as simple as it is clear. It can be summed up thus: each person is born with a certain number of each, linked in matrimony so that they balance each other out in life. When one of the spouses is stronger than the other, it alone guides the individual, without him being able to say that, because he has not practiced a given virtue, or has committed a given sin, he is free of one or the other; the norm is that both are practised simultaneously, to the advantage of the bearer of both, and sometimes to the greater glory of earth and heaven. It's a pity I am unable to exemplify this with one or more cases from the lives of others; I haven't the time.

As far as I am concerned, it is certain that I was born with some of these couples, and naturally I still have them. It has happened to me, here in Engenho Novo, one night when I had a bad headache, that I wished that the Central line train would explode way out of earshot, and block the line for several hours, even if someone died; and on the following day, I have missed the train on the same line, by having gone to give my cane to a blind man without a stick. *Voilà mes gestes, voilà mon essence.*

LXIX

The Mass

One of the gestures that best expresses my essence was the devotion with which I ran next Sunday to hear mass at Santo Antônio dos Pobres. José Dias wanted to go with me, and began to get dressed, but he was so slow with his braces and trouserstraps, that I couldn't wait for him. Moreover, I wanted to be alone. I felt the need to avoid any conversation that might turn my thoughts aside from my purpose, which was to reconcile myself with God after what happened in Chapter LXVII. Nor was it only to ask pardon for the sin, it was also to thank Him for my mother's recovery, and, since I am confessing all, to make Him forgo the payment of my promise. Jehovah, even though He is divine, or for that very reason, is a much more humane Rothschild, who doesn't insist on prompt payment: he waives debts entirely, if the debtor truly wishes to mend his ways and cut down on his expenses. Well, that was just what I wanted; from now on I would make no promises that I could not pay, and those that I did make I would pay straight away.

I heard mass; at the elevation of the Host, I thanked God for the life and health of my mother; then I asked pardon for my sin and remission of the debt, and I received the final blessing of the officiant as a solemn act of reconciliation. At the end, I remembered that the church had set up in the confessional a reliable registry office, and in confession the most authentic of instruments for the settling of moral accounts between man and God. But my incorrigible timidity closed that door to me; I was afraid of not finding words to tell the confessor my secret. How man changes! Today I'm going so far as to publish it.

L X X

After Mass

I prayed some more, crossed myself, shut my missal and went towards the door. There were not many people, but the church is not large either, so that I had to move slowly, and could not go straight out. There were men and women, old and young, silks and cheap cotton, and probably pretty eyes and ugly ones, but I saw neither one nor the other. I was going in the direction of the door, carried by the current, hearing the greetings and whispers of conversation. In the square in front of the church, where it was light, I stopped and looked at everyone. Then I saw a girl and a man, who were coming out and then stopped; the girl was looking at me and speaking to the man, and the man was looking at me, listening to the girl. I heard these words:

"But what do you want?"

"I want to know how she is; you ask, Papa."

It was Miss Sancha, Capitu's schoolfriend, and she wanted news of my mother. The father came over; I told him she had recovered. Then we came out, he pointed out his house, and as I was going in the same direction, we went together. Gurgel was a man of forty or a little more, who was starting to go plump in the belly; he was very obsequious; when I came to his door, he was determined that I should have lunch with him.

"Thank you; Mamma is expecting me."

"We'll send a black to say that you're having lunch with us, and will be home later."

"I'll come another day."

Miss Sancha, looking at her father, listened and waited. She was not bad looking; you could only notice the resemblance in the nose, which also had a plump end, but there are features that detract from the beauty of one person while enhancing it in another. She was simply dressed. Gurgel was a widower and worshipped his daughter. As I refused lunch, he insisted that I rest for a few minutes. I couldn't refuse and went up. He wanted to know how old I was, about my studies and my faith, and gave me advice should I become a priest; he told me the number of his store, on the Rua da Quitanda.* Finally, I said goodbye, and he came to the top of the steps; his daughter sent her regards to Capitu and my mother. From the street I looked up; the father was at the window, waving me goodbye with an expansive gesture.

* A street in the central business quarter of Rio de Janeiro.

L X X I

Escobar's Visit

At home, they had already lied to my mother, saying that I had come back and was changing my clothes.

"Eight o'clock mass must be over ... Bentinho should be back by now ... Has something happened, brother Cosme? ... Send someone to see ..." She voiced her alarm over and over, but then I came back and with me came tranquility.

It was a day of pleasant surprises. Escobar came to see me and to inquire after my mother's health. He had never visited me before, nor were our relations as close as they afterwards became; but knowing why I had left three days before, he took advantage of the Sunday to come and see me, and ask if the danger had passed. When I said it had, he sighed with relief.

"I was worried," he said.

"Did the others find out?"

"I think so: some did."

Uncle Cosme and José Dias liked the lad; the dependent said that he had once seen his father in town. Escobar was very polite; and though he spoke more than was his habit later, even so it was not as much as most young men of our age; that day I found him a little more expansive than usual. Uncle Cosme invited him to dine with us. Escobar thought for a moment and then said that his father's agent was expecting him. I, thinking of Gurgel's words, repeated them:

"We'll send a black to say you're having lunch with us, and will be along later."

"Don't trouble yourselves!"

"It's no trouble," said Uncle Cosme.

Escobar accepted, and dined with us. I noted that the quick movements that were natural to him, and which he controlled in class, were also under control now, in the living room and at table,

We spent an hour together, on openly friendly terms. I showed him the few books I possessed. He much admired my father's portrait; after looking at it for a short while, he turned and said to me:

"One can tell that he had a good heart!"

Escobar's eyes, which were pale as I have already said, were of the softest; that was how José Dias defined them, after he had gone, and I will not change the word, in spite of the forty years that have passed. The dependent was not exaggerating. His clean-shaven face had white, smooth skin. His forehead, though, was a little low, so that his parting almost came down to the left eyebrow; but it was still high enough not to clash with his other features, or diminish their charm. Truly, it was an interesting face, with an delicate mouth always ready for a laugh, and a thin, curved nose. He had the habit of twitching his right shoulder from time to time, but rid himself of it when one of us pointed it out to him one day in the seminary; the first example I've seen that a person can perfectly well cure himself of small defects.

I have always felt a certain pride when my friends have pleased everybody. At home, everyone came to like Escobar; even cousin Justina thought that he was an estimable lad, in spite of . . . "In spite of what?" asked José Dias, seeing that she did not finish the phrase. He got no reply, nor was he likely to; cousin Justina could probably find no obvious or important defect in our guest; the *in spite of* was a kind of safety clause in case she discovered one some day; either that or it was the product of an old habit, which made her criticize when she had found no object of criticism.

Escobar said goodbye straight after dinner; I took him to the door, where we waited for a tram to pass. He told me that the agent's warehouse was in the Rua dos Pescadores, and was open until nine o'clock; but he did not want to stay out late. We parted very affectionately: he waved goodbye from the bus. I stood at the door to see if he would look back again when he was far off, but he didn't.

"Who's the great friend then?" asked someone from a nearby window.

There's no need to say that it was Capitu. There are things that can be divined, in life as in books, whether they are novels or true stories. It was Capitu, who had been watching us for some time from behind the shutters, and now had opened the window and appeared. She saw our effusive, affectionate farewells, and wanted to know who was so important to me.

"That's Escobar," I said going to beneath the window, and looking up at her.

LXXII

A Reform in the Drama

Neither I, nor you, nor she, nor anyone else in this story could have said more in reply, so true it is that destiny, like all dramatists, does not reveal the twists of the plot or its dénouement. They come in their own time, until the curtain falls, the lights go out, and the spectators go home to their beds. To that extent, it might be a good thing to reform things somewhat, and I would like to propose, as an experiment, that all plays should begin with their endings. Othello would kill himself and Desdemona in the first act, the three following ones would be given over to the slow and decreasing progress of jealousy, and the last would be left with the initial scenes of the threat from the Turks, the explanations of Othello and Desdemona, and the good advice of the subtle Iago: "Put money in thy purse." In this way, the spectator, on the one hand, would find in the theater the regular puzzle that the newspapers give him, for the final acts would explain the dénouement of the first, as a kind of witty conceit; and, on the other hand, he would go to bed with a happy impression of tenderness and love:

> She lov'd me for the dangers I had pass'd,
> And I lov'd her that she did pity them.

LXXIII

The Stage Manager

Destiny is not only a dramatist—it is also its own stage manager. That is, it sets up the characters' entrances on stage, gives them letters and other objects, and makes the offstage noises corresponding to the dialogue: a roll of thunder, a carriage, a gunshot. When I was young they performed here a play in some theater or other, which ended with the Last Judgement.* The principal character was Ahasuerus, who in the last scene ended a monologue with this exclamation: "I hear the archangel's trumpet!" No trumpet was heard. Embarrassed, Ahasuerus repeated the words, louder this time, to cue the stage manager—still nothing. Then he went to the back of the stage, looking tragic, but in fact to whisper into the wings, in a low voice: "The cornet! the cornet! the cornet!" The audience overheard his words and burst into laughter, until, at the moment when the trumpet really sounded, and Ahasuerus shouted for the third time that it was the archangel's trumpet, a wag in the stalls below corrected him: "No sir, it's the archangel's cornet!"

This explains my standing beneath Capitu's window and seeing a man on horseback pass, a dandy as we said at the time. He was mounted on a fine sorrel horse, firm in the saddle, the reins in his left hand, his right on his waist, patent leather boots, an elegant figure and posture: his face was not unfamiliar to me. Others had passed by, and others would come later; they were all on the way to see their sweethearts. At that time people went courting on horseback. Reread Alencar: "Because a student [says one of his characters in a play staged in 1858] can't be without these two things, a

---

* The play in question is *Ahasuérus*, by Edgar Quinet (1803–75). In it, Ahasuerus, the Jewish king, becomes the Wandering Jew, condemned to wander endlessly until the Last Judgement.

horse and a sweetheart."* Reread Álvares de Azevedo: one of his poems, of 1851, tells us that he lived in Catumbi, and to go and see his sweetheart in Catete, he had rented a horse for three milreis ...† Three milreis! How everything disappears into time's abyss!

Well, the dandy on the bay horse did not pass by like the others; he was the trumpet of the Last Judgement that sounded, and at the right moment; that is the way of Destiny, which is its own stage manager. The horseman was not content with passing by, but turned his head towards us, towards Capitu, and he looked at Capitu and Capitu at him; the horse went on, and the horseman kept looking backwards. This was the second time the fangs of jealousy bit into me. Admittedly, it was natural to look at elegant passers-by; but this fellow usually passed that way in the afternoon. He lived in the old Campo da Aclamação, and then ... and then ...†† Just try to reason with a burning heart like mine at that moment! I didn't even say anything to Capitu; I came away from the street in a hurry, ran down the corridor, and next thing I knew I was in the living room.

LXXIV

The Trouserstrap

In the living room Uncle Cosme and José Dias were talking, the one seated, the other walking up and down and stopping

* José de Alencar (1829–77) was a friend and mentor of Machado. He was the most important novelist of the Romantic period in Brazil, and in the late 1850s wrote a series of plays influenced by the French realist drama of the time. This quotation is from *O crédito* (*Credit*), first performed in 1858.

† A quotation from "Namoro a cavalo" ("Courting on horseback"), by the important Romantic poet Álvares de Azevedo (1831–52).

†† The Campo da Aclamação was a large open area near the center of Rio de Janeiro, now occupied by the Praça da República.

from time to time. Seeing José Dias reminded me of what he had said to me at the seminary: "Just waiting to find some local beau to marry her ..." Of course it was an allusion to the man on horseback. This recollection worsened the impression I'd had in the street; or was it rather those words, stored in the unconscious, that made me see the cunning in their eyes? I had the desire to grab José Dias by the collar, take him into the corridor and ask him if he had spoken of a reality or only a hypothesis; but José Dias, who had stopped when he saw me come in, went on walking and talking. I was impatient, and wanted to go next door; I imagined that Capitu would come away from the window alarmed and would not be long in appearing, to ask what had happened and explain ... And the two went on talking, until Uncle Cosme got up to go and see the invalid, and José Dias came over to me, in the other window recess.

A minute ago I had had the desire to ask him what was going on between Capitu and the local beaux; now, imagining that he might be coming over to tell me just that, I was afraid of what he would say. I wanted to stop his mouth. José Dias saw something different from my habitual expression, and asked me with concern:

"What is it, Bentinho?"

So as not to look him in the face, I let my eyes fall. As they fell, they saw that one of his trouserstraps was unbuttoned, and, as he insisted on knowing what the matter was, I replied by pointing with my finger:

"Look at your trouserstrap, it needs buttoning."

José Dias bent down, and I ran out.

L X X V

Despair

I escaped from the dependent, I escaped from my mother by not going to her room, but I did not escape from myself. I ran to my room, and came in after myself. I talked to myself, I chased after myself, I threw myself on the bed and rolled around with myself, weeping and stifling my sobs on the edge of the sheet. I swore I would not go and see Capitu that afternoon, nor ever again, and that I would become a priest once and for all. I saw myself already ordained, in front of Capitu, who would weep repentently and beg for my forgiveness, but I, cool and serene, would have nothing but contempt, cold contempt for her; I turned my back on her. I called her perverse. Twice I became aware that I was biting on my own teeth, as if I had her between them.

From my bed I heard her voice: she had come to spend the rest of the afternoon with my mother, and no doubt with me too, as she had before; but, however shaken I was, she couldn't make me come out of my room. Capitu laughed aloud, spoke loudly, as if she was telling me she was there; I remained deaf, alone with myself and my contempt. It made me want to sink my nails into her neck, bury them deep, and watch the life drain out of her with her blood...

L X X V I

Explanation

After some time, I felt calm, but dejected. As I was stretched out on the bed, staring at the ceiling, I remembered my mother's advice that I should not lie down after dinner to avoid congestion of the blood. I got up quickly, but I didn't leave my room. Capitu was laughing less now, and was speaking in a lower voice; she must be upset at my having shut myself away, but even that did not move me.

I had no supper, and slept badly. On the following morning I felt no better: I felt different. My pain was now mixed with the fear that I had overstepped the mark, and had failed to examine the matter. Though my head was aching a little, I pretended I was worse than I was, so as not to have to go to the seminary, and so that I could speak to Capitu. She might be angry with me, she might no longer love me, and prefer the man on horseback. I wanted to resolve everything, hear her and judge her; she might have a defense and an explanation.

She had both. When she found out why I had shut myself away the previous day, she told me that I was doing her a grave injustice; she couldn't believe that after our exchange of oaths, I could think her so fickle as to believe ... And at this point she burst into tears, and made a gesture as if of separation; but I came to her straight away, took her hands and kissed them with such feeling and warmth that I felt them tremble. She wiped her eyes with her fingers, and I kissed them again, for themselves and for the tears; then she sighed, and shook her head. She confessed that she did not know the young man, any more than she knew others that passed by of an afternoon, on horseback or on foot. If he had looked at her, that was precisely the proof that there was nothing between the young man and her; if there had been, it would have been natural to dissemble.

"And what could there be, anyway, since he's getting married?" she concluded.

"He's getting married?"

He was getting married, and she told me to whom, to a girl from the Rua dos Barbonos. This reason convinced me more than any, and she felt it in my demeanor; but that did not stop her saying that, to prevent more misunderstandings, she would stop looking out of the window.

"No! no! No! I wouldn't ask that of you!"

She consented to withdraw the promise, but she made another, and it was that at the first suspicion on my part, everything would be over between us. I accepted the threat, and swore that she would never have to carry it out: it was the first suspicion and the last.

LXXVII

Pleasure in Old Sufferings

Recounting this crisis in the love of my youth, I feel something that I don't know if I can explain properly, and it is that these sufferings have become so spiritualized with time, that they have dissolved into pleasure. This is not clear, but then not everything is clear in life or in books. The truth is that I feel a particular enjoyment in telling the story of this painful event, when it is also certain that it reminds me of others that I wouldn't remember for the world.

LXXVIII

One Secret for Another

Anyhow, at about that time I felt a certain need to tell someone what was happening between me and Capitu. I didn't tell everything, only a part, and Escobar was my confidant. When I returned to the seminary, on Wednesday, I found him anxious; he said that he had been intending to come and visit me, if I spent another day at home. He asked with concern what had been the matter, and if I was completely well.

"Yes."

He listened, fixing me with his eyes. Three days later he told me that people were finding me very absent-minded; I should disguise it as much as possible. He, for his part, had reasons to be distrait too, but he tried to keep attentive.

"So you think . . . ?"

"Yes, sometimes it seems as if you're not hearing anything, staring into space; put up a pretense, Santiago."

"I have reasons . . ."

"I believe you; no one gets distracted for no reason at all."

"Escobar . . ."

I hesitated; he waited.

"What is it?"

"Escobar, you are my friend, and I am yours; here in the seminary you are the person that I feel closest to, and outside, apart from my family, I really have no friends."

"If I say the same thing," he replied with a smile, "it won't seem so spontaneous; it'll look as if I'm repeating you. But it's true that here I have no intimate friends, you are the first, and I think they have already noticed; but that doesn't matter to me."

I was moved, and felt the words rushing into my mouth.

"Escobar, can you keep a secret?"

"If you ask it's because you have doubts, and in that case . . ."

"I'm sorry, that's just my way of putting it. I know that you're a serious person, and I'll make believe I'm confessing to a priest."

"If you need absolution, you're absolved."

"Escobar, I can't be a priest. I'm here, and my family believe it and expect it of me; but I can't be a priest."

"Neither can I, Santiago."

"You neither?"

"One secret for another. I have no intention of finishing the course either; my desire is to go into business, but say nothing, nothing at all; it's just between us. And it's not that I'm not religious; I am, but business is my passion."

"Is that all?"

"What more could there be?"

I gave two turns around the room, and whispered the first words of my secret, in such a faint, low voice that I didn't hear it myself; I know, however, that I said "a person" hesitantly. A person? There was no need to say anything more for him to understand. A person must be a girl. And don't think that he was astonished to find me in love; he even found it natural and his eyes fixed me again. Then I told him sketchily what I could, but slowly so as to have the pleasure of dwelling on the subject. Escobar listened with interest; at the end of our conversation, he declared that it was as if my secret were buried in a cemetery. He advised me not to become a priest. I could not offer the Church a heart that did not belong to heaven, but to earth; I would be a bad priest—no priest at all, in fact. On the contrary, God protects those who are sincere; since I could only serve Him in the wider world, that was where I should stay.

You can't imagine the pleasure that I got from confiding this secret. It was one happiness on top of another. That youthful heart that listened to me and approved of my plans, gave the world an extraordinary new aspect. It was grand and beautiful, life was a wonderful race to be run, and I no more nor less than the darling of heaven; that was the sensation I had. And note that I didn't tell him everything, nor yet the best of it; I didn't tell him the story of combing her hair, for example, nor others like it; but I did tell him a great deal.

Needless to say, we returned to the subject. We came back to it many times; I praised Capitu's moral qualities, a subject appropriate for a seminarist's admiration: her simplicity, her modesty, her industry, and her religious habits. I didn't touch on her physical charms, nor did he ask about them; I only hinted that he should get to know her by sight.

"It's not possible now," I said to him in the first week, when I returned from home; Capitu is going to spend a few days with a friend in the Rua dos Inválidos. When she comes back, you can come. But you can come before, you can come any time; why didn't you come for dinner yesterday?"

"You didn't invite me."

"Do I have to invite you? Everybody at home has taken a great liking to you."

"I liked everyone too, but if had to choose between them, I confess that your mother is an adorable lady."

"She is, isn't she?" I replied enthusiastically.

L X X I X

A Preface to the Chapter

I certainly liked to hear him speak that way. You know what I thought of my mother. Even now, as I interrupt my writing to look at her portrait on the wall, I think she had that quality written in her face. There is no other way of explaining Escobar's opinion, when he had scarcely exchanged two or three words with her. One was enough to see into her innermost being; yes, yes, my mother was adorable. However much she might be forcing me into a career that I didn't want, I could not but feel that she was adorable, like a saint.

In any case, was it really true that she was forcing me into an ecclesiastical career? Here I come to a point that I hoped would come later, so much so that I was already considering at what point I should dedicate a chapter to it. Really, I should not have said now what I only thought I discovered later; but since I have touched on the matter, it's better to be finished with it. It is grave and complex, delicate and subtle, one of those chapters in which the author has to take heed of his child, and the child should listen to the author, so that they each tell the truth, the whole truth, and nothing but the truth. It should also be noted that it is exactly this point which makes the saint more adorable, with no disrespect (quite the contrary!) for the human and earthly part in her. Enough of writing the preface: on to the chapter itself.

L X X X

Here is the Chapter

Here is the chapter. My mother was God fearing; you know of that, of her religious habits, and of the pure faith that inspired them. Nor are you unaware that my ecclesiastical career was the subject of a promise made when I was conceived. This has all been recounted in its proper place. Furthermore, you know that, in order to tie the moral bond tighter, she confided her projects and motives to relatives and members of the family. The promise, made devoutly, and accepted with compassion, was kept by her, with joy, in the depth of her heart. I think I tasted its happiness in the milk she gave me when she suckled me. If my father had lived, it is possible that he might have altered the plans, and as he had a vocation for politics, it is probable that he would have pushed me exclusively in that direction, even if the two occupations were not and still are not incompatible; more than one priest has entered into the struggle between the parties and the governance of men. But my father had died in ignorance, and she remained behind, as the only debtor in the terms of the contract.

One of Franklin's maxims is that, if you have to pay at Easter, Lent is short. Our Lent was no longer than the others, and my mother, though she had me taught Latin and Church doctrine, began to put off my entry into the seminary. It's what is called, in commercial terms, rescheduling a debt. The creditor was a multimillionaire, didn't depend on that amount to eat, and allowed the payment to be put off, without even raising the interest rate. One day, however, one of the household who had endorsed the promissory note, spoke of the necessity to pay the agreed sum; it's in one of the first chapters. My mother agreed and I betook myself to São José.

Now, in that same chapter, she shed some tears, which she then dried without explaining them, and which none of those present, Uncle Cosme, cousin Justina, nor the dependent José Dias understood at all; I, behind the door, understood them no better than they did. On careful examination, and in spite of the distance in time, it can be seen that they were tears of anticipated longing, the pain of separation—and it may also be (this is the beginning of the point), it may also be that she repented of her promise. Catholic and devout, she knew very well that promises must be kept; the question is whether or not it is appropriate and fitting to keep them all, and naturally she inclined to reply in the negative. Why would God punish her, denying her a second child? The divine will might have been that I should live, without there being any need to dedicate me to Him *ab ovo*. It was a belated argument; she should have thought of it on the day I was conceived. At any event, she had reached a first conclusion; but since this was not enough to destroy everything, everything went on as planned, and I went to the seminary.

If faith had nodded for a moment, that might have resolved the matter in my favor, but faith kept watch with her wide, naive eyes. My mother, had she been able, would have exchanged her original promise for another, giving part of her own life to keep me with her, out of the clergy, married, and a father; that's what I presume, just as I suppose that she rejected the idea as disloyal. That is how I understood her in her daily life.

It happened that my absence was soon tempered by Capitu's solicitude. She was beginning to make herself necessary to my mother. Little by little she became persuaded that the girl would make me happy. Then (and this is the end of my point), the hope that our love, making the seminary impossible for me, would cause me to refuse to stay there in spite of God or the devil: this intimate and secret hope began to invade my mother's heart. In that case, I would break the contract without her being to blame. She would keep me to herself without any action that could be called hers. It was as if, having entrusted someone with the amount of a debt to take it to the creditor, the bearer had kept the money for himself, and delivered nothing. In ordinary life, the action of a third party does not free the contractor from an obligation; but the advantage of making a contract with heaven is that intentions are valid currency.

You must have had conflicts like this, and if you are religious, you must have sometimes tried to find a way to reconcile heaven and earth by identical or analogous means. Heaven and earth can be reconciled in the end; they are almost twins, heaven having been created on the second day and earth on the third. Like Abraham, my mother took her son to the mountain of the Vision, with the wood for the burnt offering, the kindling and the knife. And she tied Isaac to the bundle of wood, took the knife and lifted it up. When she was about to strike, she heard the voice of the angel ordering him in the name of the Lord: "Lay not thy hand upon the lad; for now I know that thou fearest God." That must have been my mother's secret hope.

Naturally, Capitu was the angel of the Scriptures. The truth is that my mother needed her continually near her. Her growing affection manifested itself in extraordinary ways. Capitu became the flower of the household, the sun in the morning, the cool of the evening, the moon at nighttime; she spent hours and hours there, listening, talking, and singing. My mother was sounding out her heart, searching in her eyes, and my name, between the two of them, was like the password to a future life.

L X X X I

Something my Mother Said

Now that I have recounted what I found out later, I can put in here something my mother said. Now we can understand why, on the next Saturday, when I got home and found out that Capitu was at the Rua dos Inválidos with Miss Gurgel, she said:

"Why don't you go and see her? Didn't you say that Sancha's father offered you his house?"

"Yes."

"Well then? But only if you want to. Capitu should have come back today to finish off some needlework with me; her friend must have asked her to stay the night."

"Maybe they've been flirting," cousin Justina insinuated.

I didn't kill her because I didn't have steel or cord, a pistol or a dagger at hand; but the look I gave her, if it could have killed, would have made up for all these things. One of the mistakes of Providence was to have given men only their arms and teeth as offensive weapons, and their legs as means of flight or defense. For the first of these, the eyes should be enough. A single movement of them would make an enemy or a rival stop or fall to the ground, they would carry out swift vengeance, with the added advantage that, to delude justice, these same murderous eyes would be full of mercy, and would make haste to weep for the victim. Cousin Justina escaped mine; but I did not escape from the effect of her insinuation, and on Sunday at eleven, I ran to the Rua dos Inválidos.

Sancha's father received me looking dishevelled and unhappy. His daughter was ill; she had come down with a fever the day before, and it was getting worse. As he loved his daughter a great deal, he thought he saw her already dead, and announced to me that he would kill himself too. Here's a chapter as funereal as a cemetery, full of deaths, suicides, and murders. I was longing for a bright ray of sunshine and blue sky. It was Capitu who brought them to the doorway, coming to tell Sancha's father that his daughter had asked for him.

"Is she worse?" asked Gurgel in alarm.

"No, but she wants to talk to you."

"Stay here for a while," he said to her, and turning to me: "She's Sancha's nurse, and she'll have no other; I'll be back in a moment."

Capitu showed signs of exhaustion and concern, but no sooner did she see me than she changed completely, and became the same girl I knew, fresh and sprightly, and no less surprised. She could hardly believe it was me. She spoke to me, wanted me to speak to her, and in fact we did converse for some minutes, but in such low, hushed voices that even the walls didn't hear, and they, as we know, have ears. Or in any case, if they heard anything, they didn't understand, neither they nor the furniture, which was as sad as its owner.

L X X X I I

The Sofa

Of the furniture in the room, only the sofa seemed to have understood our moral situation, for it offered the services of its wickerwork so insistently that we accepted and sat down. The particular opinion I have of sofas dates from that moment. They unite intimacy and decorum, and reveal the whole house without one having to leave the living room. Two men sitting on a sofa can debate the destiny of an empire, and two women the charm of a dress; but only by some aberration of the laws of nature will a man and a woman talk of anything other than themselves. That was what we did, Capitu and I. I can vaguely remember that I asked her if she would have to stay long. . .

"I don't know; the fever seems to be abating . . . but . . ."

I also remember, vaguely, that I explained my visit to the Rua dos Inválidos by telling her the simple truth, that is, that it was my mother's advice.

"Her advice?" murmured Capitu.

And she added with her eyes shining singularly brightly:

"We are going to be happy!"

I repeated these words just with my fingers, squeezing hers. The sofa, whether it saw or not, continued to provide its services to our clasped hands, and to our heads, which were touching, or nearly.

L X X X I I I

The Portrait

Gurgel came back to the living room and told Capitu that his daughter was calling for her. I got up quickly and could not keep my composure: I fixed my eyes on the chairs. For her part, Capitu got up naturally and asked him if the fever had got worse.

"No," he said.

Capitu was not in the least startled; there was no air of mystery about her; she turned round to me, and asked me to give her regards to my mother and cousin Justina, and that she would see me soon; she held out her hand to me and went off down the corridor. All my envy went with her. How could she control herself so easily when I could not?

"She's quite a young lady," observed Gurgel, looking at her too. I murmured in agreement. It was true: Capitu was growing by leaps and bounds, her figure was filling out, and she was fast taking on new strength and energy: in her mind and spirit, the same thing was happening. She was a woman inside and out, to left and right, a woman from every side, from top to toe. This burgeoning seemed to be taking place more quickly, now that I did not see her every day; every time I came home I found her taller, with a fuller figure; her eyes seemed to have a new reflectiveness, and her mouth a new air of authority. Gurgel, turning to the wall, where there hung the portrait of a girl, asked me if I thought Capitu was like the portrait.

One of my habits in life has always been to agree with the probable opinion of whoever is speaking to me, so long as it doesn't offend or irritate, or otherwise obtrude itself on me. Before looking to see if Capitu really was or was not like the portrait, I replied yes. Then he said that it was a portrait of his wife, and that people who had known her said the same thing. He, too, thought that they had similar features, principally the forehead and the eyes. As for their temperaments, they were identical: like sisters.

"And to top it all, her friendship with Sanchinha; even her mother was no closer to her ... Life produces these strange resemblances."

LXXXIV

A Call

In the hall and the street, I still asked myself if he really might have suspected something, but thought not and began to walk home. I was very pleased with the visit, with Capitu's happiness, with Gurgel's praises, so much so that I didn't reply immediately to a voice calling me:

"Senhor Bentinho! Senhor Bentinho!"

Only when the voice grew louder and its owner came to the door, did I stop and see what it was and where I was. I was already in the Rua de Matacavalos. The house was a china shop, bare and poor; the doors were half shut, and the person calling me was a poor man, gray-haired and shabbily dressed.

"Senhor Bentinho," he said in tears, "do you know that my son Manduca is dead?"

"Dead?"

"He died half an hour ago—he'll be buried tomorrow. I sent a note to your mother just now, and she was so kind as to send me some flowers to put on the coffin. My poor son! He had to die, and it was a good thing he did, poor lad, but even so it still hurts. What a life he had! ... Not long ago he remembered you, and asked if you were in the seminary ... Do you want to see him? Come in, come and see him ..."

It's painful for me to say this, but it is better to sin by saying too much than too little. I wanted to say no, that I did not want to see Manduca, and I even made a move as if to get away. It was not fear; I might have gone in on another occasion quite readily and with a certain curiosity, but I was so happy at that moment! To see a dead body on my way back from seeing my sweetheart ... There are things that don't mix or fit in with each other. Even the news itself upset me. My golden thoughts all lost their color and metallic sheen, turning into dull, ugly ashes, and I felt utterly confused. I think I went so far as to say that I was in a hurry, but probably I didn't speak in clear words, or even in human speech, because he, leaning in the entrance way, was motioning me in, and I, without the heart to enter or run away, let my body do what it could, and it ended up going in.

I don't blame the man; for him, the most important thing at the moment was his son. But don't blame me either; for me, the most important thing was Capitu. The trouble was that the two things came together in the same afternoon, and the death of one poked its nose into the life of the other. That was the whole trouble. If I had come by before or after, or if Manduca could have waited a few hours to die, no discordant note would have come to interrupt the sweet melodies of my soul. Why die exactly half an hour before? Any time is appropriate for dying; you can perfectly well die at six or seven in the afternoon.

L X X X V

The Dead Boy

Such were the confused feelings with which I entered the china shop. It was dark, and inside the house there was less light, now that the windows into the courtyard were closed. In a corner of the dining room I saw the mother crying; at the door into the small bedroom two children were looking inside with a scared expression, their fingers in their mouths. The corpse was lying on the bed; the bed...

Let's put the pen down for a while and come to the window to give the memory a breath of fresh air. In truth, it was an ugly picture, because of death itself, and the dead boy, who was horrible ... Here and now, things are quite different. Everything I can see out there is living and breathing, the goat chewing next to a cart, the hen pecking about in the roadway, the train of the Central line that puffs, whistles, lets off steam and passes by, the palm tree that shoots up into the sky, and finally even the church tower, though it has neither muscles nor leaves. A boy, over there in the alleyway, is playing with a paper kite is not dead, nor is he dying, even though his name is Manduca too.

It is true that the other Manduca was older than this one, a little older. He would be about eighteen or nineteen, but you might have thought he was anything from fifteen to twenty-two, for his face did not reveal his age, which was hidden in the folds of . . . Well, I might as well say it all: he's dead, his relatives are dead, and if there are any left none of them are important enough to be annoyed or hurt. To say it all, then; Manduca suffered from a cruel illness, leprosy, no less. When he was alive he was ugly; dead, he seemed hideous. When I saw, stretched out on the bed, the miserable body of my neighbor, I was appalled and turned my eyes away. I know not what hidden hand compelled me to look again, even fleetingly; I gave way, looked, looked again, until I backed away completely and came out of the room.

"He suffered such a lot!" sighed his father.

"Poor Manduca!" his mother sobbed.

I thought about how to get away, said that they were expecting me at home, and said goodbye. The father asked if I would do him the favor of going to the funeral; I replied with the truth, which was that I didn't know, and would do what my mother wished. I came out quickly, went through the shop, and bounded into the street.

LXXXVI

Love, My Lads!

It was so close that within three minutes I was home. I stopped in the corridor to catch my breath; I was trying to forget the dead body, pale and deformed, and everything else I haven't said so as not to give a repugnant aspect to these pages, but you can imagine it. I put everything out of my mind in a few seconds; all I needed to do was to think about the other house, about life and Capitu's fresh, lively face .... Love, my lads! And above all, love pretty, charming girls; they are the remedy for evil, they give a sweet smell to rottenness, they exchange life for death ... Love, my lads!

L X X X V I I

The Chaise

I had got to the top step, and an idea entered my head, as if it had been waiting for me between the bars of the gate. I heard in my memory Manduca's father's words asking me to go to the funeral the next day. I came to a halt on the step. I thought for a moment; yes, I could go to the funeral, I would ask my mother to rent a carriage for me...

Don't think that it was the desire to ride in a carriage, however much I enjoyed driving round. When I was small, I remember that I often went that way with my mother when she went to see friends or on more formal visits, and to mass, if it was raining. It was an old chaise of my father's, which she kept for as long as she could. The coachman, who was our slave and as old as the chaise, when he saw me at the door, dressed and waiting for my mother, would say laughing:

"Old João's goin' to take young master!"

And I almost always told him:

"João, really slow the animals down; go slow."

"Mistress Glória don't like it."

"Slow down, all the same!"

You'll understand that it was to savor riding in the chaise, not out of vanity, because the people inside could not be seen. It was an old obsolete chaise, a two-wheeler, narrow and short, with two leather curtains at the front, which drew to each side when one got in or out. Each curtain had a spyglass, through which I liked to look.

"Sit down, Bentinho!"

"Let me look out, Mamma!"

When I was smaller, I would stand up and put my face to the glass, and see the coachman with his big boots, astride the left-hand mule, and holding the other by the reins; in his hand he carried the thick, long whip. Everything was cumbersome, the boots, the whip and the mules, but he enjoyed it and so did I. On either side, I watched the buildings go by, some with shops, open or shut, with or without people in them, and in the street the people coming and going, crossing in front of the chaise with great strides or short steps. When there was something in the way, either people or animals, the chaise would stop, and then there was a particularly interesting spectacle; people stopped on the pavement or at the doors of the houses, looked at the chaise and talked to each other, no doubt about who was inside. As I grew older I imagined them guessing and saying: "It's that lady in the Rua de Matacavalos, who has a son, Bentinho . . ."

The chaise went so well with my mother's secluded life, that when there were no others left in Rio, we continued to go about in it, and it was known in the street and the neighborhood as the "old chaise." In the end my mother consented to us abandoning it, though it was not sold at once; she only let it go because the stabling costs forced her to it. The reason for keeping it when it was of no use was purely sentimental: her husband's memory. Everything that had belonged to my father was kept as if it were part of him, a remnant of him, the unsullied, pure soul of the man. But these habits were also the fruit of a conservatism which she admitted to her friends. My mother well expressed this faithfulness to old habits, old ways, old ideas, old fashions. She had her museum of relics, disused combs, a piece of a mantilla, some copper coins dated 1824 and 1825, and, so that everything should be ancient, she tried to make herself old; but I have already said that, in this respect, she did not achieve all she wanted.

LXXXVIII

An Honest Pretext

No, the idea of going to the funeral did not come from think-ing about the carriage and its pleasures. It had another origin: it was that, if I accompanied the funeral the next day, I would not go to the seminary, and could visit Capitu again, for a longer time. That's what it was. The idea of the carriage might have come later, as an accessory, but that was the principal, imme-diate thought. I would go back to the Rua dos Inválidos, on the pretext of asking after Miss Gurgel. I was counting on everything coming out just as it had that day, Gurgel distressed, Capitu with me on the sofa, our hands clasped, her hair. . .

"I'll ask Mamma."

I opened the gate. Before I went through, just as I had heard the voice of the dead boy's father in my memory, now I heard his mother's, and I repeated in a low-pitched voice:

"Poor Manduca!"

LXXXIX

The Refusal

My mother was puzzled when I asked her to go to the funeral.

"You'll lose a day at the seminary . . ."

I reminded her of the friendship Manduca felt for me, and they were such poor people ... I used every argument that came to mind. Cousin Justina gave her opinion in the negative.

"You think he ought not to go?" asked my mother.

"I don't think so. What's this great friendship? I never saw any signs of it."

Cousin Justina won. When I told the dependent, he smiled, and told me that her hidden motive was probably that she thought I should not give the funeral "the lustre of my presence." However that may be, I was annoyed; the next day, thinking of the motive, I was not so put out; later on, I took a certain pleasure in it.

X C

The Polemic

On the following day, I went past the dead boy's house, without going in or even stopping—or, if I did stop, it was only for a brief moment, even briefer than the time it takes to write this. If I'm not mistaken, I even walked faster, fearful that they would call me in, as on the previous day. Since I wasn't going to the funeral, better to keep a distance. I walked on, thinking about the poor devil.

We were not friends, nor had we known each other long. Intimacy—what intimacy could arise between his sickness and my health? We had a brief, distant relationship. As I went on my way, I thought about it, and remembered something of it. It all came down to a polemic we had had, two years before, about ... You'll hardly believe what it was about. It was the Crimean War.*

* The Crimean War (1853–56) opposed the Ottoman Empire, Britain and France to the Russian Empire. One of the chief objects of the allies was to prevent Russia gaining Constantinople (Istanbul), and thus entry to the Mediterranean.

Manduca lived at the back of the house, stretched out on the bed, reading to kill time. On Sunday afternoons, his father used to dress him in a dark nightshirt, and bring him into the back of the shop, from where he could see a small stretch of the street, and the people passing by. That was all the amusement he got. I went there and saw him once, and I was not a little shocked; the illness was eating away at part of his flesh, and his fingers were slowly seizing up; he looked anything but attractive. I was thirteen or fourteen. The second time I saw him there, we spoke about the Crimean War, which was raging at the time and was all over the papers; Manduca said that the allies would win, and I said they would not.

"Well, we'll see," he replied. "Only if justice is vanquished in this world, which is impossible; and justice is on the side of the allies."

"No, sir, the Russians are in the right."

Naturally, we were following what the local newspapers were saying, as they transcribed the foreign ones; but it may also be true that each of us had an opinion corresponding to his temperament. I have always been somewhat Muscovite in my ideas. I defended Russia's rights, Manduca did the same with the allies, and on the third Sunday I went into the shop we touched on the subject again. Then Manduca proposed that we should exchange our arguments in writing, and on the Tuesday or Wednesday I received two sheets of paper containing the exposition and defense of the allies' cause, and that of the integrity of Turkey, all concluding with this prophetic phrase:

"The Russians will never enter Constantinople!"

I read it and set out to refute it. I can't remember a single one of the arguments I employed, and perhaps it is of no interest to know what they were, now that the century is about to expire; but the impression I have is that they were irrefutable. I took the paper to him myself. They showed me into his bedroom, where he was lying stretched out on the bed, barely covered by an old patchwork quilt. Whether it was the taste for polemics, or for some other reason I cannot divine, I didn't feel all the horror exuded from the bed and the sick boy, and it was with sincere pleasure that I gave him the paper. For his part, however disgusting Manduca's face might be, the smile that illuminated it disguised the physical illness. There are no words in our or any other language completely and accurately to express the conviction with which he took the paper from me and said he would read it and reply to it; it was not fanatical or overeager, there were no gestures, nor would the illness allow them; it was simple, grand, profound, an infinite enjoyment of victory, before he knew my arguments. He already had paper, pen, and ink beside his bed. Some days later I got his reply; I can't remember whether it had anything new in it or not; the vehemence of the words was greater, and the end was the same:

"The Russians will never enter Constantinople!"

I replied in my turn, and for some time we carried on a fiery polemic, in which neither of us gave way, each one energetically defending his clients. Manduca wrote at greater length and replied more promptly than I. Of course, I had a thousand other things to amuse me, my studies, my games, my family, and health itself, which stimulated me to other exercises. Manduca, apart from the small stretch of street on Sunday afternoons, only had this war, the talk of the city and the world, but which no one would go to talk to him about. Chance had given him an adversary in me; since he took pleasure in writing, he flung himself into the debate, as if into a new, radical cure. His long, sad hours were now short and happy; his eyes forgot how to cry, if indeed they wept before. I felt this change in him even in the attitude of his father and mother.

"You've no idea how he's been lately, since you've been writing those papers to him," the shopkeeper said to me one day, at the street door, "He talks and laughs a lot. As soon as I send the shop assistant to take you his papers, he's thinking about the reply, and if it will take a long time, and to be sure to ask the messenger boy when he passes. While he's waiting, he rereads newspapers and takes notes. Then, as soon as he gets your papers, he plunges into reading them, and soon begins to write the reply. There are times when he doesn't eat, or hardly; so much so, that I want to ask you something: if you wouldn't mind not sending them at lunch or dinner time . . ."

It was I who tired of it first. I began to delay my replies, until I sent them no longer; he still persisted two or three times after I ceased, but when he received no replies, either out of exhaustion or so as not to be a nuisance, he stopped sending his arguments. The last one, like the first, like all the others, affirmed the same eternal prediction:

"The Russians will never enter Constantinople!"

They certainly did not, neither then, nor later, nor up to the present day. But will the prediction remain valid forever? Might they not enter some day? A difficult question. Manduca himself, to enter the tomb, took three years to decompose, so sure is it that nature, like history, is no joke. His life resisted as Turkey did, and if at last it gave way it was because it lacked an alliance like the Anglo-French one, since the simple conjunction of medicine and pharmacy cannot be called that. He died in the end, as nations do; in our own case, what we want to know is, not if Turkey will die, because death spares no one, but if the Russians will one day enter into Constantinople; that was the question that preoccupied my leprous neighbor, under his miserable, ragged, filthy patchwork quilt . . .

X C I

A Consoling Discovery

Of course the reflections I've set down here were not made then, on the way to seminary, but now in my study in Engenho Novo. Then, I really made no reflection at all, unless it was this: that one day I had provided some relief for my neighbor Manduca. Now, on further consideration, I think that not only did I provide some relief: I even gave him some happiness. And this discovery consoles me; now I will never forget that I gave two or three months of happiness to a poor devil, and made him forget his illness and the rest. It's something when my life's accounts come to be settled. If there is some kind of prize in the next world for unintentional virtues, this one will pay for one or two of my many sins. As for Manduca, I don't think it was a sin to have anti-Russian opinions, but if it was, he will have been expiating now for forty years the happiness he had for two or three months—from which he will conclude (too late) that it would have been much better just to groan, and have no opinions at all.

X C I I

The Devil's Not as Black as He's Painted

Manduca was buried without me. The same thing has happened to many others, without my feeling anything, but this case upset me particularly for the reason already mentioned. I also felt a kind of melancholy as I recalled the first polemic of my life, the joy with which he received my papers and got to work to refute them, not counting the desire to go in the carriage ... But time quickly erased all those regrets and rebirths of old memories. Nor was it only time; two people came to assist it, Capitu, whose image came to sleep with me that same night, and another which I will tell you of in the next chapter. The rest of this chapter is only to ask that, if someone reads my book with more attention than is demanded by the price of a copy, he should be certain to conclude that the devil is not as black as he's painted. What I mean is...

What I mean is that my Matacavalos neighbor, easing his illness with his anti-Russian opinions, gave to his rotting flesh a spiritual glow that consoled him in his sufferings. No doubt there are greater consolations, and one of the most excellent of all is not to suffer from this or any other illness, but nature is so divine that it amuses itself with such contrasts, and it beckons the most loathsome and unhappy with a flower. Perhaps, even, the flower turns out more beautiful that way; my gardener tells me that violets, to have a lovely scent, need pig's manure. I've never gone into it, but it must be true.

X C I I I

A Friend for a Dead Boy

As for the other person who had the power to erase my thoughts, it was my friend Escobar, who came to Matacavalos one Sunday, before midday. A friend thus took the place of a dead boy, and this same friend took my hand in his for about five minutes, as if he had not seen me for many months.

"Will you have dinner with me, Escobar?"

"That's exactly what I came for."

My mother thanked him for his friendship towards me, and he replied very politely, though a little hesitantly, as if he couldn't easily find words to express himself. You have already seen that he was not like that, words obeyed him, but people are not the same all the time. What he said, in summary, was that he esteemed me for my good qualities and refined manners; at the seminary everybody liked me, as was natural, he added. He emphasized my manners, the good example I gave, the "rare, sweet mother" that heaven had given me . . . All this with a choking, tremulous voice.

Everybody came to like him. I was as happy as if Escobar had been my invention. José Dias loosed a couple of superlatives at him, Uncle Cosme beat him twice at backgammon, and cousin Justina could find no fault to lay at his door; later, it's true, on the second or third Sunday, she confessed to us that my friend Escobar was a little inquisitive and that he had eyes like a policeman, that took everything in.

"It's his eyes," I explained.

"I'm not saying they're anyone else's."

"They are reflective eyes," said Uncle Cosme.

"Assuredly," added José Dias, "however, it may be that there is some truth in what Dona Justina says. One thing does not rule out the other, and reflection is well matched with natural curiosity. He is inquisitive, certainly, but . . ."

"He seems a very serious young man to me," said my mother.

"Exactly!" chimed José Dias so as not to disagree with her.

When I told Escobar of my mother's opinion (naturally, without recounting the others') I saw that he took extraordinary pleasure in it. He thanked me, said that we were too good, and also praised my mother, a dignified, distinguished, and youthful lady, very youthful . . . What would her age be?

"She's over forty," I replied vaguely, out of vanity.

"Impossible!" exclaimed Escobar. "Forty! She hardly seems to be thirty; she's very youthful and pretty. And you have to take after someone, with those eyes God gave you; they're just like hers. Was she widowed many years ago?"

I told him what I knew of her life and my father's. Escobar listened attentively, asking for more, requesting explanation of anything I omitted, or what was merely unclear. When I told him I remembered nothing of the country, being so young when I came to the city, he told me of two or three memories from when he was three years old, and which were still fresh in his memory. And did we have no plans to go back to the country?

"No, we'll never go back now. Look, that black over there, he's from there. Tomás!"

"Massa!"

We were in the orchard, and the slave was working; he came up to us and waited.

"He's married," I said to Escobar. "Where's Maria?"

"She's poundin' corn, yes, sir."

"Do you remember the plantation, Tomás?"

"Yes, sir, I 'member."

"All right, off you go."

I showed him another, then another and another, here Pedro, there José, then Damião...

"All the letters of the alphabet," interrupted Escobar.

It was true, they were different letters, and only then did I notice it; I pointed out other slaves, some with the same first names, distinguished by a nickname, either describing the person, like Crazy João, or Fat Maria, or others from their place of origin, like Pedro Benguela, Antônio Mozambique...

"And are they all here at home?" he asked.

"No, some are working in the streets, and others are hired out. It wasn't possible to keep them all at home. And these are not all the ones from the plantation; the majority stayed there."

"What surprises me is that Dona Glória should have got used to living in a town house, where everything is cramped; the house there must be big."

"I don't know, but I expect so. Mamma has other houses larger than these; but she says she wants to die here. The others are rented. Some are really big, like the one on the Rua da Quitanda ..."

"I know that one; it's lovely."

"She also has them in Rio Comprido, in Cidade Nova, one in Catete ..."

"She'll never be without a roof over her head," he concluded, smiling agreeably.

We went towards the bottom of the garden. We went past the washing place; he stopped for a moment, looking at the stones for beating the clothes and making some reflections on cleanliness; then we went on. What reflections he made I cannot remember; I can only remember that I thought they were clever, I laughed, and so did he. My happiness brought his out, and the sky was so blue, the air so clear, that nature itself seemed to laugh with us. Happy times are like that. Escobar confessed to this harmony of the inner and outer worlds, in words so lofty and subtle that I was moved; then, concerning the accord between moral and physical beauty, he talked of my mother again: "a double angel," he said.

X C I V

Arithmetical Notions

I won't relate the rest, though there was a great deal of it. Not only did he know how to praise and think, he also knew how to calculate, speedily and accurately. He was one of Holmes' arithmetical types $(2 + 2 = 4)$.* You can't imagine the ease with which he added and multiplied in his head. Division, which was always a difficult operation for me, was no trouble to him: he would shut his eyes a little, raise them, and mutter the numbers— and that was it! This, with as many as seven, thirteen, twenty digits. His vocation was such that he loved the very signs for the numbers, and was of the opinion that the digits, since there were only ten of them, were much more efficient than the twenty-six letters of the alphabet.

"There are useless, unnecessary letters," he would say. "What different uses do *d* and *t* have? They have almost the same sound. You can say the same of *b* and *p*, of *s*, *c* and *z*, of *k* and *g*, etc.

* In his *Autocrat of the Breakfast-table* (1858), Oliver Wendell Holmes says that all practical and economic knowledge comes from the formula $2 + 2 = 4$, and all philosophical propositions from $a + b = c$.

They're just calligraphic nonsense. Look at the digits: no two have the same function: 4 is 4, and 7 is 7. And look how beautifully a 4 and a 7 make something else, which is written 11. Now, double 11 and you have 22; multiply it by an equal number, that's 484, and so forth. But the greatest perfection is in the use of zero. The value of zero is nothing, of itself; but the function of this negative sign is, precisely, to increase. A 5 on its own is 5; put two zeros on to it, and it's 500. So, what is worth nothing can add on a great deal of value, which you can't say of double letters, for I can *approve* just as well with one or two *p*s."

Brought up with the spelling of my forefathers, I disliked hearing such blasphemies, but I didn't dare argue. Still, one day, I did proffer some words in my defense, to which he replied that it was a prejudice, and added that arithmetical ideas could go up to infinity, with the advantage that they were easier to handle. Thus, I could not resolve a philosophical or linguistic problem in a moment, whereas he could add up any quantity of numbers in three minutes.

"For example . . . give me a case, give me some numbers I don't know, and cannot know beforehand . . . look, give me the number of houses your mother has and the rents on each of them, and if I can't tell you the total sum in two minutes—in one—you can hang me!"

I accepted the wager, and the following week, I gave him, on a sheet of paper, the figures for the houses and their rents. Escobar took the paper, cast his eyes over it to memorize the figures, and while I was looking at my watch, he lifted his eyes up, shut his lids, and muttered: Oh! the wind itself is not so swift! No sooner said than done; in half a minute he shouted:

"1,070 milreis a month in all!"*

I was astounded. Just think that there were no less than nine houses, and that the rents varied from 70 to 180 milreis. Well, all this that I would have spent three or four minutes doing—and on paper—Escobar did in his head, with no trouble at all. He looked at me in triumph, and asked if it wasn't right. Just to prove the

* See the note on page 31 (Chapter XVI) for the value of currency.

point, I took the piece of paper with the total sum out of my pocket, and showed it to him: exactly right, not the smallest mistake: 1,070.

"This proves that arithmetical ideas are simpler, and so more natural. Nature is simple. Art is complicated."

I was so taken with my friend's mental agility, that I could not refrain from embracing him. It was in the courtyard; other seminarists noticed our exuberance; a priest who was with them did not approve.

"Modesty," he said to us, "does not permit such effusive gestures; your esteem can be expressed with moderation."

Escobar remarked that the priest and the others were speaking out of envy, and said that we should perhaps keep apart from one another. I interrupted him to say no; if it was envy, so much the worse for them.

"Let's cock a snook at them!"

"But . . ."

"Let's be even firmer friends than we have been up to now."

Escobar grasped my hand in secret, so hard that my fingers still hurt from it. An illusion, no doubt, perhaps the effect of the long hours I've been writing without a break. I'll put down the pen for a while . . .

X C V

The Pope

Escobar's friendship became great and fruitful; that of José Dias refused to lag far behind. The next week he said to me, at home:

"It's certain now that you'll soon be able to leave the seminary."

"How's that?"

"Wait till tomorrow. I'm off to play cards with them—they've sent for me. Tomorrow, in your room, in the garden, or in the street on the way to mass, I'll tell you about it. The idea is so holy that it wouldn't look bad on the altar. Tomorrow, Bentinho."

"But is it certain?"

"*Most* certain!"

The next day he unveiled the mystery. At first sight, I confess I was dazzled. It had a grand, spiritual quality which answered to my seminarist's notions. It was nothing less than this: my mother, he thought, repented of what she had done, and would like to see me out here in the world, but thought that the moral ties of the promise bound her irrevocably. We had to break those ties, and the means was in Scripture, in the power of unbinding given to the apostles. So, he and I would go to Rome to ask absolution of the Pope . . . What did I think?

"I think it's a good idea," I replied after some seconds' reflection, "It might be a good solution."

"It's the only one, Bentinho, the only one! I'll go and talk to Dona Glória right away, today, I'll lay it all out before her, and we can go two months from now, or before . . ."

"Better say something next Sunday; let me think it over first . . ."

"Oh, Bentinho!" the dependent interrupted. "Think what over? What you really want . . . Should I say it? You won't be upset with your old friend? What you want to do is consult a certain person."

In point of fact there were two people, Capitu and Escobar, but I flatly denied that I wanted to consult anyone. Who, anyway, the Rector? Why should I want to confide in him on such a matter? No, not the Rector, nor my teachers, nobody; I only wanted time to reflect, a week, and on Sunday I would give my reply; I could tell him now that it didn't seem a bad idea to me.

"Doesn't it?"

"No."

"Then let's make up our minds today."

"It's no joke, going to Rome."

"If you've got the means, there's nothing easier. In our case, money's not lacking. Well, you might spend a bit on yourself . . .

but not on me; a pair of trousers, three shirts, and my daily bread, that's all I need. I'll be like St. Paul, who lived from his trade while he preached the holy word. In my case, I'm going, not to preach it, but to seek it out. We'll take letters from the Internuncio and the Bishop, letters for our ambassador there, letters from Capuchins . . . I'm quite aware of the objection that can be made; they'll say that you can ask for the dispensation from here, from far away; but, apart from other things I'll not mention, you only have to reflect that it is much more solemn and beautiful to see the object of the favor himself enter the Vatican, and prostrate himself at the Pope's feet: the promised Levite, who is going to ask God's dispensation for the sweetest and gentlest of mothers. You can picture it, you kissing the feet of the prince of the apostles; His Holiness, with an evangelical smile, leans over, asks the question, hears the answer, absolves, and blesses. The angels look on, the Virgin tells her most holy Son that all your desires, Bentinho, should be satisfied, and that what you love on earth should likewise be loved in heaven . . ."

I'll say no more, because I have to end the chapter, and he did not end his speech. He spoke to all my feelings as a Catholic and a lover. I saw my mother's soul relieved of its burden, I saw Capitu's joyful heart, both of them at home, I with them, he with us, all by means of a little journey to Rome. I only knew where it was in geographical terms: spiritually, too, but I had no idea how far it would be away from Capitu's desires. That was the essential point. If Capitu thought it was a long way, I wouldn't go; but I had to know what she thought, and the same with Escobar, who would give me good advice.

X C V I

A Substitute

I expounded José Dias' idea to Capitu. She listened attentively to me, then looked sad:

"If you go," she said, "you'll completely forget me."

"Never!"

"You will. They say Europe is so beautiful, and Italy most of all. Isn't that where the singers come from? You'll forget me, Bentinho. Isn't there some other way? Dona Glória is dying for you to leave the seminary."

"Yes, but she thinks she's tied by the promise."

Capitu could think of no other way, but neither could she persuade herself to adopt this one. In any case, she asked me, if I did go to Rome, to swear that I would be back in six months.

"I swear."

"Do you swear by God?"

"By God, by anything you want. I swear that at the end of six months I'll be back."

"And if the Pope hasn't released you yet?"

"I'll send a message saying just that."

"And what if you lie?"

These words hurt me a great deal, and I couldn't immediately think how to reply. Capitu treated the matter as a joke, laughing and calling me a sly dog. Afterwards, she said she believed I would keep my word, but even so she did not consent at once; she was going to see if there was not some other way, and wanted me to do the same.

When I went back to the seminary, I told everything to my friend Escobar, who heard me with the same attention, and at the end had the same sadness on his face that she had had. His eyes, usually so elusive, almost ate me up with avid attention.

Suddenly, I saw a flash of light in his face, the reflection of an idea. I heard him say eagerly:

"No, Bentinho, that's not necessary. There's a better way—not better, because the Holy Father is always better than anything— but there's something that will produce the same effect."

"What is it?"

"Your mother made a promise to God to give him a priest, did- n't she? Well, give him a priest, but not you. She can easily take an orphan lad, get him ordained at her expense, and a priest is pre- sented at the altar, without you . . ."

"I see, I see, that's it."

"Don't you think so?," he went on, "Consult the protonotary about it; he'll tell you if it's not the same thing, and I'll consult him myself, if you want; and if he hesitates, we'll speak to the bishop."

I reflected:

"Yes, I think that's the way; it is true that the promise is kept, if the priest is not forfeited."

Escobar observed that, from the financial point of view, it was an easy matter; my mother would spend the same as on me, and an orphan would not be in need of any great luxuries. He quoted the total of the house rents, 1,070 milreis, not to mention the slaves . . .

"That's the way," I said.

"And we'll leave together."

"You too?"

"Me too. I'm going to improve my Latin and leave; I won't bother with theology. Even Latin is unnecessary; what use is it in business?"

"*In hoc signo vinces,*" I said laughing.

I was in joking mood. Oh, how hope brightens everything! Escobar smiled, and seemed to like my reply. Then we began to think about our own affairs, each of us staring into the distance, probably. That was what he was doing, when I came out my reverie, and again thanked him for thinking of the plan; there could be no better solution. Escobar listened to me, delighted.

"Once again," he said gravely, "religion and liberty link hands."

X C V I I

Leaving

That was how it all happened. My mother hesitated a little, but ended up giving way, after Father Cabral, having consulted the bishop, came back to tell her that yes, it could be done. I left the seminary at the end of the year.

I was then a little over seventeen . . . This should have been the middle of the book, but my inexperience has let my pen run away with me, and I have come almost to the end of the paper, with the best of the story still to tell. There's no way for it now but to take it in great strides, chapter after chapter, with few corrections, not much reflection, everything in resumé. This chapter already covers months, others will cover years, and so we will get to the end. One of the sacrifices I make to this harsh necessity is the analysis of my emotions at age seventeen. I don't know if you were ever seventeen. If you were, you must know that it is an age when the half-man and the half-boy make a curious whole. I was *most* curious, as my dependent José Dias would say, and quite right too. What that superlative quality did for me I could never say here, without falling into the error that I have just condemned; the analysis of my emotions at that time did in fact enter into my plans. Even though I was the son of the seminary and of my mother, I already felt, beneath my chaste modesty, some impulses of a more daring, bolder nature; they came from my blood, but also from the girls who in the street or from windows wouldn't leave me alone. They thought I was handsome, and said so; some wanted to see my beauty closer up, and vanity is the beginning of corruption.

XCVIII

Five Years

Reason won out, and I went off to my studies. I passed my eighteenth, nineteenth, twentieth, twenty-first birthdays; at twenty-two I was a Bachelor of Law.

Everything around me had changed. My mother had decided to grow old; even then her white hairs came reluctantly, little by little, only here and there; her bonnet, clothes, and flat, muffled shoes were the same as in days gone by. Perhaps she no longer went around the house so much. Uncle Cosme was suffering from his heart and had to rest. Cousin Justina merely got older. So did José Dias, though not enough to prevent him doing me the courtesy of coming to my graduation, coming down the mountains with me as sprightly and exuberant as if it were he who had just graduated. Capitu's mother had died, and her father had retired from the same post in which he had wanted to make his exit from life itself.

Escobar was beginning to trade in coffee, after having worked for four years in one of the leading firms in Rio de Janeiro. It was cousin Justina's opinion that he had cherished the notion of inviting my mother to marry again; but, if such an idea did exist, one should not forget the great difference in age. Perhaps he intended nothing more than to link her to his first commercial undertakings, and in fact, at my request, my mother did advance him some sums of money, which he gave her back, as soon as he could, not without this dig: "Dona Glória is timid, and has no ambition."

The separation did not cool our friendship. He was the go-between in the exchange of letters between Capitu and me. As soon as he met her he encouraged me in my love for her. The business relationship he entered with Sancha's father brought him still closer to Capitu, and made him serve both of us, as a friend. At first, she was reluctant to accept him, preferring José Dias, but

José Dias didn't suit me, because of a residue of the respect I had for him as a child. Escobar won; though she was embarrassed, Capitu handed him her first letter, which was the mother and grandmother of the others. Even when he was married, he did not withdraw his favors ... For he married—guess who—he married the good Sancha, Capitu's friend, almost her sister, so much so that he, when he wrote to me, sometimes called her his "little sister-in-law." That's the way that friends and relations, adventures and books are made.

X C I X

The Son Is the Image of His Father

My mother, when I came back a Bachelor of Law, almost burst with happiness. I can still hear José Dias' voice, recalling St. John's Gospel, and saying on seeing us embracing:

"Woman, behold thy son! Son, behold thy mother!"

My mother, amidst her tears:

"Brother Cosme, he's the image of his father, isn't he?"

"Yes, he's got something, his eyes, the shape of his face. He's his father, only a bit more modern," he concluded jokingly. "And tell me now, sister Glória, wasn't it better that he didn't persist in becoming a priest? Imagine this dandy making a good priest!"

"How's my substitute?"

"Coming along; he'll be ordained next year," answered Uncle Cosme. "You must go to his ordination; me too, if this devil of a heart will let me. You must feel yourself in his soul, as it were, as if you yourself were being consecrated."

"Exactly!" exclaimed my mother. "But look carefully, brother

Cosme, see if he isn't the image of my dear departed. Look, Bentinho, look right at me. I always thought you looked like him, now it's much clearer. The moustache detracts from it a little . . ."

"Yes, sister Glória, the moustache, it's true . . . but he's very like."

And my mother kissed me with a tenderness I can't put into words. Uncle Cosme, to please her, called me doctor, José Dias, too, and everybody at home, cousin Justina, the slaves, guests, Pádua, his daughter, and she herself kept repeating the title to me.

C

"You will be Happy, Bentinho!"

In my room, as I unpacked my trunk and took my Bachelor's degree from its case, I thought about my happiness and glory. I saw my marriage and a successful career, while José Dias helped me, silently and zealously. At that point, an invisible fairy came down into the room, and said, in a voice both soft and warm: "You will be happy, Bentinho; you're going to be happy."

"And why shouldn't you be happy?" asked José Dias, straightening his back and staring at me.

"Did you hear?" I asked, as I got up too, astonished.

"Hear what?"

"Did you hear a voice saying I will be happy?"

"That's a good one! You said it yourself . . ."

Even now I could swear that it was the fairy's voice; obviously, fairies, having been expelled from stories and poems, have gone into people's hearts and speak from inside. This one, for instance—I've often heard her clearly and distinctly. She must be a cousin of the Scottish witches: "Thou shalt be king, Macbeth!" "You will be happy, Bentinho!" In the end, it's the same prediction, set to the same universal, eternal tune. When I had got over my astonishment, I heard the rest of José Dias' speech:

" . . . You will be happy, as you deserve, just as you deserved that diploma, which is a favor from nobody. The proof is that you got a distinction in every subject; I've already told you that I heard the most unstinting praise from the professors themselves, in private. What is more, happiness is not only glory, it's something else as well . . . Ah, you've not confided in old José Dias! Poor José Dias is pushed away in a corner, like an old sock, no good for anything any more; now it's the new friends, the Escobars of this world . . . I'm not denying that he's a very refined young man, hardworking, a first-class husband; but, when all's said and done, an old man knows how to love too. . .

"But what is it?"

"What do you think? Who doesn't know all about it? . . . That neighborly intimacy was bound to end in this, and it is truly a blessing from heaven, for she is an angel, the *angelest* . . . Pardon the solecism, Bentinho, it's a way of underlining the young lady's perfection. Years ago, I thought differently; I confused her childish ways with expressions of character, and didn't see that that mischievous girl, already with her thoughtful eyes, was the capricious bloom which would produce such a sweet, wholesome fruit . . . Why didn't you tell me what others know, and is well known and approved of here at home?"

"Does Mamma really approve?"

"Well, what do you think? We have spoken about it, and she did me the favor of asking for my opinion. Ask her what I said to her in clear, positive terms; ask her. I told her that she could not ask for a better daughter-in-law, good, discreet, accomplished, a friend of the family . . . and a good housewife, I don't need to tell you. After her mother's death, she took charge of everything. Pádua, now he's retired, does nothing but get his pension and hand it over to his daughter. She's the one who takes care of the money, pays the bills, keeps track of expenses, looks after everything, food, clothes, fuel; you saw her yourself last year. And as for her beauty, you know better than anyone . . ."

"But did Mamma really consult you about our marriage?"

"Not in so many words; she did me the favor of asking if Capitu wouldn't make a good wife; it was I who, in my reply, spoke of daughters-in-law. Dona Glória didn't deny it, and even gave a knowing smile."

"Always when Mamma wrote to me, she spoke of Capitu."

"You know that they are fond of one another, and that's why her cousin gets sulkier every day. She might get married all the quicker."

"Cousin Justina?"

"Don't you know? It's only gossip, of course; but anyway, Dr. João da Costa lost his wife a few months ago, and they say—I don't know, the protonotary told me—they say that the two of them are half inclined to leave widowhood behind and get married again. It might turn out to be nothing, but it might suit, even though she always thought the doctor was a bag of bones ... Only if she's a cemetery," he commented laughing; then seriously: "I only say that in fun ..."

I didn't hear the rest. I only heard the voice of my internal fairy, who kept repeating, now wordlessly: "You will be happy, Bentinho!" And Capitu's voice said the same thing, in different terms, and Escobar's, both of whom confirmed José Dias' news by their own impressions. Finally, my mother, some weeks later, when I went to ask her permission to marry, gave me the same prophecy along with her consent, except that it was in a mother's version: "You will be happy, my son!"

C I

In Heaven

Let's get on with it, and be happy, before the reader, half-dead with waiting, picks himself up and goes to amuse himself elsewhere; let's get married. It was in 1865, a March afternoon—it was raining, by the way. When we got up to Tijuca, where our love-nest was, heaven took the rain away and lit the stars, not just the ones we know, but also those which will only be discovered many centuries hence.* It was a great favor, and not the only one. St. Peter, who holds the keys of heaven, opened its gates to us, invited us in, and after touching us with his staff, recited some verses from his first Epistle: "Likewise, you wives, be in subjection to your own husbands . . . Whose adorning let it not be that outward adorning of plaiting of hair, and of wearing of gold, but let it be the hidden man of the heart . . . Likewise ye husbands, dwell with them, giving honor unto the wife as unto the weaker vessel, and as being heirs together of the grace of life . . ."† Then, he made a sign to the angels, and they chanted a part of the Song of Songs, so harmoniously, that they would have given the lie to the Italian tenor's theory, if this had happened on earth; but it was in heaven. The music went with the words, as if they had been born together, just as in a Wagner opera.†† Afterwards, we visited a part of that infinite place. Don't worry, I'll not describe it, nor does human language have have the proper tools for such a task.

After all, everything may have been a dream; nothing could be more natural for an ex-seminarist than to hear Latin and Scripture everywhere. It is true that Capitu, who did not know Latin or Scripture, did learn certain words by heart, such as these: "With great delight I sat down under the shadow of him I had so much desired."††† As for St. Peter's words, she told me the next day that she accepted everything, that I was the only decoration, the only adornment, that she would ever put on. To which I replied that my wife would always have the best adornments the world could offer.

* Tijuca was a partly landscaped forest area relatively close to the center of Rio de Janeiro, with romantic associations: a traditional place for honeymoons.

† First Epistle of St. Peter, ch. 3, vv. 1–4.

†† According to Wagner's theory of the total work of art (*Gesamtkunstwerk*), an opera, in its words, music and production, should be under the control of a single person.

††† Song of Solomon, Ch. 2, v. 3.

C I I

The Married Woman

Imagine a clock that only had a pendulum and no face, so that you could not see the figures for the hours. The pendulum would go from side to side, but no external sign would show the march of time. Such was that week in Tijuca.

From time to time we went back to the past, and amused ourselves by recalling our sorrows and calamities, but that, too, was a way of not emerging from ourselves. So we lived anew the long period we had to wait as lovers, our adolescent years, the accusation that appears in the early chapters, and we laughed at José Dias who plotted to separate us and ended by applauding our union. From time to time, we talked about going to town, but the days we agreed on always brought rain or sunshine, and we wanted an overcast day, which refused to come.

Nevertheless, I thought that Capitu was a little impatient to go down. She agreed to stay, but she kept mentioning her father and my mother, saying that they would have no news of us, one thing and another, until we became a little ruffled. I asked her if she was already bored with me.

"Me?"

"It looks like it."

"You'll always be a child," she said putting my face in her hands and putting her eyes close up to mine. "Did I wait for so many years to get bored in seven days? No, Bentinho; I say it because it's really true, I think they may be anxious to see us, and might imagine some illness, and I confess, on my part, that I'd like to see Papa."

"Well, we'll go tomorrow."

"No, not until there's an overcast day," she answered, laughing.

I laughed too, and took her at her word, but her impatience continued, and we went down in the sunshine.

The contentment with which she put her married woman's hat on, and the married woman's air with which she gave me her hand when she got into or out of the carriage, or her arm to walk in the street, all showed me that the cause of Capitu's impatience were the external signs of her new state. It was not enough for her to be married between four walls and a few trees: she needed the rest of the world, too. And when I found myself down in town again, walking the streets with her, stopping, looking, talking, I felt the same thing. I invented walks so that I could be seen, recognized, and envied. In the street, many turned their heads around in curiosity, others stopped, and some asked: "Who are they?". Some knowing person would reply: "That's Dr. Santiago, who married that young lady there a few days ago: she's Dona Capitolina. They married after a long childhood romance; they live in Glória, and their families reside on Matacavalos." Then both would say: "She's a fine figure of a woman!"

C I I I

Happiness Has a Good Heart

"Fine figure of a woman" is vulgar; José Dias found a better phrase. He was the only person from down here who visited us in Tijuca, bringing love from our families and words of his own, which were music itself; I'll not put them here to save paper, but they were delicious. One day, he compared us to birds brought up under the eaves of neighboring houses. Imagine the rest, the chicks getting their wings and flying up into the sky, and the sky itself wider so as to make room for them. Neither of us laughed: both of us were moved and convinced, forgetting everything, even that afternoon in 1857 . . . Happiness has a good heart.

C I V

The Pyramids

José Dias now divided himself between me and my mother, alternately taking dinner at Glória and lunch at Matacavalos. Everything was going well. After two years' marriage, apart from the great disappointment of not having a child, everything was going well. True, I had lost my father-in-law, and Uncle Cosme couldn't last long, but my mother's health was good: ours was excellent.

I was the lawyer for some important firms, and the work kept coming. Escobar had contributed a great deal to my first steps in the courts. He intervened with a famous lawyer for him to admit me to his office, and arranged some cases for me, all of this spontaneously.

In any case, the relationship between our families was already set up; Sancha and Capitu continued their schoolgirl friendship after marriage, Escobar and I ours from the seminary. They lived in Andaraí, and were always inviting us to go there; and though we couldn't go as often as we wanted, we went there to dine sometimes on Sundays, or they came to us.* Dinner hardly describes it. We always went very early, straight after lunch, to enjoy the whole day to the full, and we only came away at nine, ten, eleven, when we could really stay no longer. Now, when I think of those days in Andaraí and Glória, I am sorry that life and the rest of it are not as solid as the Pyramids.

Escobar and his wife lived happily; they had a little daughter. At one time, I did hear talk of the husband having an adventure, something to do with the theater, I can't remember whether it was an actress or a dancer, but if it was true, it created no scandal. Sancha was modest, and her husband hardworking. As I was say-

* Andaraí was a middle-class suburb in the foothills.

ing to Escobar one day that I regretted not having a child, he replied:

"Don't worry, old man. God will give one when He wills it, and if He doesn't it's because He wants them for Himself, and it's better for them to stay in heaven."

"A child, a son, is the natural complement of life."

"It will come if it's needed."

It didn't. Capitu begged for it in her prayers, and more than once I caught myself praying and begging, too. Now it was no longer as it had been when I was a child; now I paid in advance, just as I paid the house-rent.

C V

Arms

Apart from that, everything was going well. Capitu loved fun and amusement, and, at first, when we went for an outing or to the theater, she was like a bird out of its cage. She dressed charmingly and modestly. Although she was fond of jewelry, like other girls, she didn't want me to buy her many or very costly ones, and one day got so upset that I promised not to buy her any more; but this didn't last long.

Our life was more or less placid. When we were not with the family or with friends, or if we were not going to a play or a private party (and these were few and far between), we spent the evenings at the window of our house in Glória, looking at the sea and the sky, the shadow of the mountains and the ships, or passers-by on the beach. Sometimes, I would recount the history of the city to Capitu, or tell her about astronomy; an amateur's gleanings, which she listened to attentively, not that she didn't nod off a little sometimes. Since she couldn't play the piano, she learned after our marriage, so fast that quite soon she would play in friends' houses. In Glória it was one of our amusements; she sang, too, but not much and not often, because she hadn't a good voice; one day, she realized that it was better to give up, and kept her resolution. She enjoyed dancing, and adorned herself with loving care when she was going to a ball. Her arms ... Her arms are worth a sentence or two.

They were beautiful, and on the first night she went with them bare to a ball, I don't believe they had their equal in the whole city, not even yours, lady reader, if yours had been born yet: but they were probably still in the marble they came from, or in the hands of the divine sculptor. They were the loveliest arms of the night, so much so that they filled me with pride. I could hardly speak to other people for looking at them, however much they might touch other frock coats. But at the second ball we went to it was different; when I saw that men couldn't stop looking at them, seeking them out, almost begging for them, and brushed their black sleeves against them, I was embarrassed and annoyed. I didn't go to the third, and in this I had the support of Escobar, in whom I had frankly confided my irritation; he agreed with me at once.

"Sanchinha won't go either, or she'll go in long sleeves; I think it's indecent otherwise."

"Don't you think so? But don't say why; they'll call us seminarists. Capitu has already done so."

That didn't stop me telling Capitu about Escobar's agreement. She smiled and answered that Sanchinha's arms were not shapely, but she soon gave way, and didn't go to the ball. She went to others, but she went with them half-dressed in chiffon, or some such cloth, which neither covered nor uncovered them entirely, like Camões' veil.*

* A reference to Canto II, stanza 37 of Luís de Camões' *Os Lusíadas* (The Lusiads) (1572), the great Portuguese epic poem, in which the nymph Dione is described as wearing a "cendal," or silken cloth, which neither hides nor reveals the parts that "shame naturally covers."

C V I

Ten Pounds Sterling

I've already said that she was thrifty—and if I haven't I have now—and not only with money but with worn-out objects, that you keep out of respect for the past, as a memory or for old times' sake. A pair of shoes, for example, little flat shoes with black ribbons that were tied at the instep and ankle, the last ones she had used before she wore more formal shoes: she brought them home, and once in a while took them out the chest of drawers, with other old things, telling me that they were part of her childhood. My mother, who had the same temperament, liked to hear her talking and doing things in this way.

As for saving money itself, I'll tell one story, and that's enough. It was, precisely, on one of those occasions when I was giving her an astronomy lesson, at our house in Glória. You know that sometimes I made her nod off a little. One night she was lost to the world, staring at the sea, with such intensity and concentration that I became jealous.

"You're not listening, Capitu."

"Me? I heard you perfectly."

"What was I saying?"

"You . . . you were talking about Sirius."

"Sirius my foot, Capitu. It's twenty minutes since I mentioned Sirius."

"You were talking . . . talking about Mars," she hurriedly corrected herself.

It was Mars, in fact, but of course she had only caught the sound of the word, not the sense. I became serious, and had an impulse to leave the room; Capitu, when she saw this, became the most affectionate of creatures, took my hand, and confessed that she had been counting, that is, adding up some money to find a certain quantity that was missing. She had been converting paper money into gold. At first I thought it was a stratagem to put me in a good humor, but soon I was calculating too, now with pencil and paper on my knee, and I found the difference she had been looking for.

"But what pounds are these?" I asked when I had finished.

Capitu looked at me laughing, and answered that I was the one to blame for breaking the secret. She got up, went into the room, and came back with ten pounds sterling in her hand; it was the leftovers from the money I gave her monthly for household expenses.

"All that?"

"It's not much, only ten pounds; it's what your miserly wife could put together in a few months," she concluded clinking the gold in her hand.

"Who was the broker?"

"Your friend Escobar."

"Why didn't he say anything to me?"

"It was just today."

"Has he been here?"

"Just before you came; I didn't say anything so that you would-n't suspect."

I wanted to spend double on some present to celebrate this, but Capitu stopped me. On the contrary, she consulted me about what we were going to do with these pounds.

"They're yours," I replied.

"They're ours," she corrected me.

"You keep them, then."

The next day, I went to see Escobar at his warehouse, and laughed about their secret. Escobar smiled, and said that he had just been just about to go to my office to tell me everything. His little sister-in-law (he still gave Capitu this name) had spoken to him about it during our last visit to Andaraí, and had told him the reason for keeping it secret.

"When I told Sanchinha about it," he concluded, "she was amazed: 'How can Capitu save money, when everything's so expensive?' 'I don't know, dear; all I know is that she managed to save ten pounds.'"

"See if she can learn, too."

"I don't think so; Sancha doesn't waste money, but she's not thrifty; what I give her is enough, but just enough."

I, after some moments of reflection:

"Capitu is an angel!"

Escobar nodded in agreement, but unenthusiastically, as if he regretted that he couldn't say the same of his wife. You would think the same, so true is it that the virtues of people near to us make us feel a certain vanity, pride or consolation.

C V I I

Jealousy of the Sea

If it had not been for astronomy, I would not have discovered Capitu's ten pounds so soon, but that is not why I'm returning to the subject; it is so that you don't think that a teacher's vanity made me suffer from Capitu's inattention, and become jealous of the sea. No, my friend. My object is to explain to you that I felt that jealousy because of what might have been in my wife's head, not outside or above it. It's well known that people's distraction may be to blame, or half to blame, or a third, a fifth, or a tenth to blame, since there is an infinite gradation where blame in concerned. The simple memory of a pair of eyes is enough to make us stare at others which remind us of them and delight us by making us imagine them. There is no need for real or mortal sin, or an exchange of notes, a word, a nod, a sigh or even a tinier, slighter sign. An unknown man or woman passing the corner of the street can make us put Sirius into Mars, and you know, dear reader, the difference between them in terms of size and distance; but astronomy leads us into this kind of confusion. That was what made me go pale and silent and want to run from the room to come back God knows when; probably ten minutes later. Ten minutes later, I would have been back in the room, at the piano or the window, going on with the interrupted lesson:

"Mars is at a distance of . . ."

Such a short time? Yes, such a short time, ten minutes. My jealous fits were intense, but short; it didn't take much to make me want to destroy everything, but in the same little time I would put the sky, the earth and the stars back in their places.

The truth is that I grew even fonder of Capitu, if such a thing were possible, and she still more tender, the air milder, the nights clearer, and God more God-like. And it wasn't exactly the ten pounds sterling that did this, nor the thrifty qualities they revealed, which I was aware of, but the caution that Capitu took to show me on one day the care she took every day. Escobar also became dearer to my heart. Our visits became more frequent, and our conversations more intimate.

C V I I I

A Son

Well, not even this quenched my desire for a son, pale and thin as you like, but a son, a son of mine, belonging to me. When we went to Andaraí and saw Escobar's and Sancha's daughter, familiarly known as Capituzinha, to distinguish her from my wife, since they had baptized her with the same name, we were filled with envy. She was a charming little thing, chubby, talkative, and inquisitive. Her parents, like other parents, recounted her pranks and clever sayings, and we, as we came back to Glória at night, sighed with envy, mentally begging heaven to allay it . . .

. . . Our envy died, hopes were born, it was not long before their fruit came into the world. He wasn't thin or ugly, as I had begged, but a handsome, robust, healthy boy.

I cannot find words to express my happiness when he was born; I have never felt anything comparable, and I don't think there can be anything to equal it, or resemble it in the least. I felt dizzy; it was a kind of madness. I didn't sing in the street out of a natural sense of shame, nor at home, so as not to disturb Capitu, who was convalescing. I didn't fall down in the street, because there is a god that looks after recent fathers. Out of the house, I could think of nothing else but the boy; at home, observing him, looking at him, asking him where he came from, and why I was so entirely in him, and several other silly things that I didn't put into words, but which I thought of or rhapsodized about at every minute of the day. I may have lost some cases in court out of carelessness.

Capitu was no less tender towards him and me. We held each others' hands, and when we were not looking at our son, we talked about ourselves, our past and our future. The hours of greatest enchantment and mystery were when she was feeding the child. When I saw my son sucking his mother's milk, and all that union of nature for the nourishment and life of a being who had been nothing, and which our destiny had affirmed would come to be, I was in a state I can't describe, nor shall I; I can't remember, and I fear that anything I said would come out obscure.

Excuse these details. There is no need to talk about the dedication of my mother and Sancha, who went to spend the first days and nights with Capitu. I tried to refuse Sancha's kindness; she replied that it was nothing to do with me; Capitu, too, before she was married, had gone to look after her at the Rua dos Inválidos.

"Don't you remember that you went to see her there?"

"I remember; but what about Escobar . . ."

"I'll come and have dinner with you, and at night I'll go back to Andaraí; a week, and it'll all be over. You can tell you're a novice at being a father."

"You too; where's the second one?"

This was typical of our family jokes. Today, when I have retired into my shell, I don't know if that kind of language still exists: but it must. Escobar was as good as his word; he dined with us, and went back at night. At evening, we would go down to the beach or to the Promenade, he engrossed in his calculations, I in my dreams. I saw my son as a doctor, a lawyer, a businessman, I put him into several universities and banks, and even accepted the idea that he might be a poet. The possibility of being a politician was thought of, and I thought he would be an orator, a great orator.

"It's possible," Escobar commented, "no one could have foretold what Demosthenes would be."

Escobar often went along with my childish notions; he too guessed at what the future might hold. He even spoke of the possibility of marrying the child with his daughter. Friendship exists; it was all there in the hands with which I grasped Escobar's when I heard this, and in the total absence of words with which I signed the pact; the words came later, tumbling over one another, their rhythm determined by my heart, which was beating hard. I accepted the idea, and proposed that we should work to this end, by educating them together in the same way, and by a well-directed childhood in common.

It was my idea for Escobar to be the boy's godfather; the godmother had to be and would be my mother. But the first part was changed by the intervention of Uncle Cosme, who, when he saw the child, said to him amongst other endearments:

"Come on then, take a blessing from your godfather, you rascal."

And, turning round to me:

"I won't refuse the offer; and the christening had better be soon, before my illness removes me for good."

I told Escobar the story discreetly, so that he would understand and forgive me; he laughed and was not offended. More than that, he wanted the christening lunch to be at his house, and it was. I still tried to delay the ceremony to see if Uncle Cosme would succumb to his illness first, but it seems that it was more bothersome than fatal. There was nothing for it but to take the boy to the font, where he was given the name of Ezequiel; it was Escobar's, and this was my way of making up for his not being godfather.

C I X

An Only Son

E zequiel, when the last chapter began, had not been conceived; when it ended, he was Christian and Catholic. This one is designed to bring him up to the age of five, a handsome boy, with his clear eyes, already lively, as if they wanted to flirt with all the girls in the neighborhood, or nearly all.

Now, if you consider that he was an only child, that no other came, certain or uncertain, alive or dead, the sole, only one, you can imagine the worries he gave us, the sleep we lost, the frights that his teething and other crises gave us: the smallest fever, all the usual problems of childhood. We attended to everything, according to necessity or urgency: there was no need to say this, but there are readers so obtuse that they are incapable of understanding anything, if you don't tell them everything, and then the rest. Let's proceed to the rest.

C X

Childhood Traits

T he rest will take up many chapters still; there are lives that need less, and still are finished and complete.

At the age of five or six, Ezequiel gave no signs of disappointing my dreams on Glória beach; on the contrary, you could imagine every possible vocation in him, from idler to apostle. Idler can be understood in a good sense, that of a man who thinks and keeps himself to himself; he sometimes shut up within himself, and reminded one of his mother, ever since she was a girl. So, too, he would become excited and insisted on going to persuade the neighborhood girls that the sweets I brought him were real; he didn't do it before he had eaten his fill, but neither do the apostles carry the good news until their hearts are full of it. Escobar, the good businessman, gave it as his opinion that the principal cause of this latter tendency was perhaps to suggest implicitly to his neighbors that they might undertake a similar mission when their parents brought them sweets; he laughed at his own joke, and announced that he would take him into partnership.

He liked music no less than sweets, and I asked Capitu to play on the piano the refrain of the black man selling coconut sweets in Matacavalos. . .

"I can't remember it."

"Don't say that; don't you remember that black man selling sweets, in the afternoons . . ."

"I remember a black man selling sweets, but not the tune."

"Nor the words?"

"Nor the words."

My lady reader, who must still remember the words if she has read me attentively, will be amazed at such forgetfulness, the more so as she will still remember the cries of her childhood and adolescence; she will have forgotten some, but not everything stays in our minds. That's what Capitu said, and I could find nothing to say in reply. However, I did something she did not expect: I ran to my old papers. In São Paulo, when I was a student, I asked a music teacher to transcribe the tune of the refrain; he did it with pleasure (all I had to do was repeat it to him from memory) and I kept the piece of paper; I went to look for it. A little later I interrupted a ballad she was playing, with the scrap of paper in my hand. I explained it to her; she ran over the sixteen notes.

Capitu found a peculiar, almost delicious flavor in the tune; she told her son the story of the refrain, and so played it and sang it.

Ezequiel took advantage of the music to ask me to give the lie to the words by giving him some money.

He played at being doctor, soldier, actor, dancer. I never gave him oratories; but wooden horses and a sword hanging at his side were his passion. I'll say nothing of the battalions passing in the street, and which he ran to see; all children do that. What not all of them have are the eyes that he had. In none have I ever seen the eager pleasure with which he watched the passing soldiers and listened to the drum-beats as they marched.

"Look, Papa! look!"

"I'm looking, my boy!"

"Look at the commander! Look at his horse! Look at the soldiers!"

One day he started blowing into his hands as if they were a bugle; I gave him a toy trumpet. I bought him little lead soldiers, and pictures of battles which he looked at over and over, asking me to explain a piece of artillery, a fallen soldier, another with his sword raised—all his admiration was for the one with his sword raised. One day (what an innocent age!) he asked me impatiently:

"But, Papa, why doesn't he bring his sword down once and for all?"

"Because he's painted, my son."

"Why did he paint himself then?"

I laughed at the mistake, and explained to him that the soldier in the picture had not painted himself, but the engraver, and I had to explain what an engraver was, and an engraving: Capitu's curiosity, in a word.

These were his principal childhood traits: one more and I'll finish the chapter. One day, at Escobar's house, he saw a cat with a mouse between its teeth. The cat would not release its prey, nor could it find anywhere to get away from us. Ezequiel said nothing, stopped, squatted down, and looked. When we saw him so attentive, we asked him from far off what it was; he signalled to us to keep quiet. Escobar said:

"I'll bet it's the cat that's caught a mouse. It's the devil, the way the mice still infest the house. Let's go and see."

Capitu wanted to see her son as well; I went with them. It was true, it was a cat and a mouse, a very banal situation, with nothing interesting or amusing about it. The only peculiar thing about it was the fact that the mouse was alive, struggling, and my little lad was enraptured. Anyway, it was soon over. As soon as it sensed other people, the cat started to run off; the boy, without taking his eyes off it, motioned to us again to be quiet; and the silence could not have been greater. I was going to say religious, crossed it out, but I'm putting it back now, not only to convey the completeness of the silence, but because there was in the action of the cat and the mouse something like a ritual. The only noise was the final squeaks of the mouse, and they were in any case very weak; its legs gave slight, uncoordinated movements. A little annoyed, I clapped my hands to make the cat run away, which it did. The others didn't even have time to stop me; Ezequiel was dismayed.

"Oh, Papa!"

"What's the matter? By now the mouse has been eaten."

"Yes, I know, but I wanted to see."

The two of them laughed; even I thought it amusing.

C X I

Quickly Told

I thought it amusing, and even now I won't go back on that, in spite of the time that has gone by, the things that have happened, and a certain sympathy for the mouse that I find I have; it was amusing. I'm not sorry to say it; those who love Nature as she wishes to be loved, without partially rejecting or unjustly excluding anything, find nothing inferior in her. I love the mouse, and don't not love the cat. I once thought of having them live together, but I realized they are incompatible. It's true that one gnaws my books, the other my cheese; but it's no trouble to forgive them, as I forgave a dog which robbed me of my rest in worse circumstances. I'll tell the story quickly.

It was when Ezequiel was born; his mother had a fever, Sancha was constantly at her bedside, and three dogs were barking in the street all night. I looked for the local watchman, and I might as well have looked for you, dear reader, who are only just now learning of this. So I decided to kill them; I bought poison, had three meatballs meat made, and I myself inserted the drug into them. At night, I went out; it was one o'clock; neither the patient nor her nurse could sleep with the racket made by the dogs. When they saw me, they ran off; two went down towards Flamengo beach, and one stayed a short distance away, as if waiting. I went towards him, whistling and snapping my fingers. The wretch barked some more, but trusting in my signs of friendship, he gradually quietened down, finally going completely silent. As I went on, he came up to me, slowly, wagging his tail, which is their way of laughing; I already had the poisoned meatballs in my hand, and was going to give him one, when that special laughter, affection, confidence or whatever it is, froze my will; I can't describe how I felt, touched with pity, and I put the balls back in my pocket. The reader might think that it was the smell of the meat that made the dog quieten down. I don't say it wasn't so; I think he didn't suspect treachery in my gesture, and entrusted himself to me. In any case, the conclusion is that he got off.

C X I I

Ezequiel's Imitations

Ezequiel would not have done such a thing. He would not have made up poisoned meatballs, I presume, but he wouldn't refuse them either. What he certainly would do is go after the dogs with stones, as far as his legs would carry him. And if he had had a stick, he would have used that. Capitu adored her future warrior.

"He doesn't take after us; we love peace," she said to me one day, but Papa when he was a child was like that, too; Mamma told me."

"Yes, he won't be a wimp," I replied, "I can only find one little defect in him; he likes imitating others."

"Imitate how?"

"Imitate their gestures, their habits, their attitudes; he imitates cousin Justina, José Dias; I've even found something of Escobar about the way he moves his feet and eyes . . ."

Capitu stopped for a moment, thinking and looking at me, and in the end said that we should correct him. She saw now that it was a bad habit of his, but she thought it was only imitating for imitation's sake, as happens with many adults, who take on others' mannerisms; but so that it would go no further . . ."

"There's no need to be too harsh. We've plenty of time to correct him."

"You're right, I'll wait and see. Weren't you like that too, when you got angry with someone?"

"Yes, I admit it, when I got angry—a child's way of getting vengeance."

"Yes, but I don't like having that kind of imitation in the house."

"And did you love me in those days?" I said patting her cheek.

Capitu's reply was a soft mocking laugh, one of those laughs which can't be described, and hardly painted; then she stretched her arms out and flung them over my shoulders, so full of charm that they seemed—to use a worn image—a garland of flowers. I did the same with mine, and was sorry that there was no sculptor there to copy our posture in a piece of marble. It is true that only the artist would get any glory from it. When a person or a group turn out well, no one wants to know about the model, only the work, and it is the work that endures. No matter: we would know it was us.

C X I I I

*Third-Party Embargoes**

Talking of this, it's natural for you to ask me if, having been so jealous of her, I didn't go on being so in spite of my son and the passing years. Yes, sir, I did. I went on being so, to such a point that the least gesture alarmed me, the tiniest word, any kind of insistence on a point; often mere indifference was enough. I came to be jealous of everything and everyone. A neighbor, a waltz partner, any man, young or old, filled me with terror or mistrust. It is true that Capitu liked to be seen, and the most appropriate means to that end (a lady said to me one day) is to see in one's own right, and one cannot see without showing that one is seeing.

The lady who told me this had taken a fancy to me, I think, and naturally it was because she did not find her affection returned that she explained her insistent eyes in that way. Other eyes sought me out too, not many, and I'll not say anything about them, since I have already at the beginning confessed to future adventures, but they were still future. At that time, however many beautiful women I came across, none would receive the least part of the love I bore Capitu. I even loved my mother only half as much. Capitu was everything and more than everything; I thought about her constantly, at work or anywhere. We went to the theater together; I only remember twice when I went without her, an actor's benefit, and the first night of an opera, which she didn't go to because she was ill, but was determined I should go. It was too late to offer Escobar the box; I went, but I came back at the end of the first act. I found Escobar at the front door.

---

* This refers to an action moved by a third party, not directly involved in a legal dispute, but who regards him or herself as adversely affected by it, to safeguard his or her interests.

"I was coming to talk to you," he said.

I explained that I had gone out to go to the theater, and had come back because of my concern for Capitu, who was ill.

"What of?" asked Escobar.

"She was complaining of her head and stomach."

"Then I'll go. I was coming about that business of the embargoes . . ."

These were some third-party embargoes; an important incident had happened, and since he had dined in town, he hadn't wanted to go home without telling me about it, but now he would tell me another time . . .

"No, tell me now, come up; she may be better. If she's worse, you can leave."

Capitu was better, in fact quite well. She confessed that she only had a slight headache, but had made it sound worse than it was so that I would go and enjoy myself. She didn't sound cheerful, which made me think she was lying, so as not to alarm me, but she swore it was the simple truth. Escobar smiled and said:

"My little sister-in-law is as ill as you or me. Let me tell you what's happened."

C X I V

Which Explains What has Already Been Explained

Before going on to the embargoes, let's explain something that has already been explained, but not very well. You have seen (Chapter CX) that I asked a music teacher in São Paulo to transcribe the tune of the sweet-seller's refrain from Matacavalos. In itself, it is a trivial subject, and is not worth the trouble of one chapter, let alone two; but there are things like this which provide interesting lessons, even agreeable ones. Let's explain what has already been explained.

Capitu and I had sworn not to forget that refrain; it was at a moment of great tenderness, and the divine notary has knowledge of things that are sworn in such moments, and writes them down in the eternal books.

"Do you swear?"

"I swear," she said, extending her arm tragically.

I took advantage of the gesture to kiss her hand; I was still at the seminary. When I went to São Paulo, wanting one day to remember the tune, I realized that I was on the way to forgetting it; I managed to remember it, and hurried to the teacher, who did me the favor of writing it out on the scrap of paper. I did this so as not to break my oath. But can you believe that, when I went back to the old papers, that night in Glória, again I couldn't remember the tune or the words? My sin was to be so particular about the oath: as for forgetting, anyone can forget.

The truth is that no one knows if they will keep an oath or not. Who knows what the future holds? Therefore, our political constitution, which has substituted a simple affirmation for an oath, is profoundly moral.* It did away with a terrible sin. To break one's word is always disloyal, but for someone who is more fearful of God than men it will not matter if he lies once in a while, so long as he does not put his soul in purgatory. Don't confuse purgatory with hell, which is eternal shipwreck. Purgatory is a pawn shop, which loans money against all the virtues, short term and at high interest. But the periods can be renewed, until one day one or two middling virtues pay off all the sins, great and small.

* The constitution of the Brazilian Republic, which replaced the Empire in 1889, separated Church and State, and thus did not require deputies and office holders to take oaths of office by religious formulae.

C X V

Doubts Upon Doubts

Let's proceed to the embargoes ... And why should we go on to the embargoes? God knows what an effort it is to write the briefs out, and more still to recount them. Of the new circumstance that Escobar brought to my attention I can only say what I said then, that is, that it was useless.

"Useless?"

"Almost useless."

"Then it's of some use."

"As backing for the reasons we already have it's worth less than the tea you're going to have with me."

"It's late for tea."

"We'll have it quickly."

We did so. While we were having it, Escobar was looking at me warily, as if he thought that I was rejecting this new circumstance to avoid having to write it out; but such a suspicion was unworthy of our friendship.

When he had gone, I told Capitu of my doubts; she dissolved them with that subtle art she had, a way with her, a charm all of her own, capable of dissolving the sadness of Olympio himself.*

"It must have been the business of the embargoes," she concluded; "and if he came here at this hour, it must be because he's worried about the case."

"You're right."

One thing leads to another, and I talked of other doubts. At this time, I was a well full of them; they croaked inside me, like real frogs, even to the point of sometimes keeping me awake at

---

* A reference to Victor Hugo's poem "Tristesse d'Olympio," in which Olympio (an *alter ego* of the poet) wishes that the happy moments of life could be made eternal.

night. I told her that I was beginning to find my mother cool and aloof with her. Even here, Capitu's subtle arts worked!

"I've already told you what it is: that's the way with mothers-in-law. Your little Mamma is jealous of you; as soon as it passes and she begins to miss you, she'll go back to what she was. When she wants to see her grandson . . ."

"But I've noticed that now she's cool with Ezequiel, too. When he goes with me, Mamma no longer makes such a fuss of him.

"Who's to say she's not well?"

"Should we go and have dinner with her tomorrow?"

"Yes, let's . . . No . . . All right then."

We went to have dinner with my old mother. Now she could be called that, even though her hairs were not all white, or even completely white, and her face was still comparatively fresh; it was a kind of fifty-year-old youthfulness, or flourishing old age, as you will . . . But let's not be melancholy: I don't wish to speak of the moisture in her eyes, when we arrived and left. She hardly entered into the conversation; nor was she any different from usual. José Dias spoke of marriage and its beauties, of politics, Europe and homeopathy, Uncle Cosme of his aches and pains, cousin Justina of the neighbors, or of José Dias, when he was out of the room.

When we came back home, at night, we went on foot, and spoke of my doubts. Again Capitu told me we should wait. All mothers-in-law are like that; there comes a day when they change. As she talked to me, her tenderness grew. Thenceforth, she was more and more affectionate with me; she didn't wait for me at the window, so as not to awaken my jealousy, but as I was going in, I saw at the top of the steps, through the gate, the delightful face of my wife and companion, as full of laughter as it had been all through our childhood. Sometimes Ezequiel was with her; we had accustomed him to seeing the kiss we gave when I left for work and when I came back, and he would cover my face with kisses.

C X V I

Son of Man

I sounded José Dias out on my mother's new manner; he was astonished. There was nothing the matter, nor could there be, such was the incessant praise he heard for the "beautiful and virtuous Capitu."

"Now, when I hear it, I join the chorus; but I felt *most* ashamed at the beginning. For someone like me, who went so far as to disapprove of this marriage, it was hard to confess that it was a veritable blessing from heaven. What a dignified lady that mischievous girl from Matacavalos has become! It was her father who separated us somewhat, when we didn't know one another, but it's all worked out for the best. Yes indeed, when Dona Glória praises her daughter-in-law and mother of her godson . . ."

"So Mamma? . . ."

"Absolutely!"

"But why hasn't she come to see us in so long?"

"I think she's been suffering more from her rheumatism. It's been very cold this year . . . Imagine how miserable she must be, when she used to be active all day; now she has to sit down beside her brother, who's not too well himself . . ."

I wanted to say that this explained the interruption of her visits, and not her coolness when we went to Matacavalos; but I didn't take my intimacy with our dependent that far. José Dias asked to see our "little prophet" (that was what he called Ezequiel) and made the usual fuss of him. This time he spoke in the biblical manner (he had been leafing through the book of Ezekiel the day before, as I found out afterwards), and asked him: "How are things, son of man?", "Tell me, son of man, where are your toys?", "Would you like a sweet, son of man?"

"What son of man is that?" asked Capitu, irritated.

"It's the biblical way of putting it."

"Well, I don't like it," she replied sharply.

"You're right, Capitu," agreed the dependent. "You can't imagine how many crude, coarse expressions there are in the Bible. I put it that way for a change. How are you, my angel? My angel, how do I walk down the street?"

"No," interrupted Capitu; "I'm trying to rid him of that habit of imitating others."

"But it's very funny; when he imitates my gestures, I seem to see a miniature version of myself. The other day he even imitated a gesture of Dona Glória's so well that she kissed him for it. Come on, how is it I walk?"

"No, Ezequiel," I said, "Mamma says no."

Even I thought it was a bad habit. Some of the gestures kept on coming back, like those of Escobar's hands and feet; lately, he had even caught his way of turning his head around when he talked, and of letting it drop when he laughed. Capitu scolded him. But the boy was a mischievous little devil; hardly had we started to talk about something else, when he jumped into the middle of the room, saying to José Dias:

"This is the way you walk."

We had to laugh, I more than anybody. The first person to frown, reprimand him, and bring him to his senses was Capitu.

"I won't have that, do you hear?"

C X V I I

Close Friends

By that time Escobar had left Andaraí and bought a house in Flamengo:* I saw it there, some days ago, when I had the urge to see if the old sensations were dead or just asleep; I can't really tell, because in sleep, when it is heavy, the dead look like the living, except that the living still breathe. I was breathing a little heavily, but it might have been because of the sea, which was a little rough. Anyway, I passed on, lit a cigar, and found myself in Catete; I had come up by the Rua da Princesa, an old street ... Old streets! Old houses! Old legs! We were all old, and needless to say in the bad sense: old and done for.

The house is old, but it hasn't been altered at all. I don't know if it still has the old number. I won't reveal it, so that no one can go and dig out the story. Not that Escobar lives there still, or is even alive; he died a little later, as I will recount. While he was alive, since we were so close, we had, so to speak, only one house; I lived in his house, he in mine, and the stretch of beach between Glória and Flamengo was like a private right of way, for our use alone. It made me think of the two houses on Matacavalos, with the wall between them.

A historian in our language, I think it was João de Barros, puts into the mouth of a barbarian king some gentle words, when the Portuguese were proposing to establish a fort nearby; the king said that good friends should remain distant from one another, not close, so as not to become angry with one another, like the waves of the sea that were beating furiously on the rocky coastline they could see from there.† May the writer's shade forgive me, if I

---

* Flamengo is an area of Rio de Janeiro further from the center, and just beyond Gloria, on Guanabara Bay. Escobar has moved up in the world.

† João de Barros (c. 1496–1570), the Portuguese historian, relates this story in the first part of his *Décadas*. It is supposed to have taken place at the fort of São Jorge da Mina, in present-day Senegal, in 1484.

doubt that the king said that, or that what he said is true. It was probably the writer himself who invented it to adorn his text, and he did right, for they are truly striking words. I do believe that the sea beat on the stones, as is its habit, since the days of Ulysses and before. But I am sure that the comparison is not a just one. Certainly there are enemies who live close by, but there are also friends who are both near and true. And the writer forgot— unless it had not yet been invented—forgot the adage: "out of sight, out of mind." Our hearts could not have been closer than they now were. Our wives lived in each others' houses, we passed our evenings here or there chatting, playing cards or gazing at the sea. The two little ones spent their days either at Flamengo or Glória.

As I observed that the same thing could happen to them as had happened between Capitu and me, they all agreed, and Sancha added that they were already beginning to look alike. I explained:

"No; it's because Ezequiel imitates other people's gestures."

Escobar agreed with me, and suggested that sometimes children who play a lot together end up looking like each other. I nodded my head, as I often did in matters on which I had no opinion one way or the other. Anything was possible. The truth is that the two of them were very fond of each other, and might have ended up married; but they did not end up married.

C X V I I I

Sancha's Hand

All things come to an end, reader; it's an old truism, to which we may add that not everything that lasts, lasts for very long. This second part does not readily find believers; on the contrary, the idea that a castle in the air lasts any longer than the air of which it is built is difficult to get out of anyone's head, and it's as well that this is so, so that the habit of constructing these near-eternal structures is not lost.

Our castle was solid, but one Sunday ... The previous day we had spent the evening at Flamengo, not only the two inseparable couples, but also the dependent and cousin Justina. It was then that Escobar, speaking to me in the window, invited us for dinner there the next evening; he wanted us to talk about a family project, a project for the four of us.

"For the four of us? A quadrille?"

"No, you'll never guess what it is, and I won't tell you. Come tomorrow."

Sancha didn't take her eyes off us during the conversation next to the window. When her husband went out, she came across to me. She asked me what we had been talking about; I told her it was a plan, but I didn't know what for. She asked me to keep a secret, and told me what it was: a trip to Europe in two years' time. She said this with her back to the room, almost sighing. The sea was crashing on the beach; there was a strong undertow.

"Are we all going?" I asked finally.

"Yes."

Sancha lifted her head and looked at me with so much pleasure that I, thanks to her close friendship with Capitu, would have been quite happy to kiss her on the forehead. However, Sancha's eyes were not inviting me to fraternal enthusiasm, they seemed warm and imperious, saying something else, and it was not long before they removed themselves from the window, where I stayed looking at the sea, lost in thought. The night was clear.

From that very place I sought Sancha's eyes, next to the piano: mine met hers half way. The four of them stopped and faced each other, each pair waiting for the other to pass on, but neither did: like two stubborn people meeting each other in the street. Caution separated us; I went to look outside again. And there I began to search my memory to see if I had ever looked at her with the same expression; I was unsure. I was sure of one thing, that I had thought of her one day, as one thinks of any pretty passer-by;

but could it be that she had guessed ... Perhaps the mere thought had shone in my face, but before, she had fled from me out of annoyance or timidity; now, because of an invincible urge ... Invincible; the word was like the priest's blessing at mass, which one receives and repeats inside oneself.

"That sea tomorrow will be a real challenge," said Escobar's voice, right next to me.

"Are you going in tomorrow?"

"I've gone in rougher seas, much rougher; you've no idea what a really good angry sea is like. You have to swim well, as I do, and have lungs like these," he said, slapping his chest, "and these arms; feel them."

I felt his arms, as if they were Sancha's. This is a painful confession to make, but I cannot suppress it; that would be to avoid the truth. Not only did I feel them with that idea in mind, but I felt something else as well; I thought they were thicker and stronger than mine, and I envied them; what's more, they knew how to swim.

When we left, I again spoke with my eyes to the lady of the house. Her hand squeezed mine hard, and stayed there for longer than usual.

Modesty required that then, as now, I should see in Sancha's gesture nothing more than an approval of her husband's project and an expression of gratitude. That's the way it should have been, but a peculiar fluid that flowed through my whole body removed from me the conclusion I have just written. I felt Sancha's fingers again, as they gripped mine and mine hers. It was a dizzy moment, a moment of sin. It took no time on the clock; when I put my watch to my ear, I heard only the ticking of virtue and reason.

"... A most delightful lady," José Dias concluded a speech he had been making.

"Most delightful!" I repeated with some warmth, which I then moderated, correcting myself: "Really, it is a lovely night!"

"As every night in that house must be," the dependent went on.

"Not out here: there's an angry sea; listen."

We could hear the roaring sea—as one could hear it from the

house too—there was a violent swell, and in the distance one could see the billowing waves. Capitu and cousin Justina, who were walking ahead, stopped at one of the turns in the beach, and we went on, the four of us conversing; but I could hardly talk. There was no way of completely forgetting Sancha's hand, nor the look we exchanged. First I thought of them in one way, then in another. God's minutes were interrupted by the devil's moments, and so the pendulum swung between my perdition and my salvation. José Dias said goodbye to us at our door. Cousin Justina was to sleep at our house; she would go back next day, after lunch and mass. I retired to my study, where I stayed longer than usual.

Escobar's photograph, which I had there next to my mother's, spoke to me as if it were he himself. I sincerely struggled against the impulses I had brought from Flamengo; I thrust aside the image of my friend's wife, and accused myself of disloyalty. Besides, who could tell me that there was any intention of that kind in her goodbye gesture, or the previous ones? Everything could be put down to her lively interest in the trip. Sancha and Capitu were such friends that it would be an added pleasure for them to travel together. Even if there was any sexual intent, who could prove to me that it was no more than a fleeting sensation, destined to die with night and sleep? Remorse often springs from such trivial sins, and lasts no longer than this. I clung to this hypothesis, which could be reconciled with Sancha's hand, the memory of which I could feel in my own, warm and slow, squeezed and squeezing...

In all sincerity, I felt ill at ease, caught between my friend and the attraction I felt. It may be that timidity was another cause of this crisis: it is not only heaven that gives us our virtues, timidity, too, and that's not counting chance—but chance is mere accident; it is best if virtue comes from heaven. However, since timidity comes from heaven, which gives us this disposition, virtue, its daughter, is, genealogically speaking, of the same celestial family. That is what I would have thought if I had been able to; but at first my thoughts simply wandered in confusion. It was not passion or a serious inclination. Was it just a caprice? After twenty minutes it was nothing, nothing at all. Escobar's portrait seemed to speak to me; I saw his frank, open manner, shook my head and went to bed.

C X I X

Don't Do It, My Dear!

My lady reader, who is my friend and has opened this book to amuse herself between yesterday's cavatina and today's waltz, now wants to shut it hastily, as she sees us approach an abyss. Don't do it, my dear; I'm changing course.

C X X

Documents

The following morning I awoke free of the abominations of the previous day; I called them hallucinations, had my breakfast, leafed through the newspapers, and went to study some documents relating to a lawsuit. Capitu and cousin Justina went out for nine-o'clock mass at Lapa. The figure of Sancha disappeared completely in the midst of the allegations made by the opposing party, as I read them in the documents, false allegations, inadmissible, with no support in law or precedent. I saw that it was easy to win the case; I consulted Dalloz, Pereira e Sousa . . .

Only once did I look at Escobar's portrait. It was a fine photograph taken a year previously. He was standing, with his frock coat buttoned, his left hand on the back of a chair, his right hand on his chest, looking into the distance to the left of the onlooker. He looked both elegant and natural. The frame I had had made for it did not cover up the dedication, written beneath, not on the back: "To my dear Bentinho, with affection, Escobar 20-4-70." These words strengthened the thoughts I had had that morning, and drove away the memories of the previous day. In those days my sight was good; I could read the words from where I was sitting. I went back to the documents.

C X X I

The Catastrophe

Right in the middle of them, I heard hurried footsteps on the stairs, the bell rang, I heard the sound of hands clapping, there was knocking at the gate, voices, everyone came running, myself included. It was a slave from Sancha's house calling me:

"Come over there . . . massa swimming, massa dying."

He said no more, or I didn't hear the rest. I dressed, left a message for Capitu and ran to Flamengo.

On the way, I began to guess the truth. Escobar had gone in for his swim, had gone a little farther out than usual in spite of the rough sea, had been swept away in the waves and killed. The canoes that came to the rescue only just managed to bring in his body.

C X X I I

The Funeral

The widow ... I'll spare you the widow's tears, my own and those of the others. I left at about eleven; Capitu and cousin Justina were waiting for me, the one looking downcast and stunned, the other merely irritated.

"Go and keep poor Sanchinha company; I'll make the arrangements for the funeral."

That's what we did. I wanted the funeral to be full of pomp and ceremony, and a large crowd of friends came. The beach, the streets, the Praça da Glória, were full of carriages, many of them private. The house was not large enough to hold everyone; many people stayed on the beach, talking of the tragic event, pointing out the place where Escobar had died, hearing how the body had been brought in. José Dias also heard talk of the dead man's business affairs: there were different views as to the amount of his estate, but it was agreed that his liabilities must be few. They praised Escobar's qualities. Here and there they were talking about the recent Rio Branco ministry; we were in March 1871: I have never forgotten the month or the year.*

As I had determined to make a speech in the cemetery, I wrote some lines and showed them at home to José Dias, who found them truly worthy of the deceased and of me. He asked me for the paper, and slowly recited the speech, weighing the words, and confirmed his original opinion; he spread the news around Flamengo. Some acquaintances came to ask me:

"So, we're going to hear from you?"

---

* This government, led by the Visconde do Rio Branco, was one of the longest and most important of the Empire. Its most notable act was the passing of the Law of the Free Womb, by which all slaves born after 28 September 1871 would be free on their twenty-first birthday. It was the first legal acknowledgement that slavery (finally abolished on 13 May 1888) would end.

"Four or five words."

There would not be many more. I had written them out, fearing that the emotion might prevent me improvising. As I rode around in the tilbury for an hour or two, I had done nothing but remember our time at the seminary, how I came to know Escobar, our closeness, our friendship, begun, continued and never interrupted, until a stroke of fortune separated two people who seemed destined to stay united for many years. From time to time I wiped my eyes. The driver ventured two or three questions about my moral state; getting nothing out of me, he went on with his job. When I got home, I put those emotions onto paper; that would be my speech.

C X X I I I

Undertow Eyes

Finally, the time came for commending his soul to God, and for the final goodbye. Sancha wanted to say farewell to her husband, and the despair of the scene dismayed everyone. Many men were weeping too; all the women. Only Capitu, supporting the widow, seemed able to control herself. She consoled her, and tried to get her away. There was general confusion. In the midst of it, Capitu looked for some moments at the body with such a fixed gaze, with such a passionately fixed gaze, that it's small wonder that into her eyes there came a few silent tears ...

Mine stopped immediately. I stood looking at hers; Capitu wiped them hastily, looking sidelong at the people in the room. She redoubled her caresses for her friend, and tried to take her away; but it seems that the body held her back, too. There was a moment when Capitu's eyes fixed on the body, like those of the widow though without her tears or cries, but large and wide open, like the waves on the sea out there, as if she too wanted to swallow up that morning's swimmer.

C X X I V

The Speech

"Come, it's time ..."
 It was José Dias reminding me to shut the coffin. We shut it, and I took hold of one of the handles; there was a final burst of weeping. I give you my word that, when I got to the door, and saw the bright sunlight, people and carriages everywhere, heads uncovered, I had one of those impulses of mine which I never carry out: to throw the coffin, body and all, into the street. In the carriage I told José Dias to be quiet. In the cemetery I had to repeat the same ceremony as at the house, undo the straps, and help bear the coffin to the grave. You can imagine what an effort this was. Once the body was down in the grave, they brought the lime and the shovel; you know all about it, you'll have been to more than one funeral, but what neither you, nor any of your friends, nor any other person can know, reader, is the crisis that overcame me when I saw everyone's eyes on me, their feet still, ears attentive, and after some moments of total silence, a vague murmur, some enquiring voices, gestures, and someone, José Dias, saying into my ear:
 "Go on, speak."
 It was the speech. They wanted the speech. They had a right to

the advertized speech. Mechanically, I put my hand in my pocket, took out the paper and read it stumblingly, not all of it, not in order and not clearly; my voice seemed to be going back into my mouth instead of coming out of it, and my hands were trembling. Nor was it only the new emotion that affected me in this way, it was the text itself, the memories of my friend, my affection for him, my praise of the man and his merits; all these things I was obliged to say and said badly. At the same time, fearing that they might suspect the truth, I was struggling to hide it. I think that few heard me, but the general reaction was of understanding and approval. The hands that stretched out to shake mine expressed fellow feeling; some said: "Very fine! well said! magnificent!" José Dias thought that my eloquence had been in keeping with the emotion of the occasion. A man, who seemed to be a journalist, asked my permission to take the manuscript and publish it. Only my great inner turmoil can explain my refusing such a simple request.

C X X V

A Comparison

Priam thinks himself the most unfortunate of men, for having kissed the hand of the man who killed his son.* It's Homer that tells the story, and he's a fine author, even though he does tell it in verse—but there are true narratives in verse, even in bad verse. Compare Priam's situation with mine; I had just praised the virtues of the man who had, in death, been the object of such a look ... It seems impossible that some Homer could have failed

---

* *Iliad*, Canto XXIV, lines 376–79.

to get a much better effect out of my situation, or at least as good. And don't tell me that Homers are lacking, for the reason that Camões gives; no, sir, they are lacking, it's true, but it's because the Priams seek out obscurity and silence.* The tears, if they shed them, are wiped away behind the door, so that the faces can appear fresh and serene; the speeches are cheerful rather than melancholy, and all goes on as if Achilles had not killed Hector.

C X X V I

Thoughts

A little after leaving the cemetery, I tore up the speech and threw the pieces out of the carriage window, in spite of José Dias' attempts to stop me.

"It's worthless," I said, "and as I might be tempted to have it printed, it's best it's destroyed once and for all. It's no good—useless."

José Dias demonstrated at length that the contrary was true, then he praised the funeral, and finally entered on a panegyric of the dead man, a great soul, an active mind, with an upright heart, and a friend, a good friend, a worthy friend, worthy of the most loving wife that God had given him . . .

At this point in the speech, I let him carry on talking to himself and began to think. My thoughts were so dark and confused that I felt out of my depth. In Catete I ordered the carriage to stop, told José Dias to go and fetch the ladies at Flamengo, and take them home; I would go on foot.

---

* In Canto V, stanza 97 of *Os Lusíadas* (see note 47), Camões complains that the lack of poets such as Homer and Virgil in Portugal is due, not to any lack of noble subjects, but to the lack of an appreciative audience.

"But ..."

"I'm going to pay a visit."

The reason for this was to finish my thoughts, and reach a decision suitable to the moment. The carriage would go faster than my legs: these could choose their own pace, they could slow down, stop, turn back, and allow the head to go on thinking as it wanted to. I went on walking and brooding. I had already compared Sancha's gesture of the previous day and her present despair: they were irreconcilable. She really was a most loving widow. Thus all the illusion conjured up by my vanity disappeared. Wasn't it the same with Capitu? I tried to visualize her eyes again, the position I saw her in, the press of the people that would naturally force her to dissemble, if there was anything to dissemble for. What is here present in logical, deductive order, had first been a confused medley of ideas and sensations, thanks to the jolting of the carriage and José Dias' interruptions. Now, however, my head was clear and I could remember correctly. I came to the conclusion that it was my old passion that was blinding me still, and making me lose my head as always.

When I arrived at this final conclusion, I was also getting to the door of my house, but I turned back, and went back up the Rua do Catete. Was it the doubts upsetting me, or the need to upset Capitu with my long delay? Let's say it was both things; I walked for a long while, until I felt myself calm down, and turned howewards. The clock in a bakery was striking eight.

C X X V I I

The Barber

Near home there was a barber, who knew me by sight; he loved the fiddle, and didn't play it altogether badly. At the moment I was passing by, he was playing some piece or other. I stopped in the street to listen to him (anything will do as a pretext for an anguished heart); he saw me, and went on playing. One customer and then another came by, in spite of the time and of it being Sunday, to entrust their faces to his razor; but he didn't attend to them. He missed them without missing a single note; he went on playing for me. This courtesy made me come openly to the shop door, and stand there facing him. At the back, lifting the chintz curtain that hid the back of the house, I saw a dark-haired girl in a light dress, and with a flower in her hair. She was his wife; I think she had seen me from within, and came to thank me with her presence for the favor I was doing her husband. Unless I am mistaken, she even said this with her eyes. As for the husband, he was now playing with more feeling; without noticing his wife, or the customers, with his cheek glued to the instrument, his soul passed into the bow, and he played and played . . .

Divine art! A group of people was beginning to form, and I left the shop door, and went walking home; I came into the lobby and went noiselessly up the stairs. I have never forgotten this episode of the barber, either because it is linked to a grave moment in my life, or because of this maxim, which compilers of such things may lift and insert in school compendiums if they wish. The maxim is that we forget our good actions only slowly, and in fact never truly forget them. Poor barber! He lost two beards that evening, which were tomorrow's daily bread, all to be heard by a passer-by. Suppose now that this latter, instead of going away as I did, had stayed at the door listening to him and making eyes at his wife; then, completely given up to his bow and his fiddle, then he really would have played with a desperate intensity. Divine art!

CXXVIII

A Handful of Events

As I was saying, I went noiselessly up the stairs, pushed open the door, which was ajar, and came on cousin Justina and José Dias playing cards in the sitting room nearby. Capitu got up from the sofa and came over to me. Her face was now serene and pure. The others stopped their game, and we all talked about the tragic event and the widow. Capitu criticized Escobar's imprudence, and didn't disguise the sadness her friend's grief caused her. I asked her why she hadn't stayed with Sancha that night.

"There are a lot of people there; even so, I did offer, but she didn't want me to. I also told her that it would be better for her to come here, and spend some days with us."

"She refused that too?"

"Yes."

"Still, the sight of the sea must be painful to her, every morning," reflected José Dias, "and I don't know how she'll be able ..."

"But it'll pass; what doesn't?" interrupted cousin Justina.

When we started a conversation on this topic, Capitu went out to see if her son was asleep. As she passed by the mirror, she arranged her hair so carefully that one would have thought it affectation, if we didn't already know that she was very fond of herself. When she came back her eyes were red; she told us that, when she looked at her sleeping son, she had thought about Sancha's little daughter, and the widow's suffering. Without taking any notice of our visitors, or looking to see if there were any servants about, she embraced me and said that, if I wanted to think of her, I must take care of my own life first. José Dias thought it a "most beautiful" phrase and asked Capitu why she didn't write poetry. I tried to laugh the episode off, and so we ended the night.

The following day, I was sorry I had torn the speech up, not that I wanted to publish it, but it was a souvenir of the deceased. I thought of putting it together again, but I could only find loose phrases, that made no sense next to one another. I also thought of writing another, but it was difficult now, and I might be caught out by those who had heard me in the cemetery. As for picking up the pieces of paper I had thrown into the street, it was too late; they would already have been swept away.

I made a list of the gifts I had received from Escobar, books, a bronze inkwell, a walking stick with an ivory top, a bird, Capitu's album, two landscapes of Paraná and other things. He had also had some from me. We often exchanged presents and keepsakes in this way, on birthdays or for no particular reason. All this made my eyes mist over ... Then the daily papers came; they gave the news of the accident and Escobar's death, his education and commercial activities, his personal qualities, the condolences of the business community, and spoke, too, of his estate, of his wife and daughter. All this was on the Monday. On Tuesday the will was opened, and it named me second executor; the first was his wife. He left me nothing, but the words he had written to me in a separate letter were a sublime expression of friendship and esteem. This time, Capitu wept a great deal; but she composed herself quickly.

The will, the inventory, everything happened almost as quickly as it's set down here. After a little time, Sancha retired to her relatives' home in Paraná.

C X X I X

To Dona Sancha

Dona Sancha, I ask you not to read this book; or, if you've read it thus far, drop the rest. All you need to do is shut it;

better still, burn it, to avoid the temptation of opening it again. If, in spite of the warning, you go to the end, it's your fault; I can't answer for the harm that may be done. Whatever I have already done by recounting our gestures on that Saturday, is done with, since events, and I myself, have given the lie to my illusion; but anything that might affect you from now on cannot be wiped away. No, my friend, read no more. Go on growing old, without husband or daughter, for I am doing the same thing, and it's the best one can do once youth has passed. One day, we will go from here to heaven's gate, where we will meet again, renewed, like young plants, *come piante novelle,*

> *Rinovellate di novelle fronde.* *
> The rest is in Dante.

C X X X

One Day ...

So then, one day Capitu wanted to know what was making me silent and irritable. And she proposed Europe, Minas, Petrópolis, a series of balls, a thousand of those remedies recommended for the melancholy. I didn't know what to reply; I refused the diversions. As she insisted, I replied that business was bad. Capitu smiled to cheer me up. What did it matter if things were bad? They would get better again, and meanwhile the jewels and objects of any value would be sold, and we would go and live in some back alley. We would live quietly, forgotten by the world;

* The last lines of Dante's *Purgatorio* ("like plants / renewed with fresh leaves").

then we would come back to the surface. The tenderness with which she said this would have moved a stone. But it was no good. I curtly replied that there was no need to sell anything. I went on being silent and irritable. She proposed a game of cards or draughts, a walk, a visit to Matacavalos; and, as I agreed to nothing, she went to the drawing-room, opened the piano, and began to play. I took advantage of her absence, took my hat and went out.

... I beg your pardon, but this chapter should have been preceded by another, recounting an incident that happened a few weeks earlier, two months after Sancha's departure. I'll write it now; I could insert it before this one, before I send the book to the press, but it's a great nuisance to alter the page numbers; I'll leave this as it is, and then the narration will go straight on to the end. Anyway, it's short.

C X X X I

Before the Previous One

So, my life was again sweet and tranquil, my lawyer's practice was doing well, Capitu was lovelier, and Ezequiel was growing. It was the beginning of 1872.

"Have you noticed that Ezequiel has an odd expression in his eyes?" Capitu asked me. "I've only seen two people like that, a friend of Papa's and the late Escobar. Look, Ezequiel; look straight ahead, just so, turn round to Papa, you've no need to roll your eyes, just so ..."

It was after dinner; we were still at table, Capitu was playing with her son, and he with her, or each with the other, for, in truth, they were fond of each other; but it is also true that he was even fonder of me. I looked closely at Ezequiel, and thought that Capitu was right; they were Escobar's eyes, but they didn't seem any the odder for that. After all, there can't be more than half a dozen expressions in the world, and many similarities would come about naturally. Ezequiel didn't understand what was happening, looked startled at her and at me, and finally jumped into my lap:

"Can we go for a walk, Papa?"

"Soon, my son."

Capitu, remote from us both, was now staring at the other side of the table; but when I said to her that, as far as their beauty was concerned, Ezequiel's eyes came from his mother, Capitu smiled, shaking her head with an air that I have never seen in another woman, probably because I loved none as much as her. Each person is worth the value put on them by the affection of others, and that is where popular wisdom has found the proverb that beauty is in the eye of the beholder. Capitu had half a dozen gestures that were unique on earth. That particular one went straight to my heart. That explains why I ran to my wife and companion and covered her face with kisses; but this further incident is not completely necessary to the understanding of the last chapter or of those that follow; let's stick to Ezequiel's eyes.

C X X X I I

The Outline and the Coloring

Not only the eyes, but the other features, the face, the body, the whole person, were gradually rounded out with time. They were like a primitive sketch which the artist fills out and colors in little by little, and the figure starts to look out of the canvas, to smile, pulsate with life, almost to speak, until the family hangs the portrait on the wall, in memory of what once was and can no longer be. Here it could be and was. Habit could still fight against the effect of the change; but the change did take place, and not as happens in the theater; it happened like the day dawning: at first, it's impossible to make out some handwriting: then you can read it in the street, at home, and then in your study, without opening the windows: the light filtering through the blinds is enough to make out the words. I read this letter, at first with difficulty and not entire, then I started to read more easily. True, I fled from it, put it in my pocket, ran home, shut myself in, didn't open the windows: I even shut my eyes. When I opened them and the letter again, the writing was clear, and the message as clear as could be.

So Escobar began to arise from his tomb, from the seminary and from Flamengo to sit beside me at table, greet me on the stairs, kiss me in my study in the morning, or ask for my customary blessing at night. All these actions were repulsive; I put up with them or carried them out, so as not to reveal myself to myself and to the world. But what I could hide from the world, I could not hide from myself, since I lived closer to myself than anyone. When neither mother nor son were with me, my despair grew, and I swore to kill them both, either at a single blow, or slowly, to divide all the moments of my deluded and anguished life by the time it took them to die. When, however, I came back home, and saw at the top of the stairs the little creature who loved me and was waiting for me, I was disarmed, and put the punishment off from one day to another.

What happened between Capitu and me in those dark days will not be put down here, since it was so petty and repetitious, and it is now too late to describe it without falling short of the truth or wearying the reader. But the main thing can be said. And the main thing is that our storms were now continuous and terrible. Before the discovery of that evil land of truth, we had other tempests, of short duration; it was never long before the sky was blue, the sun shining and the sea smooth: we would set our sails to cross it once more, and they would take us to the loveliest isles and coasts in the universe, until another squall would upset everything, and we would lower our sails, waiting for a further spell of fine weather, and when it came, it was neither slow nor uncertain, but complete, trustworthy, and sure.

Excuse these metaphors; they smell of the sea and the tide which brought death to my friend, my wife's lover, Escobar. They smell, too, of Capitu's undertow eyes. So, though I have always been a landsman, I recount that part of my life, as a sailor would recount his shipwreck.

Now all that remained for us to do was to say was the final word; we read it, however, clear and unavoidable, in each other's eyes, and every time that Ezequiel was with us, he only drove us further apart. Capitu proposed that we should put him in a school, and that he should only come home on Saturdays; the boy was not at all willing to accept this situation.

"I want to go with Papa! Papa must go with me!" he shouted.

It was I who took him one morning, a Monday. It was in the old Largo da Lapa, near our house. I look him on foot, holding his hand, as I had carried the other one's coffin. The lad was crying and asking questions at every step, if he would come back home, and when, and if I would go and see him. . .

"I'll come."

"You won't!"

"I will."

"Swear it, Papa!"

"All right."

"You haven't sworn!"

"I swear it, then."

And there I took him and left him. The temporary absence did not diminish the evil, and all Capitu's subtle arts to at least lessen it might as well not have existed; I felt worse and worse. The new situation even aggravated my suffering. Ezequiel was now out of my sight more; but his return at weekends, whether it was because I got out of the habit of seeing him, or because time went on and completed the resemblance, was the return of a livelier, noisier Escobar. Even his voice: in a short time, it seemed to be the same, too. On Saturdays, I tried not to dine at home, and only to come in when he was asleep; but I couldn't escape on Sundays, in my study, surrounded by newspapers and legal papers. Ezequiel would come in boisterous and cheerful, full of laughter and of love, for the little devil grew more and more fond of me. I, to tell the truth, now felt an aversion that I could hardly disguise, either to her or to others. Not being able to cover up this moral disposition entirely, I tried to keep out of his way, to see him as little as I could; I would have work which would make me lock myself in my study, or I would go out on Sundays to take my secret wound for a walk round the city and its outskirts.

CXXXIII

An Idea

One day—it was a Friday—I could stand it no longer. A certain idea spread its black wings inside me, beating them from one side to another, as ideas do when they are trying to get out. I think it was an accident that it was Friday, but it might have been intentional; I was brought up in terror of that day; I heard songs sung at home, either from the countryside or from old Rio, in which Friday was an unlucky day. However, since there are no almanacs in the brain, it is probable that the idea was only beating its wings out of the need it felt to emerge into the fresh air and into life. Life is so beautiful that even the idea of death needs to come to life, before it can be realized. You are beginning to catch my drift; now read another chapter.

C X X X I V

Saturday

Finally, the idea emerged from my brain. It was night, and however much I tried to shake it away from me, I could not sleep. But no night ever passed so quickly. Day dawned, when I thought it was only one or two o'clock. I went out, thinking I would leave the idea behind; it came with me. Outdoors, it had the same black color, the same tremulous wings, and though it flew around with them, it was as though it was fixed; I carried it in my retina, not that it covered up external objects, but I saw them through it; they had a paler color than usual, and my eyes would not rest on them for long.

I can't remember the rest of the day very well. I know I wrote some letters, and bought a substance, I'll not say what, so as not to awaken the urge to try it out. The pharmacy has failed, it's true: the owner became a banker, and the bank is doing well. When I felt death in my pocket I felt as happy as if I had won the grand prize in the lottery, or even more than that, for lottery prizes can be frittered away, which is not true of death. I went to my mother's house, to say goodbye, on pretence of paying her a visit. Whether it was true or an illusion, everything there seemed better that day; my mother was less sad, Uncle Cosme had forgotten his heart, and cousin Justina her tongue. I spent an hour in peace. I even thought of giving up the project. What did I need to do to live? Never to leave that house again, or clasp that moment to my bosom . . .

C X X X V

Othello

I dined out. In the evening I went to the theater. The play was none other than *Othello*, which I had never seen or read; I only knew the subject, and was pleased at the coincidence. I saw the moor's rage, because of a handkerchief—a mere handkerchief!—and here I provide material for the consideration of the psychologists of this and other continents, for I could not help observing that a handkerchief was enough to kindle Othello's jealousy and so bring forth the most sublime tragedy ever written. The handkerchiefs have gone, now we need the sheets themselves; sometimes not even the sheets are there, and nightshirts will do. These were the ideas that were passing through my head, vague and confused, as the moor rolled convulsively around, and Iago distilled his calumny. In the intervals I did not leave my seat; I didn't want to risk encountering anyone I knew. Nearly all the ladies stayed in their boxes, while the men went out to smoke. Then I asked myself if one of these women might not have loved someone now lying in a cemetery, and other incoherent thoughts came into my head, until the curtain rose and the play went on. The last act showed me that it was not I but Capitu that ought to die. I heard Desdemona's pleas, her pure, loving words; then came the moor's fury, and the death he meted out to her amidst the audience's frenetic applause.

"And she was innocent," I said over and over as I walked down the street, "what would the public do if she were really guilty, as guilty as Capitu? And what death would the moor give her then? A pillow would not be enough; he would need blood and fire, a vast, intense fire, which would consume her completely, reduce her to dust, and the dust would be thrown to the winds, extinguished for ever ..."

I wandered around the streets for the rest of the night. I dined, it's true, eating almost nothing, just enough to go on till morning. I saw the last hours of the night and the first of the day, I saw the last strollers of the night, and the first streetsweepers, the first carts, the first noises, the first light of dawn, one day coming after another, but one that would see me go, never to return. The streets I wandered around seemed to slip away from me of their own accord. I would never again see the sea from the Glória, nor the Serra dos Órgãos, the Fortress of Santa Cruz and the others. There were not so many people passing by as on normal weekdays, but they were already numerous and going to some kind of job, which they would do again another day; I would never return to mine.

I got home, opened the door slowly, went in on tiptoe, and shut myself in my study; it was nearly six. I took the poison from my pocket, sat there in my shirt sleeves and wrote yet another letter, the last, addressed to Capitu. None of the others was to her; I felt the need to write her a word which would make her suffer remorse for my death. I wrote two versions. The first I burned, as being long and diffuse. The second contained only what was needful, and was clear and short. I did not recall our past, nor our quarrels, nor any happiness; I spoke to her only of Escobar and the need to die.

C X X X V I

The Cup of Coffee

My plan was to wait for my coffee, dissolve the drug in it and swallow it. Until then, since I had not completely forgotten my Roman history, I remembered that Cato, before he killed himself, read and reread a book by Plato.* I didn't have Plato by me; but an abridged volume of Plutarch in which the life of the famous Roman was told was enough to occupy that short space of time, and, so as to imitate him completely, I stretched out on the sofa. Nor was it merely to imitate him to this extent; I needed to instill some of his courage in myself, just as he had needed some of the philosopher's thoughts, to die so fearlessly. One of the disadvantages of being ignorant is that one does not have such remedies to hand at the final hour. There are many people who kill themselves without it, and expire with dignity; but I think that many more people would put an end to their days, if they could find this kind of moral cocaine in good books. Nonetheless, wishing to avoid any suspicion of imitation, I remember well that, so that Plutarch's book should not be found next to me, and news of it should not be given out in the papers along with the color of the trousers I was wearing at the time, I decided to put it back in its place before I drank the poison.

The servant brought the coffee. I got up, put the book away, and went to the table where the cup had been placed. There were already noises from the house; it was time to do away with myself. My hand shook as I opened the paper containing the drug. Even so I had the strength to pour the substance into the cup, and began to stir the coffee, with my eyes dim, thinking back to the innocent Desdemona; the spectacle of the previous evening intruded into the morning's reality. But Escobar's photograph gave me the courage that was beginning to falter; there he was with his hand on the back of the chair, looking into the distance . . .

"Let's be done with this," I thought.

When I was about to drink, I wondered if it would not be better to wait for Capitu and her son to go out to mass; I would drink it afterwards; that would be better. When I had decided this, I began to pace up and down my study. I heard Ezequiel's voice in the hall, and saw him come in and run to me shouting:

"Papa! Papa!"

---

* Cato the Elder reread Plato's *Phaedo*, which recounts Socrates' suicide, before he killed himself, according to Plutarch in his life of Cato.

Reader, at this point there was a gesture that I won't describe because I've completely forgotten it, but believe me that it was beautiful and tragic. For the figure of the boy made me retreat until I backed into the bookcase. Ezequiel hugged my knees, stood up on the tips of his toes, as if to climb up and give me his usual kiss; and he repeated, tugging at me:

"Papa! Papa!"

C X X X V I I

A Second Impulse

If I hadn't looked at Ezequiel, it's probable I wouldn't be here writing this book, because my first impulse was to run to the coffee and drink it. I went so far as to pick up the cup, but the lad was kissing my hand, as usual, and the sight of him, like his gesture, gave me an impulse, which I am reluctant to put down here; but what does it matter, let all be said. Let me be called a murderer; I won't deny it or contradict it; my second impulse was criminal. I bent down and asked Ezequiel if he had already had coffee.

"Yes, Papa; I'm going to mass with Mamma."

"Have another cup, just a half."

"Are you having some, Papa?"

"I'll send for more; come on, drink it!"

Ezequiel opened his mouth. I put the cup to his lips, shaking so much that I almost spilled it, but prepared to make it go down his throat, if he disliked the taste or the temperature, for the coffee was cold . . . But I don't know what I felt that made me recoil. I put the cup on the table, and realized I was madly kissing the lad's head.

"Papa Papa!" Ezequiel exclaimed.

"No, no, I'm not your father!"

CXXXVIII

Enter Capitu

When I lifted my head, I saw the figure of Capitu before me. Here is another scene that will seem staged, and yet it's as natural as the first, since mother and son were going to mass, and Capitu never went out without speaking to me. Nowadays it was a dry, brief word; most times, I didn't even look at her. She always looked at me, waiting.

This time, when I saw her, I don't know if it was in my eyes, but Capitu seemed pale to me. There followed one of those silences which can, without exaggeration, be described as lasting a century, time seems to stretch out so in moments of great crisis. Capitu regained her composure; she told her son to go out, and asked me to explain . . .

"There's nothing to explain," I said.

"There's everything to explain; I don't understand your tears or Ezequiel's. What's happened between you?"

"Didn't you hear what I said to him?"

Capitu replied that she had heard crying and the sound of words. I think she had heard everything clearly, but to confess it would have meant losing the hope of silence and of reconciliation; for this reason she denied hearing anything and only confirmed what she had seen. Without telling her of the coffee episode, I repeated the words at the end of the chapter.

"What?" she said as if she had heard wrong.

"That he is not my son."

Great was Capitu's stupefaction, and the indignation that followed was no less, and both of them so natural that they would have made the first eyewitnesses in our law courts doubt what they had seen. I've heard that they exist for all kinds of cases: it's just a question of paying the right price. I don't think it's true, the more so as the person who told me had just lost an action. But, whether or not there are witnesses for hire, mine was reliable; nature itself swore on her own behalf, and I had no wish to doubt her. So, paying no attention to Capitu's words, to her gestures, to the pain that twisted her features, to anything at all, I repeated the words I had said twice with such resolution that she began to give way. After some moments, she said to me:

"Such an insult can only be explained by sincere conviction; however, you, who were so jealous of my least gesture, never showed the least shadow of suspicion. Where did you get such a notion? Tell me," she went on, seeing I said nothing in reply, "tell me everything; after what I've heard, I can hear the rest, it can't be much. What has given you such a conviction now? Come on, Bentinho, tell me, tell me! Send me away now, but tell me everything first."

"There are things that can't be said."

"That can't be said by halves; but now you've said the half, tell me everything."

She had sat down on a chair by the table. She might have been a little confused: her bearing was not that of an accused woman. I asked her once again not to insist.

"No, Bentinho, either tell me the rest, so that I can defend myself, if you think I have a defense, or I'll ask for an immediate separation: I can't take any more!"

"The separation is already decided on," I replied taking up her suggestion. "It would have been better to have done it by means of hints, or in complete silence; each of us would have gone his way, with his own wound. Since you insist, however, here is what I can say, and it's all."

I didn't say everything; I could hardly refer to the affair with Escobar without uttering his name. Capitu could not prevent herself laughing, with a laugh that I am sorry not to be able to transcribe here; then in a tone both ironic and melancholy:

"Even the deceased! Not even the dead escape your jealousy!"

She adjusted her short cape and stood up. She sighed, I think she sighed, while I, who wanted nothing more than her complete vindication, said some words I can't remember to this effect. Capitu looked at me disdainfully, and murmured:

"I know the reason for this; it's the accident of the resemblance ... The will of God must explain it all ... You're laughing? It's natural; in spite of the seminary, you don't believe in God; I do ... But don't let's talk of it any more; it's not right for us to say any more."

C X X X I X

The Photograph

I give my word that I was on the verge of thinking that I was the victim of a great illusion, the phantasmagoria of a hallucinated man, but the sudden entrance of Ezequiel, shouting: "Mamma! Mamma! It's time for mass!" brought me back to an awareness of reality. Capitu and I, involuntarily, looked at Escobar's photograph, and then at each other. This time her confusion became a pure confession. The one was the other; there must certainly be a photograph of Escobar as a child somewhere that would be our little Ezequiel. She confessed nothing, however, overtly; she repeated her last words, took her son by the hand and they went out to mass.

C X L

Return from Church

Once alone, it would have been natural to take the coffee and drink it. Well no, sir, I didn't; I had lost the taste for death. Death was one solution; I had just found another, all the better for not being definitive, and it left the door open for redress, if such a thing were possible. I did not say *pardon*, I said *redress*, that is, justice. Whatever the reason for doing so, I rejected death, and awaited Capitu's return. This took longer than usual; I even feared that she might have gone to my mother's house, but she hadn't.

"I confided all my bitterness to God," said Capitu when she came back from church; "I heard a voice inside me saying that our separation is unavoidable, and I am at your disposal."

The eyes with which she said this were veiled, as if looking out for a gesture of refusal or postponement. She was counting on my weakness or even on any uncertainty I might have as to the paternity of the boy, but everything failed. Perhaps there was a new man inside me, who came to the surface now, now that new and strong feelings had flushed him out? In that case the new man had merely been hidden. I replied that I was going to think, and we would do whatever I decided. In truth, I can tell you that everything had been thought out and concluded on.

While I was waiting, I had recalled the words of the late Gurgel, when at his house he showed me his wife's portrait, similar to Capitu's. You must remember them; if not, reread the chapter, whose number I'll not give you here, since I can't remember it, but it's not far back. They come down to saying that there are these inexplicable resemblances ... Later on in the day, and on other days, Ezequiel came with me to my study, and the lad's features gave a clear idea of those of the other; either that or I paid more attention to them. At the same time, I remembered vague, remote episodes, words, encounters, and incidents, things in which my blindness saw no cunning, and when my old jealousy was not operative. One time when I came across them alone and silent, a secret that made me laugh, a word she spoke when dreaming, all these reminiscences came back now, in such a tumult that they made me dizzy . . . And why didn't I strangle them one day, when I turned my eyes away from the street where two swallows were sitting on a telegraph wire? Inside the house, my two other swallows were floating on air, their eyes deep in each other's eyes, but so cautious that they broke off straight away, saying something cheerful and friendly to me. I recounted the loves of the swallows outside, and they thought it amusing; Escobar said that, for him, it would be better if the swallows, instead of sitting on the wires, were on the dinner table, stewed. "I've never eaten their nests," he went on, "but they must be good, if the Chinese have discovered them." And we started talking about the Chinese and the classic works that speak of them, while Capitu, confessing that we bored her, went to do other things. Now I remembered everything that at the time had seemed to be nothing.

C X L I

The Solution

Here is what we did. We picked ourselves up and went to Europe, not for a pleasure trip, nor to see anything, new or old; we stopped in Switzerland. A governess from Rio Grande, who went with us, stayed as company for Capitu, teaching Ezequiel his mother tongue, while he learnt everything else in the local schools.* With life thus organized, I went back to Brazil.

---

* Rio Grande do Sul, the southernmost province of the Empire, bordering on Uruguay.

After some months, Capitu had begun to write me letters, which I replied to curtly and drily. Hers were submissive, without hatred, affectionate maybe, and towards the end full of longing; she begged me to go and see her. I made the journey a year later, but I did not go to see her, and later made the same voyage again, with the same result. On my return, those who remembered her asked for news of her, which I provided, as if I had just been living with her; naturally the journeys were made to pretend just that, and delude public opinion. One day, finally. . .

C X L I I

A Saint

It will be understood that if, when I went on journeys to Europe, José Dias didn't come with me, it was not from any lack of desire to go; he stayed as company for Uncle Cosme, who was almost an invalid, and for my mother, who had aged suddenly. He was old, too, though sturdy. He would come on board to say goodbye to me, and the words he said to me, his gestures with his handkerchief, even the way he wiped his eyes were such that they moved me too. The last time he didn't come on board.

"Come on . . ."

"I can't."

"Are you afraid?"

"No, I can't. Now, goodbye, Bentinho, I don't know if you'll see me ever again; I think I'm going to the other Europe, the eternal one . . ."

He didn't go immediately: my mother made the journey first. Look for a tomb in the cemetery of São João Batista, a tomb without a name, and with only these words: *A Saint*. It's there. I had some difficulty with this inscription. The sculptor thought it strange; the cemetery superintendent consulted the parish priest: he made the point to me that the place for saints is on the altar and in Heaven.

"But, pardon me," I cut in, "I'm not saying that the person in the tomb has been canonized. My idea is to give with this word an earthly definition of all the virtues that the deceased possessed in life. What's more, since modesty was one of them, I want to prolong that into death also, by not inscribing her name."

"Not even her name, her parentage, the dates . . ."

"Who'll care about dates, parentage, and names, when I go?"

"You want to say that she was a saintly woman, is that right?"

"Exactly. If he were alive, Protonotary Cabral would confirm what I've told you."

"I wouldn't doubt of the truth of what you say, I only hesitate as to the formula. You knew the protonotary, then?"

"I did. He was a model priest."

"A real expert on canon law, a good Latinist, pious and charitable," the priest went on.

"And he had some social graces," I said; "at home I always heard that he was a wonderful partner for backgammon . . ."

"He was good with the dice!" sighed the priest slowly. "A real master!"

"So, do you think . . ."

"So long as there's no other meaning intended, nor could there be thought to be, yes, sir, it can be allowed."

José Dias was present at these proceedings, very melancholy. At the end, when we came out, he spoke ill of the priest, and called him fussy. He could only forgive him because he, along with the other men in the cemetery, had not known my mother.

"They didn't know her; if they had, they would have inscribed 'most saintly.'"

C X L I I I

The Last Superlative

It was not José Dias' last superlative. There were others which it is not worth transcribing here, until the last, the best of them, the gentlest, which made his death a part of his life. Now he was living with me; although my mother had left him a small legacy, he came to tell me that now, with the legacy or without it, he would not be separated from me. Perhaps he hoped to bury me. He corresponded with Capitu, asking her to send him a portrait of Ezequiel; but Capitu kept putting it off from one mail to the next, until he asked for nothing more than the young student's affection; he also asked her that she should not fail to speak to Ezequiel of his father's and grandfather's old friend, "destined by heaven to love those of the same blood." That was his way of preparing himself to be looked after by the third generation; but death came before Ezequiel. It was a brief illness. I asked for a homeopathic doctor to be sent for.

"No, Bentinho," he said, "an allopath will do; death comes in every school. Anyway, those were the ideas of my youth, and time has taken them away; I am converted to the faith of my fathers. Allopathy is the Catholicism of medicine . . ."

He died serenely, after a short agony. A little before, he heard that the sky was beautiful, and asked us to open the window.

"No, the air could do you harm."

"What harm? Air is life."

We opened the window. Truly, the sky was clear and blue. José Dias raised himself up and looked out; after some moments, he let his head fall back, murmuring "Most beautiful!" They were the last words he uttered in this world. Poor José Dias! Why should I deny that I wept for him?

C X L I V

A Belated Question

So may the eyes of all the friends that I leave behind in this world, men and women, weep for me, but I doubt they will. I have tried to make people forget me. I live at a distance, and hardly go out. It's not that I have really tied the two ends of life together. This house in Engenho Novo, even though it does reproduce the Matacavalos one, merely reminds me of it, and then more by comparison and reflection than by feeling. I've already said just that.

You will ask me why, since I owned the old house itself, in the same old street, I did not stop it being demolished and instead had this one reproduce it. The question should have been asked at the beginning, but here is the reply. The reason is that, shortly after my mother died, I wanted to move there, and first made a long visit of inspection for some days, and the whole house refused to recognize me. In the garden, the aroeira and the pitanga tree, the well with its old bucket and the washing stones knew nothing of me.* The casuarina tree was the same one I had left at the bottom of the garden, but the trunk, instead of being straight as in earlier days, now had the look of a question mark; probably it was surprised by the intruder. I ran my eyes over the scene, looking for some thought I might have left there, and could find none. On the contrary, the branches began to whisper something that I didn't at first understand, and which it seems was the song of a new morning. Beneath that clear and cheerful music, I also heard the grunting of the pigs, a kind of concentrated, philosophical mockery.

---

* Both trees are native to Brazil: the first is an ornamental tree with rose-colored fruit; the second is known as the Brazilian cherry, and has small orange-red edible fruit.

Everything was strange and hostile. I let the house be demolished, and later, when I came to Engenho Novo, I had the idea of making this reproduction according to instructions I gave the architect, as I have recounted at the opportune moment.

C X L V

The Return

Well, I was already in this house when one day, as I was dressing for lunch, I received a visiting card with this name:

EZEQUIEL A. DE SANTIAGO

"Is the person there?" I asked the servant.

"Yes, sir; he's waiting."

I didn't go straight away; I made him wait for ten or fifteen minutes in the living room. Only afterwards did it occur to me that I should be somewhat excited, and should run in, embrace him and speak to him of his mother. His mother—I don't think I've said that she was dead and buried. She was; there she rests in the earth of old Switzerland. I hurriedly finished dressing. When I came out of my room, I took on a father's air, somewhere between gentle and brusque, half Dom Casmurro. When I came into the room, I saw a young man, with his back to me, looking at the bust of Massinissa painted on the wall. I trod carefully, making no sound. Nevertheless, he heard my steps, and quickly turned round. He knew me by my photographs and ran towards me. I didn't move; it was no more, no less than my former young companion at the seminary of São José, a little shorter, less full in the body, and apart from the high coloring of his complexion, the same face as my friend. He was dressed in the modern fashion, of course, and his manners were different, but his general demeanor reproduced the dead man. It was the same, the exact, the true Escobar. It was my wife's lover; he was his father's son. He was in mourning for his mother; I too was in black. We sat down.

"You look the same as in your latest photographs, Papa," he said to me.

His voice was the same as Escobar's, with a French accent. I explained to him that in fact I had changed very little, and began asking him questions, so as to have to speak less, and keep control of my emotions. But even this brought animation to his face, and my seminary friend began to arise even more from the cemetery. Here he was before me, with the same laughter and a greater respect; all in all, the same politeness and the same charm. He was eager to see me. His mother had spoken of me often, with the greatest praise, as the purest man in the world, the most worthy of love.

"She was beautiful at her death," he ended.

"Let's go in to lunch."

If you think the lunch was unpleasant, you are mistaken. It had its moments of irritation, it's true; at first it hurt me that Ezequiel was not really my son, that he didn't complete me and continue me. If the lad had taken after his mother, I would have ended up believing everything, the more easily so because he seemed to have left only yesterday. He conjured up memories of his childhood, of episodes and words spoken, the time when he went to school.

"Do you still remember when you took me to school, Papa?" he asked, laughing.

"Am I likely to have forgotten?"

"It was in the Lapa; I was desperate, and you wouldn't stop, pulling me like I don't know what, and me with my little legs . . . Yes, I will, thank you."

He held out his glass for the wine I was offering him, took a sip, and went on eating. Escobar used to eat that way too, with his face in his plate. He told me of his life in Europe, his studies, and particularly of archaeology, which was his passion. He spoke with real enthusiasm of antiquity, told me about Egypt and its thousands of centuries, without mixing up his figures: he had his father's head for arithmetic. Even though the idea of the other's paternity was quite familiar to me, I took no pleasure in the ressurrection. At times, I shut my eyes so as not to see gestures or anything, but the young devil talked and laughed, and the dead man laughed and talked through him.

Since there was nothing for it but for him to stay with me, I made myself into a real father. The idea that he might have seen some photograph of Escobar that Capitu might have incautiously carried round with her, did not occur to me, nor, if it had, would the thought have lasted. Ezequiel believed in me, as he believed in his mother. If José Dias had been alive, he would have thought him the image of me. Cousin Justina wanted to see him, but since she was ill, she asked me to take him there. But I knew my relative. I think that the desire to see Ezequiel was so that she could see rounded out the sketch that in all likelihood she had seen in the boy. It would be a final treat; I prevented it in time.

"She's very ill," I said to Ezequiel, who wanted to go and see her, "any emotion might bring on her death. We'll go and see her when she's better."

We didn't go; death took her a few days later. There she sleeps with the Lord, or whatever the phrase is. Ezequiel saw her face in the coffin and didn't recognize her, nor would he be able to, after what the years and death had done to her. On the way to the cemetery, he remembered a few things, a street, a tower, a stretch of beach, and he was all happiness. That was what happened every time he came back home, at the end of the day; he recounted the memories brought back to him by the streets and the houses. He was astonished that many were the same as when he had left them behind, as if houses died young.

After six months, Ezequiel spoke to me of a journey to Greece, to Egypt and Palestine, a scientific journey, a promise made to some friends.

"Of which sex?" I asked laughing.

He smiled embarrassed, and answered that women were such creatures of fashion and of the present moment, that they would never understand a ruin thirty centuries old. They were two fellow students from the university. I promised him resources, and immediately gave him an advance on the money he needed. To myself I said that one of the consequences of the secret loves of the father was that I was paying for the son's archaeology; I'd rather have paid for a dose of leprosy ... When this idea passed through my brain, I felt so cruel and perverse that I took hold of the lad, and went to embrace him to my heart, but I retreated; then I looked at him, as one does a real son; the look he gave me was tender and grateful.

C X L V I

There Was No Leprosy

There was no leprosy, but there are fevers in all lands where human beings have lived, ancient or modern. Eleven months later, Ezequiel died of a typhoid fever, and was buried in the vicinity of Jerusalem, where his two university friends raised a tomb to him, with this inscription, taken from the Prophet Ezekiel, in Greek: "Thou wast perfect in thy ways."* They sent me both texts, in Latin and Greek, a sketch of the gravestone, the bill for the expenses, and the remains of the money he was carrying; I would have paid three times as much never to see him again.

As I wanted to check the text, I consulted my Vulgate, and found that it was correct, but that it also had a continuation:

* Ezekiel, ch. 28, v. 15.

"Thou wast perfect in thy ways, *from the day that thou wast created*." I stopped and silently asked: "When would the day of Ezequiel's creation have been?" Nobody replied. Here is a mystery to add to the many others in this world. In spite of everything, I dined well and went to the theater.

C X L V I I

The Retrospective Exhibition

You already know that my soul, however lacerated it may have been, didn't stay in a corner like a pale, solitary flower. I did not give it that color, or lack of it. I lived as best I could, with no shortage of female friends to console me for the first. They were passing caprices, to be sure. It was they who left me, like people who come to a retrospective exhibition, and either tire of seeing it, or the light in the room fades. Only one of these visits had a carriage at the door and a liveried coachman. The others came modestly, *calcante pede*,* and if it was raining, it was I who went to get a cab, and help them in, with profuse farewells, and even more profuse recommendations:

"Have you got the catalogue?"

"Yes; till tomorrow."

"Till tomorrow."

They didn't come back. I would stand at the door, waiting, go to the corner, look, consult my watch, and not see anybody or anything. Then, if another visitor came, I would give her my arm, we would go in, I would show her the landscapes, the historical or genre paintings, a watercolor, a pastel, a *gouache*, and she too would grow weary, and go away with the catalogue in her hand . . .

---

* On foot.

C X L V I I I

Well, and the Rest?

Now, why is it that none of these capricious creatures made
me forget the first love of my heart? Perhaps because none
had her undertow eyes, nor her sly, oblique, gypsy look. But this is
not really what remains of this book. What remains is to know if
the Capitu of Glória beach was already in the girl of Matacavalos,
or if the latter had been changed into the former because of some
intervening incident. Jesus, son of Sirach, had he known of my
first fits of jealousy, would have said to me, as in his Chapter IX,
verse 1: "Be not jealous of thy wife, lest she deceive thee with arts
she learned of thee."* But I think not, and that you will agree with
me; if you remember Capitu as a girl, you will recognize that the
one was in the other, like the fruit inside its rind.

And anyway, whatever the solution, one thing is left, and is the
sum total, or the total residue, to wit, that my first love and my
best friend, both so affectionate and so beloved—destiny willed it
that they ended up joining together and deceiving me ... May
the earth rest lightly on them! On to the *History of the Suburbs*!

---

* The quotation is from Ecclesiasticus, one of the books of the Apocrypha, which
in Greek was entitled *The Wisdom of Jesus, Son of Sirac.*

Dom Casmurro,
the Fruit and the Rind:
An Afterword

D om Casmurro (1899) completes the trilogy formed by *Quincas Borba* (1891) and *Memórias póstumas de Brás Cubas* (1881). The three books can be classified as "allegorico-satirical novels." Their style is characterized by a mixture of high and low registers, in which differing perspectives are taken on themes of his own time by Machado de Assis, who grew up in the reign of the Emperor Pedro II (1840–1889) and died in 1908, under the first Brazilian Republic. In the words of *Memórias póstumas de Brás Cubas*, it is a style in which the "pen of merriment" is dipped in the "ink of melancholy." In fact, the "merriment" and the "melancholy" are inseparable, and neither is independent of, or dominates the other.

In its time, the modernity and originality of *Memórias póstumas de Brás Cubas* stemmed from Machado's invention of a narrator who is a "dead author." Placed "on the other side of the mystery," he is beyond the judgement of the living, and recounts, in an arbitrary, cynical fashion, the commonplace adventures of his life as a member of the ruling class. Obviously, the dead are not in the habit of speaking, and the invention of a dead man, who makes half-serious, half-comic digressions with the "disdain of the dead" for the living (Ch. XXV), may well appear to the reader to be a way of criticizing traditional means of representation.

In the other books, the perspective of death, or at least that of loss and absence, again dominates the story: madness in *Quincas Borba* and loss of memory in *Dom Casmurro* define the characters and the actions. Assuming that his readers will be respectable citizens who wish to be entertained and rewarded with a reassuring impression of tenderness and love, Machado disappoints them. In all three novels, a negative irony corrodes the ideologies of his time, criticizing the realistic pretensions both of Romantic sentimentality and Naturalist determinism.

Machado invents narrators who discuss the narration itself, and so bring the reader closer to a productive, active way of reading. They are very complex types. Their way of narrating parallels the very structure of what we could call a conservative modernization, characterized by the integration of a "backward" agrarian, slave-owning country into the modern world capitalist system: in the nineteenth century, modernity came to Brazil, but colonial values remained. Since the narrators themselves have a foot in both camps, and so represent this doubleness, they do not take the side of either ideology. It is for this reason that the meaning of their ironies never ceases to surprise the reader: this, in spite of the fact that one can see them coming, because the rhetorical procedures used to generate them are often repeated.

Machado de Assis's writing takes his readers' own stereotypes into account. They never know what the next line brings, but from the very beginning they do know that their expectations will be disappointed. The narrator only needs to tell a love story, and the reader learns to expect its reverse, the sordid, trivial motivation that cheapens it; he only needs to tell us of a disreputable action, and we foresee the tragic meaning that will dignify it. The effect of this relativization of values—of making the "material" and the "ideal" equivalents—is humor, and nearly always black humor, an indirect way of amusing us with what is serious and dismaying us with comedy.

Like the narrator of *Memórias póstumas de Brás Cubas*, the narrator of *Dom Casmurro* is a self-obsessed melancholic. The type also appears in the pseudo-autobiographical monologues of English and French novels of the eighteenth century, such as Sterne's *The Life and Opinions of Tristram Shandy* (1759, 1767) or Xavier de Maistre's *Voyage autour de ma chambre* (1794), which Machado had read. According to the medical theory of the humors, such people remove themselves from society because their livers are ruined by "black bile," which makes them "bilious" or melancholy. Melancholy is the cause of their arbitrary, depressive, nihilistic statements. The genre's conventions demand that their melancholy should not be total, since the narrator also has to be able to show a certain amount of the trickster's duplicity. In *Dom Casmurro*, the narrator, Bento Santiago, also known by his nickname Dom Casmurro, has one side to him that is gloomy and subject to sudden outbursts, and that governs all the emotional and intellectual manifestations that go to make up his obsessive passion: jealousy. His other side is firm and constant, ensuring the rationality and reliability of his judgement in matters in which the "black bile" does not excite his imagination. So, he shows signs of great discernment in matters which have nothing to do with his principal passion, and at the same time a great blindness as concerns his ability to question his own judgement. For this reason, the narrator's irony is in effect turned on himself: Machado generates it through the contrast between a life which in itself is mediocre, and the refined theoretical speculations the narrator indulges in as he recounts it.

The psychological doubleness of the narrator finds its parallel in the two styles that are counterposed in his discourse. One of them is serious or elevated, with a tendency to the sublime, and containing lyric, epic and tragic elements; the other is comic or low, ironic and ingratiating in ridiculous situations, gossipy and sarcastic in shocking ones. It is by making them coexist that the narrator relativizes the meaning that each one individually represents. He makes the genre of comedy represent tragic material, and interprets what is ridiculous as serious. The reader, in general, interprets this suspension of plain meaning, this ironic dissonance, as skepticism.

The narrator is interested in and even sympathizes with his readers, and pretends to concur with their opinions, based as they are on common sense. His image is produced by his readers' interpretation, and it is not one with which he is necessarily in agreement. In a sense, he abdicates responsibility for what he says, appearing to be cynical when all he is really doing is reflecting the cynical ideas of his readers—at least his readers at that time. As he does this, he dissolves any pretensions to universality that such ideas might have, and exposes the structure of conservative modernization which determines them. Ideas are like nuts, and he breaks them open to see what they contain. In both *Memórias póstumas de Brás Cubas* and *Dom Casmurro*, literature exists in the mind, for everything happens in their narrators' heads. In both novels, the narrator is the whole book.

In the opening chapters of *Dom Casmurro*, the narrator says that his aim was to "bring back youth in old age." But, he says: "I managed neither to reconstruct what was there, nor what I had been . . . I myself am missing, and that lacuna is all-important." When he defines his self as a "lacuna," the narrator suggests that the very substance of what he writes is the time which has disappeared from his memory. He narrates, but does not remember. Like an author in search of a character, the narrator recounts a story which does not yet exist. And so, the *author* suggests to his readers that they cannot trust in the truth of what the *narrator* is saying.

A versatile and well-read man in the nineteenth-century mode, a lawyer and an ex-seminarist, Dom Casmurro is well versed in the rhetoric used in the law courts of his time. It is he who provides the arguments in the case he moves against the wife from whom he is now separated. His decision to tell the story of his life was motivated by the neoclassical medallions of Caesar, Augustus, Nero, and Massinissa, painted on the walls of his living room. The figures are copies of others which once adorned his house on the Rua de Matacavalos, now reproduced in his present residence in Engenho Novo. These images—copied from copies—represent several kinds of ambiguities, and it is they who prompt him to write about "past times," so that the narration might perhaps give "the illusion" of bringing them back.

As a fiction commenting on fiction, *Dom Casmurro* is a critique of the unity of the individual that was taken for granted in most nineteenth-century literature. The emptying out or deidentification of the narrator makes every criterion that might allow the reader to recognize him as an organic whole ambiguous and treacherous. The narrator wants to persuade the reader that he is telling the truth, but the fact that his memory is bad places limits on the way he represents himself: the process of remembering, the admirable, tender emotions felt in the past, and all the other things, strange and familiar, which enter into stories, such as the letters, dialogues, thunder, carts, shots, and the Last Judgement cited in Chapter LXXIII, are no longer determined by their context. The past no longer provides any true frame of reference. Without any real and preestablished unity, imaginary likenesses hang over Dom Casmurro's narration like the empty rind of a nonexistent fruit.

To put it another way, in *Dom Casmurro* the decisions about the narration are more fundamental than the events of the story itself, because they call readers' attention to the act of the invention of the text itself. The solitude and unhappiness of Dom Casmurro may make readers feel sorry for him as they accompany him on his visit to the bygone landscape of his past. However, when one adopts a less sympathetic perspective, one more concerned with what prevents his memory from operating in a reliable fashion, the book changes meaning and the case he moves against Capitu itself becomes suspect. The reader begins to

suspect that his solitude is perhaps the result of an overpowerful unconscious, itself dominated by the conventions of his class: the arguments
provided by this unconscious often take the form of digressions.

In *Dom Casmurro*, as in *Memórias póstumas de Brás Cubas*, the digressions are of varying length and type, somewhat mannered, pedantic, and
bookish in tone. Generally, they are parodies of or quotations from philosophy, classical mythology, the Bible, and literature in general, in the
form of sayings, parables, allegories, verses, fables, or maxims. These
digressions can embrace anything they want. An unrepentant chatterer,
Machado's narrator can talk about anything that comes into his head.

The digressive technique is principally used as a means of criticizing a
point of view by giving us alternative possibilities. For this reason, the
statements made in *Dom Casmurro* have a "realist" clarity of meaning
when they are taken in isolation, for they are the stylized product of the
discourses and incidents of a particular historical time and place, those
of Brazilian society in the second half of the nineteenth century. They
mention historical events, allude to real people of the time, talk about
ministerial comings and goings, about modern literature and modern
inventions, fashion, slavery, gas lighting, the press, the lady reader who is
getting ready to go to the opera, the Central line train . . . But the way in
which the novel arranges them and comments on them is always
ambivalent. Statements which have a clear sense when read on their
own are less clear in context, and this prevents them from forming a
unity, a total or definitive whole. They function in the manner of the
ancient technique of *adynaton*, which joins together things that cannot
be joined, such as dead people who speak, madmen who laugh at their
own madness, and absences that write.

It is useful to remind ourselves that Machado's narrator is a very cultured person. For every thing and every event, however insignificant, he
has his Tacitus or his Shakespeare at hand, ready to provide a dignifying
comparison. His digressions, too, which are made up of learned quotations, also function as a way of controlling the emotions, preventing
monotony by varying the themes and the ways they are treated. Even
the chapters are used digressively. They are quite short, and are not necessarily connected one to the other by the order of events. Their brevity
and discontinuity are a kind of allegory of the modern, multiple rhythms
of the social world of the late nineteenth century, and of the new ways
and means of organizing time and memory in reading. This fragmented
ordering of the chapters is itself a critique of the traditional "beginning,
middle, and end" way of narrating, which presupposes linear progres-

sion. The digression is thus critical and profoundly linked to the novel's way of signifying. It allows Machado de Assis to reclassify the forms given him by his own time, taking some of their conventional reality from them and showing that memory is the product of a given point of view. It is a technique that defamiliarizes the principle of causality itself, and undermines the foundation of the reader's ability to remember and recognize familiar objects.

In the conventional "beginning, middle, and end" stories of the Romantics and Naturalists that Machado implicitly criticizes, the narrator organizes, in an omniscient, linear manner, the actions of "real" people, who are coherent even in their own incoherence. This representation assumes the importance and validity of similarity, and indeed the discourse of the novel itself is understood by readers as an imitation of discourses they assume to be valid. The reading of Romantic and Naturalist stories is a kind of *re-cognition*, for they are made for and assume readers just like the narrator, that is, with a memory capable of recognizing the "real causes" by means of which the narrator links the beginning and end of the story together. When they recognize something they already know, readers become a part of this familiar world, repeating the laws of normality and unitary causation that constitute its foundation.

By making the story allow for mutually contradictory but simultaneously valid versions, Machado de Assis dissolves the unambiguous causality of that type of action and "denaturalizes" fiction. Now, in the new era of the Central line train, when modern capitalism has fragmented the metaphysical unity of "reality" and the "subject," an organic means of representation is impossible. The modern crisis in representation rejects the imperative of causality, and makes proofs based on similarity doubtful. No discourse based only on an argument from similarity can be held to be unquestionably true, for the terms of validity of any possible proof have been changed. There is no absolute law for action, and ambiguity is no longer a result merely of differences of perspective or evaluation: now, ambiguity is understood to be inherent in the structure of reality itself. *Dom Casmurro* takes on this modern crisis in fiction when it addresses the misunderstanding resulting from similarity. Capitu almost seems aware of this when she speaks of Bento's jealousy: "I know the reason for this: it's the accident of the resemblance" (Ch. CXXXVIII).

We may, at first, think that in his rejection of the unifying force of the prevailing ideology, Machado refuses to take sides at all. However, in his obsessive treatment of the senselessness of human suffering and of the struggle against "destiny" and "rules," he affirms his commitment to art itself, which, as he says in a newspaper article, is worth "all the troubles of this world."[1] In his time, when social Darwinism was widely held to be a scientific certainty, the adoption of a literary technique that allowed identity to dissolve and fragment could itself be seen as an allegory of the social maladjustments associated with Brazil's conservative modernization. The surprise experienced by his readers brought into question the very notion of "reality" at the root of this ideology.

In abandoning a narrative model that presupposed the identity of the bourgeois individual, the unity of the nation itself and the linear inevitability of progress, Machado also systematically questioned the generic opposition between "nature" and "society," and other dichotomies such as "reality" and "appearance," "reason" and "madness," "idealism" and "self-interest," dualities that gave shape to the practicality of day-to-day life in his time. As has been said, the ironic inversion of the terms of these oppositions, making them seem to be of equal value, is what produces humor.

Machado's humor is the result of a technique that connects digression and memory: Brás Cubas talks a lot, but the dead don't talk; Bento Santiago writes to remember the past, but tells us that he has a bad memory. Just as the narrators tell a story that does not exist, the events narrated and the characters' actions do not appear in the order in which they are presumed to have happened, but as if they had been accidentally filtered through the narrator's mind as it works with its own idea-associations, creating digressions that fragment the time sequence of the story. Telling the story is thus an organized subversion of everyday values founded on the formality of the law. The main targets of the novel are such ideological constructs as patriarchal morality, liberal individualism, Romantic sentimentality, progress, and positivist and determinist racism, which were commonly held—if at times contradictory— elements of the ideology of the Brazilian élite.

The short-circuiting of the meaning of these ideologies depends on the narrator's words, but also depends on the way he supposes readers will reconstruct those meanings. Machado's technique is also a matter of pragmatism. The digression which includes the reader's own assumptions thus becomes the main technical vehicle of the author's dramatic irony. It is no accident that there are constant references to theatre and the opera: they are allegories of the process of dialogue with the reader—the "audience"—by means of which the novel is composed.

One of the most important dramatic allegories in *Dom Casmurro* appears in Chapter IX. There, life is defined as an opera conducted by Satan. An essentially tragic genius, the devil is the hyperbolic doubter characteristic of Romantic negativity. In his rejection of idealism, Machado uses the devil's doubts as a means of observing our world with a critical eye. They are also means of commenting on the very work in which they appear. From Chapter IX:

> Certain motifs, indeed, weary the listener by overmuch repetition. Also, there are passages that are obscure. The composer uses the massed choruses too much, causing confusion and concealing the true meaning. The orchestral parts, however, are treated with great skill.

This diabolic theme is a symptom of the disharmony necessary to the modern novel. It invites the reader to consider the way in which Dom Casmurro, as composer, orchestrates the experience of his own life as he narrates. Right from the beginning, when the opera of jealousy has not yet begun, the author allows us to see the beginnings of a vast ambiguous structure, introducing touches which cast doubt on the one-sided certainty of the narrator.

The reader of the novel, he imagines, is a middle-class man or woman whose taste has been formed by melodrama, and who, if he is a man, probably believes in the essentially treacherous nature of women. Incorporating such stereotypes into the narrator's language, Machado encourages the reader to concur with the narrator's own convictions about "feminine nature." These stereotypes construct "woman" as the product of an ideological formation: sly, oblique, gypsy-like, capricious, calculating, fickle, treacherous. From Chapter CXLVIII:

> If you remember Capitu as a child, you will recognize that the one was in the other, like the fruit in its rind.

The images of Capitu are negative: she is criticized, in effect, for taking her own initiatives, and not taking on the role required of the submissive woman. But if we reread Chapter XVIII, we will see that the narrator's digressions, irrelevant at first sight, provide a counterpoint to the main thrust of the chapter. Through them the author dissolves the very stereotypes that the narrator places before us, making everything that he says ambiguous.

What the narrator says is ambiguous, but his manner of saying it is exactly suited to his character. There is method in his madness. Machado's syntax is characterized by a complexity full of subordination, which he learned from the Portuguese classics of the sixteenth and seventeenth centuries. In it, the original, principal idea of the sentence is continually made more specific by further analytic clauses which introduce several parallels and qualifications, which themselves function as extensions of the argument: "The composer uses the massed choruses too much, causing confusion and concealing the true meaning." The narrator continually jumps from one story to another: his capricious way of writing imitates a colloquial, urbane manner. Apparently carried away by unexpected associations of ideas, he takes his own journey through varied topics, all the time in dialogue with the reader.

The book's syntax is intimately linked to the structure of the book as a whole. By 1890, style is no longer determined by the demands of newspaper publication. Thus, Machado has no need to give additional explanations, to jog the reader's memory, as the Romantic novels of the 1850s and 1860s had to do, as they appeared episodically in the newspapers and magazines, by the week or the day. On the contrary, jerky and unpredictable, his prose tends towards the epigrammatic. Affecting a modern, frivolous cynicism in its discontinuities and fragmentary organization, it has freed itself from any sense of patriotic "mission," or of the weighty "thesis novel" of the Naturalists. It incorporates into its style modern ways of reading reality through printed matter. The short chapters imitate the rapidity and simultaneity of the mode of reading imposed by the newspaper. This kind of inclusiveness and variety causes alterations both in the content and the meaning of traditional subjects, which are transformed, with new objects in mind. For example, the old melancholy of the hypochondriacal narrator of the eighteenth-century English novel is adapted to the themes of Brazilian conservative modernization. Since it is one-sided or partial, the narrator's melancholy allows differing or opposite points of view to be represented. And the synthetic form of maxims, proverbs and moral sayings, which at the end of the nineteenth century were already out of date, typical as they were of the speech of an unquestioningly patriarchal age, is also appropriated as a paradoxical means of intregrating modern things and events into the novel. With its tensions and ambivalent principles, Machado's style is an example of the "internal inconclusiveness" that Bakhtin dealt with in his study on Dostoyevsky.[2]

When the novel is read as an allegory of life during the Brazilian Empire in the middle of the nineteenth century, Dom Casmurro's lack of a complete existence and the drama of his jealousy also point to the failure of an entire class. *Dom Casmurro* is a story with tragic echoes, which rewrites *Othello* in another form, as Helen Caldwell, along with Brazilian critics such as Lúcia Miguel-Pereira and Eugênio Gomes, has shown in her *Brazilian Othello of Machado de Assis* (1960).[3]

There is no point in wanting to know if Capitu really did commit adultery, since her "betrayal" is narrated by Bento. But one can point out how the theme of adultery is built up, and how it relates in a figured form the historical collapse of the imaginary world of a class. Treating this theme through Bento's individual experience, Machado lays bare the structure of the sexual contract in marriage as it was usually undertaken in the reign of Pedro II. His analysis of the institution is implicitly critical of the legal criteria for proof of responsibility, which are here based, not on undisputed evidence, but on rhetorical arguments, and have the form of metaphors or similes. The narrator, as we have seen, is a one-sided observer, a means used by Machado to typify the way someone of this class and period would represent himself. So, a form of writing which in this way dissolves the legal and social foundations of its time also necessarily dissolves the literary means of representing them. For this reason, the book has an "unfinished" look, with its stylistic mixture and dual point of view.

In *Dom Casmurro*, Bento Santiago's family is patriarchal, organized on the presupposition that human nature is unchanging. In it, "masculine" and "feminine" are two opposed and complementary sexual natures, which define the nature of the subject merely as a capacity to live up to fixed roles. Patriarchalism makes its members internalize the notions of family, property, religion, honor, and the privileges, pomp, and circumstance of one's position as rights and duties corresponding to a given individual nature. This internalization, which is what makes up the imaginary unity of a person, appears in the novel in the form of authoritarian memory. Dom Casmurro's memory repeats patterns inherited from the past, and models its own expectations for the future as a repetition of inherited authority. For this purpose, it adapts its actions to the demands of established institutions. The discourses of the law and of the Catholic church are the legal and metaphysical foundations of this process of modelling, for they give explicit form to the liberties and privileges which distinguish the upper-class person from those who are poor but free, and from the slave. In *Dom Casmurro*, Machado suggests, the dead govern the living.

Bento's memory is made up of the commonplaces of the patriarchal jurisprudence inculcated in him by the family group. Each family member represents a principle: Religion and Property in the case of Dona Glória; Law, Uncle Cosme; Dependency, cousin Justina, and finally, Submission in the case of José Dias.

As the principal means of mediation and interpretation of the meaning of this structure, José Dias represents the supreme allegory of this Darwinian world. As a character, he makes its mediocrity explicit: in his case, it reveals itself in the cunning which is the adaptive mechanism of the weak, their means of avenging themselves on the strong. He is an example of the bourgeois principle of common sense, acclimatized in a Brazilian patriarchal structure ruled by favor. Machado builds his character as a caricature, showing his social inferiority in the use of the superlatives with which he invests his own lack of autonomy with authority. José Dias' affectation is simply an exaggerated form of the norm, however, and he is, for example, a mirror image of Capitu both as a girl and as an adult. Both are socially inferior beings, who know how the social order functions, he a dependent and she a woman, he with no possessions at all and she poor. But he is a servant who collaborates, she someone perhaps punished for her curiosity, independence, and desire to rise in the world; a perfect example of this is Chapter XXXI, "Capitu's Curiosity." And we should remember that all these examples are given by Bento: heavily influenced by his mother, he has learned that, in a woman, independence of character is a vice. It is quite possible that he lists these details of what he calls "Capitu's curiosity" as objective evidence for such a "fact."

Since childhood, Bento, as the carrier of his mother's desires, has lived a destiny he has not chosen. Widowed herself, Dona Glória wants him, in the name of a promise made before he was born, to be castrated and angelic—a priest, not a man. As Helen Caldwell suggests, Bento Santiago's destiny is inscribed in the transparent allegory of his name: he is "consecrated" (bento = blessed) as "saint" and "Iago." With no capacity for action, he is only capable of facing obstacles by inventing another principle of authority legitimized by his own memory: for example, when he has a fantasy that the supreme paterfamilias, the Emperor, might free him from the promise.

Bento's fantasy reveals itself in its obtuse sluggishness, in the difficulty he has with abstraction—"Division, which was always a difficult operation for me . . ." (Ch. XCIV)—in his passive receptiveness. His fantasy is symmetrically inverse to Capitu's pragmatism. Their conversation in Chapter XLIII is illuminating in this respect: Bento is a confused, fearful child, who believes in his mother as a "good creature." The child is father of the man, as the narrator of *Memórias póstumas de Brás Cubas* says. *Dom Casmurro* shows that, in the patriarchal family, that is so because he is his mother's son.

Dona Glória reproduces, in the microcosm of the family, the Catholic ordering that is present in society as a whole. Her excessively religious and fearful attitude to divine power is typical of women under patriarchal rule, fearful of thunder and of the husbands of the domestic Olympus, in words paraphrased from *Memórias póstumas de Brás Cubas*. Historically, it can be defined as passivity and submission, but it is also the underside of a single social unit, made up of understated violence and a generosity entirely at the discretion of those with power. The novel reveals Bento's lack of autonomy to be the result of the social construction of his memory by this same authoritarian social order. In the decisions which are taken for him, the patriarchal structure of "honor" is always present, as an appearance to be maintained and as the principle that keeping one's word is basic. This is what happens in Dona Glória's dealing with Heaven, when she buys Bento from God, and pays Him back with a convenient poor orphan, with Father Cabral's connivance.

In colonial Portuguese society and in Imperial Brazil, the title "Dom" meant "lord, master," and was an indication of aristocracy, as in the case of "Dom Pedro II." When he refers to the title, Dom Casmurro explains that the nickname was given him by a young poet, who ironically imputed "aristocratic airs" to him (Ch. I). In this case, the word "Dom" means a social distinction represented by outward signs, meaning that anyone who carries them belongs to a hierarchical system. In the immediate context of the book, the term "Dom" means that Bento's own self-awareness has roots in the past. Dependent as he is on the opinion and recognition of others, the term also signals his obedience to predetermined roles.

When he tells his story, the narrator projects the hierarchical meaning of his title onto the events of the story. Thus, the image of his past is constructed as a figure of that unconscious law which swallows the family up into a single, authoritarian unit. This dominance, signified in the word "Dom," is like the rind of the fruit: the tough outer covering of repeated events, which contain and repress the soft pulp of Bento's subjective nature. The "rind" encloses the two sections of his memories of the past—his youth in the Rua de Matacavalos, and his married life at the house on the Bay of Guanabara at Glória beach. This latter is a significant name, and it is easy to see that it repeats the name of the person who gave birth to the fruit, and so suggests that the authoritarian principle repeats itself in the new situation. It is also in Glória that the couple become ever more intimate with Escobar and Sancha and that the son, the "son of man," Ezequiel, is born.

From their days in Matacavalos at the beginning of the novel, in 1857, to the day of Escobar's funeral, in 1871, Bento depends on Capitu. It is a relation of social dependency in which power relations are inverted. Measured by the standards of the time, there is a double inversion: the strong-willed girl who achieves dominion over the naive young man is also of an inferior social class. José Dias, good servile servant that he is, does not fail to warn Dona Glória of the fact. But the relative autonomy attained by Capitu through marriage is not guaranteed in the intimacy of the new home on Glória beach. There, Bento is still the well-beloved son of the Church and of Dom Pedro II.

Right from his youth, Bento's power of decision has been taken over. First, by his mother's choices; later, by the mediation of Capitu and José Dias; later still, by Escobar. Utterly alienated in this sense, Bento is a receptacle of the images that others create for him. His relation with others determines his lack of initiative and the instability which is a part of his untrustworthiness. In the same way, his jealousy is also the result of his lack of autonomy and reveals, once again, the authoritarian principles behind his upbringing.

As we read, the longing for what did not happen becomes the reason for the delight Dom Casmurro takes in the past. The old times are lived over again in his narration, and as this happens, they reveal the social structure, which gives meaning to the images. In the present day of the "Central line train," however, the world of his childhood is dead and gone. Mesmerized by a nostalgia for his own self, Dom Casmurro reclassifies the past that went to make up his memory, and turns his narration into the stone image of something dead: "I myself am missing, and this lacuna is everything" (Ch. II).

As he repeats himself in the imitated world of Engenho Novo, the destructive force of the past wells up in Bento in the resentment that determines the images by and through which he remembers Capitu. His infinite melancholy is eaten into by the silence of the dead. The ultimate effect of the indifferent way time gnaws at itself is that the reader, intuiting something horrible, feels a kind of nausea. An opera composed by the devil with ambiguous, treacherous notation, *Dom Casmurro* has been put on stage to amuse Saturn.

—*João Adolfo Hansen*
translated by John Gledson

Notes

1. A Semana," 8 October 1893 (*OC* III), p. 654.

2. Mikhail Bakhtin, *Problems of Dostoevsky's Poetics* (Minneapolis: University of Minnesota Press, 1984).

3. See Lúcia Miguel-Pereira, "O defunto autor" (1958), in *Escritos da maturidade* (Rio de Janeiro: Graphia, 1994), pp. 30–3 ("And maybe, in spite of her oblique manner, Capitu is innocent, and the whole tragedy only exists in Bentinho's head, whose timidity is transformed, by the action of jealousy, into sadomasochistic impulses"); Eugênio Gomes, *O enigma de Capitu* (Rio de Janeiro: José Olympio, 1967); and Helen Caldwell, *The Brazilian Othello of Machado de Assis: A Study of* Dom Casmurro (Berkeley and Los Angeles: University of California Press, 1960).